Raves for *Shadows in the D...*

S0-CFE-883

"An elf packing heat who enjoys looking like jailbait when necessary is the latest twist on the New Weird— fantasy fused with contemporary mystery tropes laced with erotic undertones—a genre Laurell K. Hamilton's Anita Blake series helped establish. This is an auspicious debut for a cool crime-solver who could teach Anita a thing or two." —*Publishers Weekly*

"With the sleekness of a supernatural Alias, Cunningham's novel is a fast, fun read with a likable, hip heroine." —*Booklist*

"Cunningham launches a new police procedural featuring a fae detective and set in a contemporary version of Earth where magic, though gone undercover is still very much alive. An excellent choice." —*Library Journal*

"Highly original and creative, this spirited read easily electrifies and stimulates. Gwen is simply delectable; touchingly human, but with just enough of the mystic to make things interesting, she's sure to engage fans of many different genres. Definitely promising, we look forward to more." —*The New Mystery Reader*

"*Shadows in the Darkness* is an amazing read, please don't pass it by!" —*Bookloons*

TOR BOOKS BY ELAINE CUNNINGHAM

Shadows in the Darkness
Shadows in the Starlight

Shadows
in the
Darkness

ELAINE CUNNINGHAM

TOR®

A TOM DOHERTY ASSOCIATES BOOK / NEW YORK

This is a work of fiction. All the characters and events portrayed in this book are either products of the author's imagination or are used fictitiously.

SHADOWS IN THE DARKNESS

A Tor Book
Published by Tom Doherty Associates, LLC
175 Fifth Avenue
New York, NY 10010

www.tor.com

Tor® is a registered trademark of Tom Doherty Associates, LLC.

ISBN 0-765-34851-9
EAN 978-0-765-34851-7

First edition: October 2004
First mass market edition: January 2006

Printed in the United States of America

0 9 8 7 6 5 4 3 2 1

To Brian Thomsen

Thanks for Gwen and Liriel!

ACKNOWLEDGMENTS

Thanks to Frank Weimann and The Literary Group for the opportunity to explore the shadows in my hometown and for a heroine who's very much at home in the darkness.

Shadows in the Darkness

Prologue

∽ Unlike her more glamorous sister to the south, the city of Providence slept—or at least gave a damn good impression of it.

Staid brick buildings huddled together against the winter chill, and the white dome of the statehouse gleamed like the bald pate of a dozing sphinx. The entire Waterfront area, the showcase of the former mayor's Renaissance City, looked as tidy and upscale as it had the day the mayor went to jail. The second time, not the first.

Charming yet colorful, historic and historically corrupt, Providence was home to an Ivy League college and more strip clubs per capita than any city in the country. It was, in short, a town that tolerated, and occasionally embraced, its multiple realities.

Tonight was such a time. Despite its somnolent mien, the city was watchful, expectant. There was a voiceless murmur in the air, an uneasy sense of shadows hiding in the darkness.

Midnight had come and gone. A bitter wind whipped across the circular basin that concluded the Waterfront walk, sending a shudder across the dark water and forcing bare-branched saplings into a brittle dance. Two burly figures shouldered their way through the gale. They climbed the broad stairs leading up the hill between the brew pub and the steak house, and turned down an otherwise empty street.

Tom Yoland, the smaller of the two, was a thick-bodied man just short of six feet. His black knit cap was pulled down over hair nearly as red as his windburned cheeks. He had the look of a fisherman who didn't like his job and didn't particularly care who knew about it. Moniz, his companion, was Latino and at least three inches taller, a big man with an aggressive swagger and the type of muscularity that indicated serious time in the weight room. Both men walked with shoulders hunched against the cold, but their coats were left open and their ungloved hands held loose and light at their sides.

The big man drew in a long breath. "Smells like snow tonight."

"Snow doesn't smell like anything," Yoland said dismissively. "You've got ice on your mustache, that's all."

"No, man. It's not the same thing."

"It's all frozen water, and who the hell cares?"

They walked in silence for a few steps. Then, "A little snow would be good, it being Solstice and all."

"How's that?"

"Solstice. The beginning of winter, the longest night of the year. It's the darkest night, too, what with the new moon."

Yoland sent his companion an incredulous glare. "What are you, the farmers' fucking almanac?"

A gust of wind sent a small flurry of city trash scuttling toward them, mostly paper cups discarded by people too hopped up on designer caffeine and self-importance to concern themselves with trash cans. Moniz absently kicked aside a vat-size cup.

"It's just that Teresa talks about this shit sometimes. How far we are from the cycles of the earth, how we've lost the ability to see things all around us. Like this star that's supposed to be visible during the day. We could see it if we looked, but we don't."

"And you mention this because?"

"Teresa might be right. I don't like thinking about what I might be missing."

"Then don't." Yoland sent a meaningful look at the shoulder harness faintly visible under the big man's coat. "We've got more important things going. How about you keep your head in?"

"Just talking. Passing time, you know?"

"And you know what? It'll pass all by itself, without the New Age bullshit to help it along. No offense to Teresa."

Moniz acknowledged this with a shrug. They continued in silence for several blocks to a narrow side street and into a small parking lot filled with high-ticket cars. On the far side of the lot, on the back side of a multistory building, was a plain wooden door. A discrete sign welcomed them to Winston's.

A blast of dance music hit them as they edged into the narrow entrance hall. Two very blond bouncers, one male and one female, blocked the way like a pair of matching Aryan pit bulls. Both wore unrelieved black, and their white-blond hair was cut short and slicked back. Someone's idea of designer muscle.

The female bouncer looked the two men up and down, a pointed and practiced gesture that quickly summed them up and dismissed them. "This is a private club," she announced. Her blue-eyed gaze was icily superior, and her tone suggested that membership was not an honor to which they could aspire.

Yoland stared her down, unimpressed. He swept off his

woolen cap, the gesture of a man who intends to stay a while. The movement, not coincidentally, opened his coat enough to show off the gun in his shoulder holster.

"Yoland and Moniz," he said curtly, indicating himself and his companion. "Mr. Leone told us to come by. He's expecting us."

That name wilted the bouncers' smug expressions. "Oh, right," the man said quickly, his tone much more cordial than his partner's had been. "Amy here will take care of you."

"Sounds good to me," Moniz murmured, treating the woman to a variation of her insulting up-and-down scrutiny.

Yoland added a smirk. "Amy? Not Gretchen? Or Brunhilda?"

She sent them both a scalding glare and led the way into the club. The throbbing music enveloped them as they inched their way through the gyrating throng.

Glitzy place, Yoland noted. The bar was a vast expanse of carved mahogany; the small tables along the walls had fancy tile inlays. At the far end of the room, three sleek young women, dressed for holiday clubbing in festively skimpy red or green dresses, danced on a raised stage. They were dancers, not strippers, which would have been too obvious for this crowd.

The club drew a young and obviously overpaid clientele. The air crackled with that brittle, frantic energy of people who are grimly determined to have fun. Yoland was willing to bet that none of these post-yuppies would leave until at least one deal had been made—a pocketful of phone numbers for future reference, a hit of Ecstasy in the ladies' room, a private dance or a party for two (or three) in one of the discreet back rooms.

The music softened, shifting to a slower, sensual dance that pulsed through the crowd like a collective heartbeat. Dancers fused into pairs. Yoland predicted that the back rooms would fill up before the number finished.

Sure enough, the crowd started to thin. Their escort picked up the pace. They moved briskly up a flight of stairs and through a VIP area that wouldn't have looked too out of place in an old-school men's club—gleaming dark wood, comfortable leather chairs.

Amy strode to a door on the back wall, rapped twice, and opened it. She stood aside to let them enter.

Inside, all pretense of respectability had been abandoned. Three very large bodyguards stood against the far wall, arms crossed, flat eyes assessing the newcomers. All wore guns at their belts, as well as coldly confident expressions that, for intimidation purposes, probably worked nearly as well as the hardware.

Tiger Leone, the club owner, was a huge man who carried a lot of muscle and even more fat. He was of mixed race, from the looks of him mostly Asian and Black, with just enough Narragansett blood in the mix to earn him a portion of the state's legitimate gambling revenue. He was seated in a huge armchair of purple velvet that must have been custom-made to accommodate his bulk, and the expression in his narrow black eyes was that of a medieval despot holding court. Tiger wore an enormous black silk shirt and cream-colored pants, way too much gold, and a pair of teenaged girls.

An aerobicized Black girl in skimpy workout gear draped herself over his shoulders, and a bottle blond who out-siliconed Pamela Anderson was perched on his lap. The blond wore pink shorts and T-shirt, both very bright and very brief. A third girl, a slim, feline brunette, curled up on the floor beside an ottoman that matched Tiger's throne. She was dressed in a strapless front-laced bodice of purple suede and a matching leather skirt, so short and so daringly slit on the sides that it was little more than a loincloth. Purple makeup encircled her catlike eyes and made her full lips look like a very ripe plum. With one long, purple nail she traced a circle around the handgun lying on the ottoman. The girl was definitely representing—all she was missing was a big gold necklace reading "Badass Fashion Accessory." Subtle, Tiger wasn't, but the overall effect—a modern-day sultan, a vice lord in his sleazy little palace—came across just fine.

The huge man nodded to the newcomers. "Right on time. I like that. You want a drink?"

Yoland shifted his gaze from the brunette. "Maybe after."

"Have yourselves a private dance, too. Consider it part of the deal."

He nodded his thanks. "We're short on time tonight, so someone's gonna have to tell us which girls are working and which ones just came to play."

The implication pleased Tiger. "No one can tell the customers from the whores just by looking," he boasted. "And some people never know, not even after they've paid and played."

Odd as that sounded, Yoland knew it to be true. Winston's had a quiet rep as a safe place to get high-quality recreational drugs, particularly those offering an erotic boost, as well as an attractive variety of like-minded, short-term friends. A few couples came to the club to spice things up, but most of the clients were young singles looking for an evening of fun.

The formula was simple: buy pretty girls or guys their drug of choice, drop a few bills for one of the private rooms available for discreet hire, go home with a smile on your face and a phone number in your pocket. Some of these encounters led to "second dates"—at the club, of course.

For employees, there was never a third date.

House rules.

The working girls and guys were rotated from club to club so that even some of the hard-core regulars didn't catch on to the hustle. Others probably figured it out but didn't want to let on, even to themselves. Winston's was the kind of place where people who "would never pay for sex" could count on getting laid. For a price. It was the sort of distinction this crowd could rationalize.

"Since you're short on time . . ." Tiger prompted. He removed his massive hand from the blond's rump and pointed to the cat-eyed girl at his feet. "Give the delivery to GiGi."

Yoland peeled back his coat and reached into an inside pocket, moving slowly so that the watchful guards wouldn't think he was reaching for his gun. He took out an amber vial and tossed it onto the ottoman. The girl picked it up and opened the lid. She spilled the contents into her hand. After a moment's study, she looked up at Tiger and nodded.

"You want to count them?" Yoland offered. "Seeing as how you're paying per pill."

"We've been doing business for what? Eight, nine months? I got no reason to doubt your word. But GiGi, she doesn't have a trusting heart, and she likes to look out for them who do. Sing for me, baby," he demanded. His leer added a dimension to the remark that Yoland didn't want to contemplate and refused to envision.

"Thirty pills, just like they said," she announced. Her voice was low and just a little bit husky, a been-there alto that sounded far too old for the rest of her. A street-waif version of Lauren Bacall, wasting time on this big-ass Bogart. The thought didn't sit well with Yoland.

Tiger shot a look at one of the henchmen. "Pay them."

Before the man could comply, a muffled, tinny rendition of—of all things—"Amazing Grace" came from the general vicinity of the blond girl's bosom. Tiger's leer returned. He reached into the girl's preternatural cleavage and produced a small cell phone.

His smile faded as he listened. His eyes flicked to the brunette, who had just finished putting the pills back into the vial. In response to her boss's unspoken command, she reached for the gun on the ottoman and trained it on Yoland. With one smooth motion she was on her feet, never taking her eyes from his.

Tiger's other girls were not quite as loyal. Both leaped up and fled shrieking to the far side of the room. His men drew their weapons and circled behind Yoland and Moniz.

"This," Tiger brandished the cell phone, "was a friend of mine." His voice was quiet, but it shimmered with suppressed violence. "He just finished doing time for possession. He says he knows you two—knows you from a 'sale' pretty much like the one you hoped was going down here." His eyes shifted to GiGi. "These assholes are cops. Get rid of them, make sure they don't get found."

The cat girl clicked off the safety on her gun. In the heavy silence, the sound seemed as explosive as the shot to come. Then she spun and put the gun to Tiger's head.

Yoland wished he could laugh at the slack astonishment on Tiger Leone's face, but that didn't seem smart, seeing that he and Moniz were outnumbered. Still, the sight was highly gratifying.

"Tell your boys to throw down," the girl said calmly, "and we'll all wait quietly until backup arrives."

Tiger sputtered for a while before he managed to form words. "Backup? But you're . . . You're not—"

"Sure I am," she affirmed. "Gellman, Lieutenant Gwen. GiGi to people who think they're my friends."

She turned a steel-edged smile toward the bodyguards, who were frozen in furious indecision. Slowly she slid the gun down Tiger's jowls and under his chins. A quick little shove forced his head up and back, giving her a nice angle toward the back of his head. A clean, killing shot.

"Do it," Tiger grunted. As the power shift took place, his massive shoulders rose and fell in a resigned sigh. He rolled his eyes toward the undercover cop.

"I don't fucking believe this," he mourned. "You were my girl—my best girl."

A hard, humorless smile lifted one side of her lips, but she didn't offer any comment.

A sliver of light appeared on the paneled wall behind Tiger's throne, a slim vertical beam from no discernible source. Before Yoland could absorb the implications of this, two of the panels flew apart, slamming into the wood on either side with a sound like gunshot.

Three thugs pounded into the room. One of the bodyguards lunged for Yoland's gun.

The cop shoulder-slammed him out of the way, shot him, and sighted down one of the onrushing men.

Moniz fired at about the same time, and two of the thugs went down. Before either cop could squeeze off a second shot, Tiger's remaining two bodyguards jumped Moniz. The three men went down in a tangle of flailing fists. A knife rose and fell, more than once.

Yoland saw all of this as if it were a movie played in slow speed, almost one frame at a time. He saw Tiger's two girls flee through the escape route, their frantic pace appearing almost leisurely. He fired again, hitting the last of the thugs in the shoulder. The man staggered but didn't go down.

Another shot came from the floor beside him. One of the bodyguards rolled off Moniz, screaming, both hands clamped to the pumping wound on his neck. Yoland kicked the third bodyguard off his partner and put a bullet in him to make sure he stayed off.

Moniz lay flat on his back, his gun held in both hands. The triumphant gleam in his eyes was icing over, and blood bubbled at the corners of his mouth. A knife was sunk hilt-deep between his ribs, deep into his lung.

A glance told Yoland the whole tale. His partner would drown in his own blood and there wasn't a damn thing he could do but break the news to pretty, witchy little Teresa. The thought occurred to him that, somehow, Teresa already knew she was a widow.

Someone punched Yoland in the gut—a mystery, since no one was within arm's reach of him. That wasn't good, but at the moment he couldn't remember why.

The thumping music from the club below abruptly stopped. A murmur of many voices took its place, a sound that rose swiftly in volume and indignation. Then police sirens sounded outside the club, and pique turned to panic. Screams and scuffles came from the dance floor as those who had reason to avoid the police—which probably included most of the employees and half the customers—remembered urgent business elsewhere.

With a furious roar, Tiger surged out of his chair, taking the female cop with him and slamming her against the wall. They grappled, and for a moment she was lost to sight behind his bulk. The gun reported, and Tiger reared back, screaming. Her second shot sent him stumbling to his knees. The third, to the floor.

Somehow Yoland found himself at eye level with Tiger, staring into the huge man's empty black eyes. He was glad that Tiger was dead but vaguely puzzled by his own proximity to the man's body.

Then the pain came—a white fire kindling in his gut. He realized that he was shot, and down.

The chaos downstairs, the battle in the room—it was all fading into a dreamlike haze. Yoland was dimly aware of the door flinging open and more of Tiger's men pouring into the room. They charged toward Gwen.

Three shots, Yoland realized. At best, she had three shots left, and that wouldn't be enough. The thought filled him with something very close to sorrow. She'd been his best girl, too, if only for a week or so, and they'd been partners for a lot longer.

Then the lights died, pitching the room into darkness. Gunfire exploded again and again, overlapping like the finale of a high-budget Fourth of July display.

Yoland's fading awareness suddenly snapped into focus, captured by a strange, soft glow. It was faintly blue, and it clung to

Gwen like the light on a mist-shrouded streetlamp. Strange as that was, weirder still was the fact that no one, not even Gwen, seemed to notice its existence.

She made her way through the darkness, sure-footed, picking her shots as she went. By the time she reached the door, the gunfire had stopped. She stumbled out into the hall, shouting for backup, unaware that she was the only one left standing. Unaware of the light surrounding her like a Madonna's halo.

Yoland remembered what Moniz had said not an hour before: They'd all been missing things. Important things. The truth of this flooded him, along with a sense of profound loss.

The light surrounding Gwen began to fade, and the room with it. Yoland took some comfort in the knowledge that at least he'd been able to see her, really see her, before the darkness came for good.

In an unlit room, in a once-stately home poised on the hills overlooking downtown Providence, a tall, black-haired man stood by the window. He stared out over the quiet winter vista with eyes that saw what others did not.

His slender frame was draped in a robe of dark silk. Beneath the robe he was naked and barefoot, and his watch and ring lay on a nearby table. There could be no metal to disrupt the flow of power, no leather to provide an unwanted link to the creature whose hide it once had been. Not on the Convergence, a time of uncommon power, a rare event that occurred when the moon and sun cycles aligned.

"The shortest day, the darkest night," he murmured in quiet exultation.

The ebb and flow of the moontides sang in his blood, and the pull of the year's turning wheel drew his Qualities more fully into the mundane world. All of his kind could do as much, but never had he felt the flow of power so keenly. Surely now he could finally claim the gift that was rightfully his, as the last member of his clan and bloodline!

He listened to the silent crescendo of starsong, waiting for the precise moment of the Solstice. When it was upon him, he reached for the blue gem on the table—the final link to his ancient birthright.

Power surged through him with a force that lifted him from his feet and hurled him backward. He hit the wall hard, his arms flung out wide. The gem fell from his benumbed hand and rolled away.

He slid down along the cracked plaster wall and slumped to the floor, staring with astonishment at the faint blue glow in the gem's heart. The pain of impact was forgotten, rendered irrelevant by the disturbing truth before him:

The clan's greatest gift had been claimed—and not by him.

That could mean only one thing: he was not, as he had so fondly believed, the last of his line.

But never in his family's long history had an heir come into the clan's power without the assistance of the gem. Whoever had usurped his hard-won place was a creature of considerable power—or at least, considerable potential. Someone who walked beneath these stars, someone whose name and face he did not know, had the power to Remember.

The thought filled him with fear, an emotion he had seldom experienced and nearly forgotten. He pushed himself to his feet and stalked over to a table that held a cut-glass decanter and a large crystal snifter. He poured enough brandy to take the coppery taste of fear from his mouth, and settled down by the fireplace to compose himself.

By his third brandy, he had forgotten why this new development had seemed so troubling.

This would not, after all, be the first time he had killed a fellow elf.

One

A cold spring rain pelted the city as Gwen Gellman maneuvered her battered blue Toyota up the hill north of Benefit Street. As she negotiated the maze of the narrow, one-way streets that characterized much of Providence's East Side, the brick buildings of Brown University and the art school gave way to old three-story frame houses, many of which had small shops or cafes in the bottom floor. She pulled into an empty spot across the street from a small Thai eatery, happy to have found a parking place so close to her destination. Tap-dancing through April showers was not her idea of a good time.

Gwen dashed across the street, dodging rain-filled potholes, and climbed the stairs leading up the side of the building. Once on the landing, she took quick stock of her appearance. A quick swipe of fingers under one eye assured her that her waterproof mascara was living up to its claims. She brushed off some of the raindrops beading on the shoulders of her leather jacket and ran both hands through her short dark-chestnut hair, not sure whether this would tame her hair or spike it and not particularly caring which outcome occurred.

A tall young woman, barefoot and semidressed in a navy

blue sports bra and capri-length bike pants, answered Gwen's knock and gazed at her uncertainly.

Gwen couldn't fault the girl. Sometimes she tried for a traditionally professional image, but today wasn't one of those days. She wore jeans so snug they looked as if they'd been spray painted on, a sleeveless black shirt that stopped a couple of inches north of her pierced navel, a leather jacket she'd bought second-hand during the Reagan administration, slim-heeled ankle boots, and far too much makeup. Her eyes, which were wide and very blue and slightly tilted at the corners, tended to remind people of Siamese cats. Gwen liked to play down the feline aspect with a few layers of judiciously applied paint, which had the added benefit of making her look older. Or at least, it made her look like a high-school kid who was trying to look older.

"Rachel York?" she asked.

"Yes . . ."

"I'm Gwen Gellman. Lauren's mother asked me to talk to you. She said you'd be home and expecting me."

The girl's brown eyes widened. "You're the private investigator?"

"That's right." Gwen waited a beat, then glanced over her shoulder at the rain.

Chagrin replaced incredulity on the young woman's face. "Oh. Sorry." She moved aside to let Gwen into the apartment.

Unlike most student apartments, this wasn't furnished with parental castoffs and Salvation Army specials. The couch was a new-looking futon with a burgundy cover and a dark oak frame. The matching coffee and lamp tables had the square, clunky look Gwen's friend Marcy called "mission style." The walls were painted a shade of orange that somehow managed to look cozy and inviting. An area rug covered the floor with geometric shapes in colors that brought to mind citrus and spice. A large abstract canvas in similar hues dominated one wall. Two small-paned windows faced the street, and between them stood a large vase—hand-thrown pottery, no doubt—that held a sheaf of willow branches covered with soft gray catkins. The painting and the vase boasted a stylized signature, the letters "LTS" entwined in curving lines. Lauren Simpson had talent, as her mother had claimed.

Gwen turned back to the roommate, who was studying her with open skepticism. She lifted one eyebrow. "Is there a problem?"

"How old are you, if you don't mind me asking?"

It was a familiar question, one that got more irritating with each repetition. Still, she managed a thin smile. "Let's put it this way: In two years, I can legally sleep with guys half my age."

Rachel looked puzzled for a moment, then years of math classes kicked in and her eyes widened. She looked Gwen up and down, taking in the mall-rat outfit and, if she was like most people, probably pegging her for about seventeen. "Thirty-four? How is that possible?"

"It's not so hard," Gwen said dryly, "especially considering that after thirty, it's all downhill."

The girl looked unconvinced, but she chuckled a little. Probably because she was young enough to take Gwen's assessment of life after thirty at face value.

"Now, about Lauren," Gwen said. "Here's what her mother told me. One of Lauren's art teachers had an opening at a small gallery downtown. Lauren went to the opening alone, planning to make a quick appearance then go to an early movie with friends."

"That would be me and our friend Deb," Rachel put in. "Lauren was supposed to meet us at the theater in the mall. When she didn't show up, we went ahead without her."

"After you got home, the gallery called. They'd found Lauren's purse after closing. You got worried and called her parents. Her mother, after asking around a bit, called me. What can you add?"

Rachel spread her hands, palms up, indicating that she was coming up empty.

"Does Lauren have any boyfriends?"

"Not at the moment, no."

"Girlfriends?"

"No! I mean, she has friends, but she's not . . ."

"Yeah, whatever. My point is, is there anyone she was likely to meet up with, someone she'd maybe take off with on the spur of the moment?"

The girl shook her head in adamant denial. "Lauren's very reliable. She wouldn't just ditch us."

"But you went to the movies without her, so you weren't too worried."

"We already had tickets," Rachel said defensively. "How were we supposed to know something was wrong? Anyone can run into a delay."

"True enough. Do you know if anything was bothering her? Maybe she's the sort of person who needs to go off alone to think things through?"

Again Rachel shook her head. "Lauren's very open. If she

had something on her mind, she'd tell me. And she puts a lot of emotion into her art. If she was feeling low, she would work it out with clay or paint or whatever. And she's really a people person. The only way Lauren would go off somewhere on her own was if the light was good and she could take along a sketch pad."

All of this agreed with the rather frantic recital of Lauren's habits and virtues Gwen had heard from Mrs. Simpson late last night. None of it helped her in the slightest. She took a deep breath and prepared to take a much-dreaded shortcut.

"I'm going to need something of Lauren's."

Rachel's face lit up. "Oh yeah. You need, like, a hairbrush or something? For DNA," she added, speaking with the certainty peculiar to those who watch a lot of television.

"That would work." Which was true, up to a point. It would keep the roommate thinking along familiar lines: detective series, pop science, logical conclusions. What Gwen needed was not genetic code but memories. For that, she needed something Lauren had had with her when she'd disappeared.

"I'd also like to have a look at her purse. There might be something in it that'll suggest where she went. A phone number, a flyer advertising a restaurant or club—like that."

"Sure. It's in her room. I picked it up from the gallery right after they called." Rachel trotted off, clearly relieved to be able to do something to help.

Gwen picked up a framed photo from a small wall shelf. It was a casual shot, probably taken by a friend, showing Rachel and Lauren in pricey ski clothes. They were mugging for the camera, standing cheek to cheek and grinning. Lauren was a pretty girl—beautiful coffee-with-cream complexion, great cheekbones, perfect teeth displayed in a Julia Roberts smile, and thick waves of black hair, shoulder length and partially covered by a fuzzy pink head-band. Her cheeks were faintly flushed with a combination of out-door exercise, youth, and high spirits.

Rachel returned in moments with a small leather purse and an immaculate brush. She noted the photo in Gwen's hand.

"You can take that. Lauren looks pretty much the same as she does in that picture, only her hair is a little longer. She had it in a French braid last night. And she was wearing . . ." She trailed off, bit her lip, thought for a moment. "Navy slacks and a cream-colored blouse. Navy coat. Pearls, I think. Yeah, definitely pearls, a necklace and earrings. She wears them a lot, because they look really good with her skin tone. She likes lots of color around her, but her clothes and jewelry are usually very simple. Classic stuff."

"Thanks. That helps."

Gwen took a large plastic bag from her pocket and held it out for the items. She didn't want to touch Lauren's purse until she was alone, just in case the answers she sought came too fast and too powerfully. That could be tough to explain to onlookers.

She thanked the girl again, promised to keep her informed, and dashed through the rain to her car. She slammed the door and dumped the contents of the plastic bag onto the passenger's seat.

For a moment she hesitated. For two days now, Gwen had felt . . . open, as if a layer of skin had been peeled away, leaving her exposed to every passing breeze. Judging from past experi-ence, she was due for what she privately called Freak Week: a few days filled with odd moments of psychic clarity and capri-cious visions.

She hated it. She'd spent the first half of her life hiding it. But her first partner had taught her to trust her instincts—all of them. This had been no easy task, considering how much time and trouble a God-fearing foster family had invested in beating them out of her.

Gwen set her shoulders, grasped Lauren Simpson's purse in both hands, and took a deep breath.

Memories flooded her—Lauren's memories, indistinct as an almost-forgotten dream. Gwen forced away a stab of panic, willed herself to sink into another woman's mind.

The rain-mottled view beyond the windshield blurred, as if the world was a watercolor painting left out in the rain. The limpid colors swam and spun and began to take the shape of two male faces. Something about them was familiar, but the vision was too hazy for Gwen to decipher. Then a third face emerged from the mist, a woman's face, surrounded by a halo of very curly red hair.

An icy shiver crackled down Gwen's spine, inspired by a memory that was very much her own. She pushed her own emotions aside and moved deeper into the missing girl's memories.

The woman held out a goblet of white wine, offering it with a friendly smile. Swirling through the pale gold liquid was a ghostly image, a white tablet that had long since dissolved—a memory within a memory. The pill tumbled lazily, and Gwen caught a glimpse of the engraving on it: on one side, the word "ROCHE"; on the other, a circle surrounding the number two.

Image gave way to sensation—an intense wash of sensuality that shivered down her spine and pooled low and hot in her body. Sensation became desire, desire became an aching compulsion. A wonderful languor began to steal over her, a silky-smoky feeling that did nothing to detract from the kindling flame. It was incredible, unexpected, compelling. Overwhelming.

Familiar.

A tendril of memory, this one entirely her own, crept into Gwen's mind and entwined with Lauren's last night.

Her scream of rage shattered the twin nightmares and flung her back into the present moment. She tossed the purse aside with shaking hands.

"No time, no time," she muttered as she stabbed the key into the ignition.

She'd almost been dragged under by Lauren's drug-induced sensations, in a way she never would have been had she been in Lauren's place. Gwen's metabolism let her chow down like a farm-hand without gaining an ounce and drink men twice her body weight under the table—a trick that had come in handy more than once in the men's club that was police work. The downside to this was that medicines didn't work very well: aspirin barely touched her headaches, Motrin was useless on the occasional sprain. Unless Lauren Simpson also had the metabolism of a fruit fly, she was in very serious trouble.

A trio of predators, people Gwen knew all too well, had mixed her wine with a double dose of Rohypnol, more commonly known as the date-rape drug.

CHAPTER

Two

൭ Gwen whipped out of the parking space and spun her car around into a U-turn, narrowly missing an oncoming minivan. Brakes screeched, and the bleating of an indignant horn followed her down the street.

She wove through traffic with the wild abandon of a Boston cab driver and pulled up short in front of a downtown hotel. A line of shops and galleries filled with expensive, impractical items fronted the hotel. She jogged around to her trunk and grabbed the plain brown package she kept on hand for such occasions. Even in these security-conscious times, most people tended to wave deliveries through without much thought.

She tossed her car keys to the valet. He deftly caught them, but his lip curled at the prospect of parking Gwen's piece-of-shit car within sight of the hotel shops.

"Fifteen minutes," Gwen promised as she strode into the gallery.

She walked past a row of chrome-and-glass shelves holding brightly glazed pottery, then through the door leading into the hotel lobby. The elevator door was closing. She caught the eye of a young businessman, the sole occupant, and sent him a look of appeal. His eyes brightened and he slapped a hand on the edge of the door to hold it open for her.

Gwen slipped past him into the elevator. "Thanks."

"No problem." He loosened his tie, a probably unconscious signal that work was not on his immediate agenda. He glanced at the package in Gwen's arms and sent her a flirtatious, sidelong glance. "Got something for me?"

She pretended to study the too-small-to-read address on the label. "Sure, if your name is Melvin Weinstein."

The man grimaced, then grinned. He leaned closer. "It could be," he confided.

"Sorry, Mel, but I just can't see myself yelling that name in the heat of the moment. Not with a straight face, anyway."

He chuckled appreciatively. "Okay, Melvin is out. What about Chris?"

The bell rang and the elevator door opened. Her would-be friend shifted slightly, subtly blocking her way out.

Gwen stifled an impatient sigh. "Popular name," she said brightly. "My ex-husband was a Chris. So's my parole officer."

He stepped back instinctively, even before his smile had a chance to freeze and fade. Gwen hurried out of the elevator and down the hall, giving the man a little waggle-fingered wave over her shoulder as she went. The room numbers were in the teens. She was, thankfully, still looking for single digits.

In the past eighteen months, four young women had gone missing in the Providence area, and all of them had disappeared from public places. One of them, the third to disappear, had been found in a hotel room. Room number three.

Gwen had commented on the connection between the

number of the victim and the number of the hotel room, but her last partner had scoffed at this notion. "You need at least two points to draw a line," he'd said.

Sweet Jesus. Instead of a new partner, they'd saddled her with a freaking math teacher.

Admittedly, she'd been arguing a tenuous connection. None of the other women had turned up in a hotel room. Two hadn't turned up at all. Garry Quaid, Tom Yoland's very reluctant replacement, hadn't seen any logical reason to connect the four disappearances. After a while, Gwen had given up. She couldn't explain what she knew or why she knew it—not to Quaid, not even to herself.

She rounded the corner to the hall where the single-digit rooms were and pulled up short. A service cart was parked outside the door of room number five, which stood open. The sound of running water drifted from the room, along with a woman's soft, slightly off-tune rendition of an old Streisand ballad.

Gwen spun on her heel and started to retrace her steps. There were at least two other hotels near the gallery. This one would have been the most convenient place to take Lauren, but there were several other places where the three rapists could have taken their latest victim before the debilitating effect of the drug reached its peak.

A new idea struck her suddenly, stopping her with the force of an arctic blast. Gwen hurried back to room six and tentatively placed one hand on the doorknob.

Emotions flooded her: fear and puzzlement and confusion, all overlaid with a drowning wave of lethargy. The sensual storm had passed, and the memory of it was a swiftly fading shadow.

Gwen glanced into the open door of room five. The house-keeper was making the bed now, her back to the door. A card key lay beside the bathroom sink. Gwen slipped into the room and picked up the card. She opened the door to room six, edged it open.

There was no sound, no movement. All of Gwen's instincts told her the room was empty of life.

She wedged her package in the door to hold it open, put the key card back where she'd found it, and went back to face what she already knew:

It was too late for Lauren Simpson.

The girl lay faceup on the bed, her arms flung out wide. She was naked except for her strand of pearls. Her ankles were daintily crossed, tied in that position by a red silk sash. Her legs were untouched up to the knees; above that point, someone had been very busy with a knife. The cuts were shallow, and there appeared to be some attempt at a pattern carved into her thighs and up across her torso. If these marks were anything like the wounds on the other woman found in another hotel room, the macabre artwork would have taken quite a bit of time. Judging from the amount of blood soaking the bed linens, Lauren had been alive throughout most of it.

The girl's pretty brown eyes were open, but her face—which was untouched by the knife—showed no sign of the horrors of her last few hours. Gwen had seen more than a few dead people, but despite the claims of novels and movies, she'd never seen a face frozen into any expression of any sort. Death tended to make people forget things.

Gwen was, on the whole, in favor of this arrangement. Some memories were not worth having.

She shoved her hands into the pockets of her jacket. Touch nothing—that was vitally important. Training taught her not to contaminate a scene, and instinct urged her to protect herself from reliving Lauren's torture and death.

But memories this powerful were slow to die and hard to hold back. The air seemed heavy with them—unquiet ghosts that pushed at Gwen with insistent, icy hands. She willed them away, fought them like a swimmer caught by a huge and unexpected wave.

Her private battle was almost her last. She didn't hear anyone come in, didn't know she was no longer alone until a hand clamped down on her shoulder.

Gwen reacted at once, throwing her elbow back into the intruder's gut and stomping down hard with the sharp heel of her boot. She spun, seized the man's still-outstretched hand in both of hers, and gave his forearm a brutal twist.

He went down on one knee, letting loose a high-pitched yelp of pain. The knife he'd been holding in his other hand dropped to the floor.

"Carl Jamison," she muttered.

The bastard had changed his appearance—a salon tan and a hair color three shades lighter made him look younger than his thirty-two years—but his voice was exactly as Gwen remembered it. She kicked him, hard, just for the pleasure of hearing it again.

He wheezed out some indecipherable oath and wildly palmed the floor for his knife. Gwen kicked the weapon out of reach, making sure to send it away from the bed. If that was the knife he'd used the night before, there would be traces of Lauren's blood on it. There could be no question about how and when her blood got there. Gwen would not give this freak a chance to walk away from what he'd done.

Again.

"Down on your face," she ordered him. "Legs spread. Hands behind your neck, fingers laced."

She kept a grip on Jamison's arm until he lowered himself to the floor and maneuvered into position. As he was lacing his fingers, he stopped short, as if something important had suddenly occurred to him. He began to raise his head. Maybe he'd suddenly realized that he hadn't seen a gun in Gwen's hand, and was checking to confirm that he was alone with a small, unarmed "teenager."

She kicked him again, this time hard enough to crack a rib. He howled and clutched at his side.

"Face down, fingers behind your neck," she reminded him.

The man sent a hate-filled glare in her direction. She returned it, with interest. Whatever he saw in her eyes convinced him to lie flat and make his hands do what they were told.

"If you even so much as twitch," she advised him, "I'll break your back. What the hell—maybe I'll do it anyway. People like you probably should be paralyzed from the waist down."

"Who the fuck are you?" he muttered.

She stooped and seized a handful of tastefully highlighted hair, jerking his head up enough to let him see her face. Her smile held an edge that could have cut glass.

"I'm number five. The one who got away, though not for lack of effort on your part."

Recognition slid over his face. "The cop?"

"Not anymore. Which sort of works out well," she said conversationally. "This way, if you were to suffer an unfortunate and entirely accidental injury, there's less fucking paperwork."

"Got it," he mumbled.

"Good." Gwen slammed his head down on the carpet and rose to her feet. She took her cell phone from an inside pocket of her jacket and dialed a number from memory.

The police dispatcher came online. Gwen asked for Quaid and gave the name of a girl he'd started seeing just before Gwen had left the force.

They patched her through. "Kate? Why are you calling me at work? What's going on?"

Quaid's voice was unmistakable—deep, a little scratchy from too many cigarettes. His Rhode Island accent was thicker than quahog chowder.

"I'm standing over the body of a nineteen-year-old girl," Gwen said without preamble. "She disappeared last night. Her parents hired me to find her. The Jamisons found her first. Carl Jamison is here with me, alive and in reasonably good condition. And, just in case you haven't figured it out by now, this isn't Kate."

There was a long moment of silence. "Gellman," he muttered. "Shit."

From the tone of his voice, Gwen suspected that his expletive was doubling as an adjective.

"Dead girl?" she reminded him.

"Right. Always the bearer of good news, aren't you?"

"Hey, I called as a professional courtesy. I just thought you might still be interested in finding the source of those date-rape drugs. Or have the area's college kids moved on to the next twisted thrill?"

"You're not on that case anymore. You're not on the force anymore."

"Thanks for the update," she said coldly. "Do you want in on this, or should I call homicide directly?"

For a moment, the phone gave her nothing but faint static. "I'll make the call. Just give me the address."

Gwen told him where to find her. She switched off her phone and settled down to wait. An occasional kick discouraged Carl Jamison's attempts at escape or conversation and just generally helped to pass the time.

Fifteen minutes later, Quaid walked in. Whatever his other faults might be, the man was prompt. Not hard on the eyes, either. Her last partner was tall but not unusually so—six feet, or an inch or two on either side—with the kind of good but non-bulky build easily rendered nondescript by street clothes. He had medium-brown hair and a pleasant but forgettable face. It was a good look for an undercover cop.

Quaid hadn't gotten any more memorable since she'd last seen him. His short brown hair was still being styled with a number five trimmer by the first available operator at SuperCuts. Khaki pants, rain-splashed navy windbreaker, brown shoes. The man could escape notice in an elevator—he was the same guy you saw a dozen times a day but never really noticed.

A new partner followed on his heels, a young Black man Gwen had never met. The kid had his own brand of camouflage, which included baggy jeans, a hooded sweatshirt, and sneakers that probably cost as much as Quaid's entire outfit. The new guy regarded Gwen with open fascination. Obviously, he'd heard some of the stories.

Quaid's gaze swept the scene, betraying no emotion until it settled on Gwen, at which point his expression went from cool to glacial. "Last person standing, as usual."

"I'm fine, thanks," she told him with equal warmth. "Nice of you to ask."

"Uh-huh. You want someone asking about you? I ran into Teresa Moniz last week. You know—Carmine's wife? She asked. Want to hear what I told her?"

"Not particularly. If you've finished busting my chops, maybe we could get on with this?"

The look he gave her suggested that he wasn't anywhere near finished, but he lifted one hand, palm up, in a sharp go-ahead gesture.

"The deceased is Lauren Simpson, a sophomore at the Rhode Island School of Design. Last night, she told her roommate she was going to an opening at a downtown art gallery. She left her purse behind. After closing, the gallery owner called her roommate, who called her mother, who called me."

"And here you are, not much more than twelve hours later." He made it a question.

"This was the logical place to go," she said, not quite keeping the bitterness from her voice, "considering how my last case ended."

Quaid received this observation in silence, and his gaze shifted to the man on the floor. Gwen hoped he was remembering the number on the door he'd gone through the last time

Jamison had struck. But after a moment Quaid's face hardened and his gaze skimmed Gwen from spiked hair to stiletto heels. On the way back up, there was a raised-eyebrow pause as he took in the jewelry framing her navel.

"If I didn't know different, I'd say you were still working vice."

"And if I were, that would make one of us," she shot back. "Since you're obviously on coffee break, sure, let's chat. If you hadn't destroyed evidence, this freak would have been out of business ten months ago." And Lauren Simpson would still be alive, filling rooms with bright colors and brilliant smiles.

Quaid splayed one hand over his heart, pantomiming wounded dignity and innocence challenged. "Is that how you remember it? According to the report, the vial was crushed during your struggle with the suspects."

"That's bullshit," Gwen retorted. "And even if it wasn't, how would you know? You were supposed to be right behind me, but you left me alone with this creep and his freak-show little family for nearly fifteen minutes."

Quaid shrugged. "You survived. As usual. To hear the Jamisons tell it, they had every reason to think you were into their game. Probably the same story Tiger Leone would tell, if he were still talking."

Gwen's eyes narrowed. She kept her gaze on the cop's face and took a quick step toward him. Quaid started to back up, a purely involuntary movement. He caught himself in time and shot her a look of pure venom.

"Good instincts," she murmured. "You should learn to go with them."

They stared at each other for a long moment. Finally, Quaid seemed to remember why he was here. He hauled Jamison up, read him his rights, and had his partner take him off.

"How did you find her?" he demanded, indicating Lauren with a sideways jerk of his head. He still hadn't taken a close look at the girl's body. Gwen wasn't sure whether that was a mark for or against him.

"The hotel adjoins the gallery where Lauren disappeared. I borrowed the maid's key card and looked in room number six. As you might recall, the Jamisons took me to room number five."

She didn't say, *I told you so.* Some things were so out there that giving voice to them was past redundancy.

Quaid's teeth clenched so hard that a muscle leaped near his jaw. After a moment he asked, "Was Jamison in the room when you entered?"

"No. He came in later."

"Did you touch anything?"

Gwen sent him a scornful look. "Please."

His eyebrows lifted. "Oh yeah. Far be it from me to question your professionalism."

"Hey, I'm not the one who 'lost' evidence that could have put these people away. That could have prevented this," she added, sweeping one hand toward the bed.

"According to your story, you spit some of the wine they gave you into a vial because you suspected it was drugged. According to the report, the vial was crushed at some point during the incident or arrest," he recited impatiently. "I don't know what your problem is. If you'd been drugged, a blood test would have proved it."

For a long moment Gwen was silent. For some reason, she'd resisted taking that step. No one had questioned her decision. She didn't show the usual symptoms, and even if she had, the time elapsed from the encounter in the bar to the booking of the suspects was enough for the drug to work its way out of her system.

"The way I saw it, you got picked up in a pick-up bar by three people looking to double date," Quaid concluded. "Nothing suggested that your little party was connected to the missing women."

And nothing had been found afterward, either. The Jamison brothers and Carl's wife Sandra had walked, making noises about false arrest as they went.

"What about the bartender from the place the second missing women was last seen? He remembered her talking to a woman with red, curly hair," she reminded him.

"Last I heard, the Orphan Annie look wasn't a crime. A fashion faux pas, maybe, but not a crime."

"Fashion faux pas?" she echoed incredulously. "I thought the boys from *Queer Eye for the Straight Guy* were still upgrading the men around New York. If the Fab Five migrated north, why are you still dressed like a mannequin from the men's department at Sears?"

A sudden clamor of footsteps in the hall forestalled Quaid's retort. He stepped aside as the homicide cops entered the room. Both of the newcomers were familiar; Ben Cerulo and Kimberly Jackson. Both were good cops and, once, both had been Gwen's friends.

Their faces, already rendered grim and pale by the sight before them, hardened when they saw her. "What's she doing here?" Cerulo demanded of no one in particular.

"Leaving," Gwen responded. She turned to her former partner. "That is, if you've got everything you need?"

"Not yet," Quaid said softly. "But then, the Jamisons weren't the only wrong people to walk away, were they?"

Three

꙰ The rest of the day rounded out the hellish morning. First came the grim task of calling Lauren's mother in Chicago, then there was another trip to Lauren's apartment to return her purse and break the news to her tearful roommate. She was still there when Quaid called her down to the station to give a formal statement.

Today's visit to her former place of employment had proved, as if more proof were needed, that she could never go back. She'd followed Quaid into the police station, trying to pretend that she didn't hear the whispers or see the angry stares.

Frank Cross, Gwen's first partner, had frequently claimed that no one on earth could hold a grudge like a pissed-off cop. The collective force of their resentment still battered at Gwen as she sauntered out of the station, wrapped in the fragile armor of her teen-slut persona. And because their memories of her downfall and its aftermath were so strong, they followed her as she drove home—eighteen miserable months of bad memories, and every minute as immediate as the six-o'clock news.

After the debacle at Winston's, after Tom Yoland's death, Gwen had waited out the usual leave of absence that followed a deadly discharge of weapon, made enlightened noises during the usual counseling, answered the usual questions from Internal Affairs. Then she'd gone back to work, expecting people to tip-toe around for a few days before things went back to normal.

But everything had changed. Conversations stopped when she entered a room. People she'd worked with for years treated her with cool distance or open hostility. That saddened her, but Gwen could have dealt with it. She'd been a loner most of her life and knew how to make that work. Alone was one thing; be-trayed was a whole different story.

Her boss had sent her undercover to get close to Tiger Leone "by any means possible" and then denied ever assigning her to the case. According to him, she'd asked for a leave of absence. The paperwork allegedly granting it had disappeared, along with just about everything else pertaining to the case.

Fortunately for Gwen, that left the department, and her boss in particular, in a very embarrassing position. It was in every-one's best interests to smooth things over as quickly as possible. Gwen was not thrown off the force, but she was definitely left in professional limbo. To make matters worse, Internal Affairs was not as eager to see the matter dropped as was her boss. The ques-tions kept coming, with no end in sight.

Tom Yoland might have spoken for her. Honestly, Gwen wasn't sure anymore. He hadn't been happy about some of her methods, and he'd been furious about her assignment to shadow Tiger Leone. They'd fought about it, and at battle's end he'd requested a new partner. So even though they were work-ing the same case, she'd gone deep undercover and hadn't seen him for months.

He'd seemed different that last night. In fact, he'd looked at her as if he had never seen her before. Maybe people just didn't look the same to each other when their eyes met over the barrel of a gun. Yoland had seemed . . . sad, maybe. Gwen didn't know what to make of that. Most likely he'd thought she'd gone wrong.

He certainly wouldn't be alone in that opinion. A lot of ugly accusations had made the rounds. No case of hers had seemed too old for scrutiny, no action too insignificant to escape suspicion. Although no criminal charges had stuck, after a while the situation started wearing her down. The last straw was Quaid's betrayal.

Gwen was convinced that he'd left her alone with the Jamisons longer than he'd had to, and that he'd neglected to secure, if not actually destroyed, potentially damning evidence. Apart from that incident, however, he seemed like a pretty decent guy and a good cop. That was the kicker: If Quaid wouldn't back her up, most likely no one would.

Her landlady's house came into view—a lovely old brick house surrounded by mature trees and a tall, wrought-iron wall. It was a serene place, a haven from whatever the day had thrown at her. The sight of it made Gwen's spirits lift. With a little luck, maybe she could leave her memories—and everyone else's— outside the gate for a few hours.

Her apartment was over the detached garage. Nothing fancy, but it did have one of those old-fashioned showerheads that made no pretense of conserving water. She couldn't wait to stand under the wonderfully punishing spray until some of the day washed away. An hour or two might make a dent.

A sleek silver sedan was parked beside the gated drive. For a moment Gwen was tempted to keep driving, to circle around until the car moved on. Her landlady wasn't expecting company; this was her day to visit the Foxwoods casino with her blue-haired, blue-blooded girlfriends. The visitor was most likely a new client. Gwen was in no mood to take on a new client, a new problem. A new heartbreak.

But part of her living arrangement included security, and she couldn't ignore the fact that some unknown person was loitering on Sylvia Black's property. Gwen swore under her breath and jerked her car to a stop behind the sedan.

She swung out of her Toyota and strode over. A slim, fair-haired woman, probably in her late thirties, lowered the window and gave Gwen the usual skeptical once-over. To her credit, she was less obvious about it than most.

"Gwen Gellman?"

"That's right."

The woman extended a perfectly manicured hand. "I'm Dianne Cody. Stephen Weiss said you might be able to help me."

Oh yeah—Stephen was nothing if not helpful. What he liked to call helpful, however, was more like Gwen's idea of controlling and manipulative. Potayto, potahto, and don't let the door hit your ass on the way out.

"Oddly enough, I should have seen this coming," she muttered. What better way to cap off a thoroughly horrible day but for her ex-boyfriend to start sending her clients—his latest "shiksa goddess," from the looks of her.

"Excuse me?" the woman inquired with icy politeness.

Gwen pulled her thoughts back to the matter at hand. "Never mind. What exactly is the problem?"

Dianne Cody hesitated. "Is there somewhere we can talk privately?"

There was no one within earshot, but Gwen didn't see any profit in pointing this out. She told the woman to follow her, then returned to her car and used the electric gate opener. They pulled into the drive and parked beside the garage. In addition to space for two cars, the bottom floor of the garage had a small room that Gwen used for an office. She led her visitor into the room and gestured to the pair of wingback chairs, castoffs from her landlady's last redecorating binge.

Her visitor sat, smoothed a nonexistent crease from her linen pants, and folded her hands in her lap. Gwen noted the matching wedding ring and diamond solitaire, and adjusted her assessment of Stephen's involvement with Dianne Cody. Stephen did not do married women. That was the sum and total of his moral code, but he was admirably consistent about it.

Gwen settled down behind her desk—a computer table, actually, complete with the usual hardware. Her notebook computer was pushed to one side. She shoved it a little farther away, brushed her hand on the leg of her jeans to remove some of the accumulated dust, and gave Mrs. Cody a go-ahead nod.

"I want you to find my daughter, Meredith. She disappeared four days ago."

Damn it to hell and back. A missing kid, four days gone. She didn't have the energy for this. But even as the thought formed, Gwen realized that her soul-deep weariness had disappeared.

"How old is Meredith?"

"She's fourteen."

Not good, Gwen thought. Girls aged ten to fourteen were in

the group most likely to be targeted for violent crimes: rape, abduction, murder. In addition, Dianne Cody's clothes and car suggested that the family had enough money to catch some enterprising scumbag's attention.

"Is there any indication of a kidnapping? A ransom note, a call demanding payment?"

"Nothing. She just . . . disappeared."

"Could this be the result of a custodial dispute?"

It was the first question to ask, since a lot of kids disappeared along with one parent. Dianne Cody's eyebrows lifted slightly: mild surprise, nothing more. "Her father and I aren't divorced or separated."

Not exactly a rousing endorsement of marital bliss, but Gwen could relate. "Have there been any problems at home recently?"

"Nothing out of the ordinary."

Sometimes it didn't have to be anything major, Gwen observed. The early teen years could be a pressure cooker, even for the pampered children of privilege.

"At fourteen, Meredith would be, what? In eighth grade?"

"No. She's a high-school freshman."

"Where?"

She named a private school in the East Side.

"When and where was Meredith last seen? School, home, the mall?"

"At home. She disappeared during the night."

"Was she alone when you last saw her?"

"Yes, of course."

"Of course," Gwen repeated, making it a question.

"It was a school night. Sometimes she has a friend over, but only on weekends."

Gwen settled back and regarded the woman with interest. Usually two or three questions were enough to prime the pump. By now, information about Meredith should be pouring out in a jumbled flood.

The mother's responses were too composed and far too brief. In Gwen's experience, parents of missing kids had a lot to say. Lauren Simpson's mother had kept her on the phone for nearly an hour, inundating her with information about her daughter, thinking it might help but mostly just needing to talk about her kid. Parents were like that, apparently, even in the best of times. But here was Dianne Cody, asking for help but doling out answers one word at a time.

That made very little sense. After all, Dianne Cody had come to her. Maybe she had a secret or two, but parents who had something to hide tended to be even more talkative, mostly elaborate disclaimers and careful explanations. Gwen moved on to the more difficult questions.

"Was your daughter involved in any high-risk behavior?"

The woman smiled thinly. "Not unless you include field hockey. Meredith is a good student, an excellent athlete."

"So to the best of your knowledge, no alcohol, no drugs."

"She has too much sense to get involved with drugs. As I told you, she's an athlete. She takes that very seriously."

"Okay." Taking another approach, Gwen folded her arms on the table and leaned forward, a posture meant to invite confidences. "Tell me about the rest of the family."

"The children?"

"Sure. Let's start there."

"Meredith is the oldest. We have two boys, ages ten and seven. Ryan Junior and Chip."

They named a kid after a golf shot. Somehow, that didn't surprise her. "Who watches the kids? A housekeeper, a nanny?"

"We have a part-time housekeeper, but I don't work outside the home."

"And Meredith's father?"

"He's an attorney."

That would explain the rings, the gorgeous linen jacket, and the spiffy car. "What kind of law does he practice?"

There was a short pause. "Why don't you just come right out and ask if he has any enemies?" Impatience and derision played a faint duet in her voice.

Interesting, Gwen thought. "Does he?"

"He's a criminal attorney. He is very good, but no one wins every case. So yes, it's possible that he might have a few disgruntled clients. It's even possible that someone might threaten our family."

"But you don't think that's what's happening here," Gwen observed.

"No, I don't. We had a threat once before, and my husband insisted the family take every precaution."

"Such as?"

"He had a new home-security system installed and bought a trained dog. The children weren't allowed to visit friends or play outside until the matter was resolved. The children's schools were made aware of the situation and extra precautions put in place. I never went anywhere alone, at my husband's insistence."

Dianne Cody's recital was offhand and slightly impatient, as if she were describing a not particularly interesting episode in someone else's life.

Even now, Gwen noted, she didn't seem to be taking these precautions seriously. Was she one of those sheltered women who believed nothing could go wrong in her little world; nothing, at least, that her husband's energy, influence, and affluence couldn't fix?

It didn't escape Gwen's notice that Mr. Cody had made all the arrangements and dictated the terms. Yet here was Mrs. Cody. Maybe she'd decided she had reason to take things into her own hands.

"This time there was no threat, no warning, nothing out of the ordinary," Gwen summarized.

"That's right. Meredith simply disappeared. She said good night and went to her room. The next morning she was gone."

"Was the security system disturbed?"

"No. It was turned on, and it was functioning properly. There was no indication that anyone attempted to enter the house."

"So what's your theory?"

Dianne Cody lifted her chin, took a deep breath. She met Gwen's eyes in a challenging gaze, as if daring her to refute what was next to come. "I suppose the logical conclusion would be that Meredith ran away. But I swear, there was no reason why she would do something like that."

Gwen nodded slowly, agreeing with the first part of Dianne Cody's assessment, if not the second. When kids ran, it was usually for a reason. With girls this age, incest was a grim possibility.

No sense asking the mother—they never knew what was going on, even if they did know.

"I'll need some information about Meredith," Gwen said, reaching into the table drawer for some of the forms she'd developed. "Her friends, her favorite haunts, and so on. I'll need a picture, as well."

"I brought all that with me." Dianne Cody took a large white envelope from her shoulder bag. "Everything is there, along with phone numbers and addresses. Her school, her coaches, her music teacher, her pediatrician, her friends, and the families she babysits for. Everyone I could think of. There's also a schedule listing Meredith's classes, practice times, and extracurricular activities."

Gwen rifled through the papers. The people who touched Meredith Cody's life had been cataloged and organized into neat, computer-generated lists.

"This is good," she said. "It will save a lot of time."

"The police have wasted four days. Four days." Her voice broke, and suddenly the weight of those four days—every minute of worry and fear, every grim possibility her imagination could conjure—was in her eyes. She turned aside, blinking rapidly. The strength of her will and the fierceness of her private battle was almost a tangible thing. It filled the room, as palpable as heat or fragrance.

Control was very important to this woman, Gwen noted. She wouldn't allow herself any lapse, any unauthorized show of emotion, not even at a time like this. It wasn't an easy way to go through life, especially for a fourteen-year-old girl.

Mrs. Cody cleared her throat and turned back, her composure

firmly in place. "The picture was taken shortly before Christmas. Meredith hasn't changed her hairstyle since then."

Gwen pulled out the photo, a professional studio portrait of a smiling girl in a red sweater. Meredith Cody was pretty, with her mother's fair coloring and a slim, athletic build. Shoulder-length blond hair skimmed her shoulders, shiny as a shampoo commercial. Her face glowed with health, and her eyes were a vivid blue that probably got a boost from cosmetic contacts. Meredith looked pampered, confident, and perhaps a little proud, more than a match for anything she might encounter in her secure little world.

And completely unprepared for whatever she might have found beyond it. She was in Gwen's world now, and may God help her.

She looked up at the girl's mother. "I'll find Meredith."

Dianne Cody's blue eyes studied Gwen's face for a long, silent moment. Finally she nodded and stood to leave. She paused at the door. "About your fee."

"Time, plus expenses. I use a sliding scale."

"According to what your client can afford," she broke in. "Stephen told me about some of your work. But in the interest of saving the time it would take you to figure out my husband's credit rating, I would rather set a flat fee now."

Gwen lifted one eyebrow and held up Meredith's photo. "It's a good thing I'm still holding this. It helps me keep focused on what's important."

Dianne Cody's face flushed. "I hope you're not implying that money is more important to me than my daughter's safety."

The long day caught up with Gwen in a sudden rush. "No,

I'm implying that you're an ice-cold, self-important bitch who just insulted me. And trust me, the fact that you know my ex-boyfriend is no point in your favor."

The woman actually smiled a little, conceding the round and, surprisingly, looking rather pleased by her defeat. Maybe her life was short on worthwhile battles and interesting opponents. Or, more likely, she was relieved to have someone take charge of a situation she herself could neither understand nor control.

"So what is it?" Gwen asked.

Dianne Cody frowned in puzzlement. "Excuse me?"

"The flat fee you had in mind."

"Oh. Ten thousand."

"I'll take it," Gwen said. After I find Meredith, I'll give you an accounting of my time and expenses. Anything left over, you get back."

A bleak expression crossed the woman's face. "The only thing I want back is my daughter." She turned and fled for her car.

Gwen watched the sedan skitter down the gravel drive. After it rounded the corner, she hit the wall-mounted button that closed the gate. She reached for her phone and punched the speed dial for Marcy's number.

"District attorney's office, answering for Ms. Bartlett," announced a crisp tenor voice.

That would be Jeff Monroe, Marcy's latest assistant. Most of Marcy's assistants were men. This criterion was not exactly politically correct, but it addressed a certain practicality: Marcy had an eye for the ladies, and Trudy, her life partner, had a jealous streak. Jeff was the best of the nonthreatening bunch. He was competent, likable, and, just in case, not quite good-looking enough to give Trudy any sleepless nights. In Gwen's opinion, he looked a lot better once the suit, tie, and shirt came off.

"Hey, gorgeous," she purred.

"Gwen!" His voice warmed considerably. "Please tell me this is a social call."

"Don't I wish."

"It never hurts to dream," he said cheerfully. "Ms. Bartlett just got back from court. I'll put you right through."

Soft chamber music floated through the line—Vivaldi's *Seasons*, only not the right one. Marcy picked up before Gwen could figure out whether this particular movement was "Summer" or "Winter."

"Gwen, I heard about the Jamison arrest. Congratulations." She paused. "I also heard about Lauren Simpson, and how you found her."

"Yeah."

Another pause followed, a sympathetic silence that invited Gwen to talk if she wanted, move on if she didn't. As a lawyer, Marcy was relentless. As a friend, she knew when not to ask questions.

"Listen, I need to get your read on one of your colleagues. A criminal attorney by the name of Cody."

Marcy switched gears without comment. "That would have to be Ryan Cody. Yes, I know him. What's this about?"

"His daughter is missing—disappeared four days ago."

A grim silence stretched between them. Both of them knew the possibilities, many of which they'd learned from experience. Some professional, some personal.

"And he came to you?"

Gwen understood all too well Marcy's incredulous tone. Most members of the legal community tended to avoid cops who left the force under a shadow.

"No. The mother did."

"Interesting," Marcy mused. "She doesn't want him to know."

That had occurred to Gwen. "That's possible, yes, and it does raise some fascinating questions. What can you tell me about this guy?"

"He's a tough opponent. I've lost a few to him."

"That must have stung." Marcy didn't like watching criminals walk away unless they were accompanied by a bailiff.

"It always does," she agreed. "But as far as I know, the guy is a straight arrow. My occasional rant to the contrary, defending criminals doesn't make you one."

"That's what they say."

"Uh-huh. Maybe this time they're right."

Gwen heard an unfamiliar note in Marcy's voice. "Is there any reason why I shouldn't take a closer look at this guy?"

"No . . ."

"Four days, Marcy," she reminded her. "Four. If the kid's still alive, chances are she won't be for much longer. I don't have time for a tap dance."

"I'm just saying you should use a little discretion until you know more about Ryan Cody."

"You make it sound as if I'm out to ruin the guy's reputation."

"That's not my intention."

Gwen silently counted to three. "Look, are you going to talk to me, or not? If you can't, fine—just say so and I'll get to work. In the dark," she added meaningfully.

Marcy sighed. "You have such a way with guilt. Okay, it's probably nothing, but here goes. A few months ago, one of Cody's former clients came after him. For a while there was extra security around the courthouse, a bodyguard in a size-forty-six suit following Cody around and pretending to be an attorney, that sort of thing. Before anything happened, the client was found dead."

"Convenient. You think Cody had something to do with that?"

"Nothing pointed to it. Apparently the client had a difference of opinion with a couple of his former associates. To all appearances, it was another example of 'Those who live by the sword, die by it.'"

"But?"

"I'm not suggesting that Ryan Cody was involved in the man's death. In fact, it never occurred to me that he might be."

"Until now."

"Well, even the most well-mannered dog will attack if it feels cornered. And they say that after a dog has attacked once, the second time comes more easily."

"I'll keep the canine metaphors firmly in mind," Gwen promised. "I should probably check out the dead client and his pissed-off associates. Mrs. Cody didn't think there was any connection to the daughter's disappearance, but I still want to take a look."

"Of course. I'll get some information together, enough to get you started, at least. Can I e-mail it to you?"

"I'll swing by your place later."

Marcy let out an exasperated huff. "Girl, what the hell do you have a computer for?"

"Show, mostly. People come into an office, they expect to see one. Can I stop by, or not?"

"Of course. It's just—"

"Seven-thirty good for you?"

"Make it seven. We're going out later."

"Deal."

Gwen hung up and dragged herself out of the chair. The long, hot shower of her dreams would have to wait, but there was time to fit in a quick one. Long ago, she'd learned that this was a good way to approach a double shift. A shower tricked your body into thinking a new day was starting. You could keep going for a long, long time with the help of coffee and a few judiciously timed showers.

"Caffeine, hot water, and the occasional psychic moment," Gwen mumbled as she trudged up the steps to her apartment. "Oh, yeah. That should do it."

Four

ᕼ Marcy Bartlett lived in a newly renovated building on North Main, in a two-bedroom condo sparsely decorated in a Danish Modern. Very sleek, very blond. It suited Marcy.

She met Gwen at the door wearing a slim black dress and the kind of pumps best reserved for the opera or theater, anywhere that dancing—or for that matter, walking—wasn't a big part of the package. Her thick ash-blond hair was cut in a wedge that tapered at the nape of her neck but kept the crown full. She'd fluffed it up for evening and brightened her makeup. Her business-length nails were painted a bright red. Rubies sparkled at her ears, and a matching ring winked as she handed Gwen a glass of red wine.

"Elderberry," Marcy said flatly, wrinkling her pert nose in good-natured disdain. Years ago, she and Gwen had stumbled upon a winery in rural Massachusetts specializing in fruit wines—blueberry, cranberry, whatever. Gwen discovered that she preferred them to vintage wines, which wasn't saying much. Still, it was nice of Marcy to keep the fruity stuff on hand for her.

She sipped the wine as she followed Marcy into the apartment. Trudy Wasserman was perched on the arm of the white sofa, also dressed in evening-out black, though her style ran more to flowing layers with asymmetrical hemlines. She was a pretty, petite woman, several inches shorter than Gwen's five and a half feet. Her light-red hair was cut in a sleek, chin-length style, and her clear gray eyes and pale, almost luminous complexion announced that her hair color was the work of Nature, not a talented colorist. She smiled at Gwen, but her eyes were not entirely friendly.

"Good to see you again," she said with polite insincerity.

"Same." Gwen lifted her wineglass as if in a toast. "Happy anniversary."

Trudy's smile brightened, turning genuine and a little girlish. "I know it's a little silly, a ten-months anniversary," she confided, "but I love celebrations."

"So, what did you get her?" asked Gwen. She glanced from Trudy's frozen smile to Marcy's stricken face. "Oh, shit. Don't tell me I've spoiled the surprise."

The redhead recovered quickly. "Well, I was saving it for later, but what the hell." She hopped off the arm of the sofa and headed for the bedroom.

Marcy groaned and sank down onto the nearest chair, covering her eyes with both hands. "God, I have *got* to start putting personal data into my PDA on a regular basis. Not that I would have remembered this. How the hell did you know about the ten-month thing?"

"I didn't," Gwen said. "But you two are going out on a school night, in the middle of exam week. Trudy's an English professor, which means she has a pile of essay exams to wade through. She's so conscientious I figured she had to be celebrating *something*."

"She bought a gift," Marcy muttered. "An anniversary gift.

Those things never go one way, do they? Jesus God, I am so screwed."

"You would have been, if you'd forgotten the occasion." Gwen reached into the pocket of her jacket and took out a small velvet box, which she tossed into Marcy's lap. Her friend glanced at it, then lowered her hands and sent an inquiring look up at Gwen.

"My landlady keeps giving me her old stuff, gifts from admirers she doesn't want to remember. This is art deco, she said. A little funky for your taste, but it looked like something Trudy might wear. Sylvia was about the same size when she was younger, so it should fit."

Marcy opened the box and glanced at the antique ring. "Christ, it's a gaudy son of a bitch!"

"Too much?"

"Hell, no. She'll love it. I owe you, big time," she said fervently.

"We'll settle up after I look at the Cody file."

"There's not much," Marcy warned her as she reached for an envelope on the coffee table. "Names and dates, a few details. If you want a copy of the police reports, I can get them, but it will take a little more time."

"This will get me started."

Trudy came in, beaming, carrying a new tennis racket. Gwen suppressed a smirk. After ten months, you'd think Trudy would have figured out that Marcy's complete lack of interest in anything with balls included her exercise program, not just her social life.

"Well, I'll leave you two to your evening. What's on the agenda?"

"Trudy got tickets for the Providence Mandolin Orchestra," Marcy said.

This time Gwen couldn't quite hide her smile.

"It might sound a little strange, but it's one of those uniquely Providence things," Trudy said earnestly. "Like the Waterfire events, or Buddy Cienci's spaghetti sauce."

"Say what you will about our former mayor, the man makes a damn good marinara sauce," Gwen said gravely.

Trudy turned to Marcy in triumph. "You see? Not everything is a political statement. To paraphrase Freud, sometimes spaghetti sauce is just spaghetti sauce."

"Freud, ethics, mandolins, and tennis." Gwen touched her fingertips to her temples as if slightly dizzied. "Much as I'd love to party with you crazy kids, I've got to get back to work."

Marcy's face turned somber. "Give me a call if you need anything."

"Count on it."

Gwen waited until she was back in her office to open the envelope. It contained a single page, but the information Marcy had pulled together was actually a bit more than names and dates.

Nearly a year ago, Ryan Cody had received threatening phone calls from Joseph Perotti, a contractor who'd been swept up years ago in a government corruption probe. Cody had defended Perotti, but not successfully. The man had completed nearly three years on a ten-year sentence, made parole, and promptly disappeared. He made the calls from hiding, and according to Marcy's information, none of the calls had been traced. Perotti died in a car crash several days after his last call to Ryan Cody. His brakes failed. The car, which was registered to one of Perotti's drinking buddies, had been in for repairs the day before. It came out that the head mechanic, Sal Almeida, was brother-in-law to one of the men Perotti had implicated during his trial.

To all appearances, it was the sort of situation that prompted people to shrug and say, "As long as they're just killing each other . . ."

There were times when Gwen had no argument with that philosophy. But once a fourteen-year-old girl was involved, things started to look different.

She made a photocopy of Marcy's information and then put Meredith Cody's picture in the scanner. While copies of the missing girl's photo slowly peeled out into the printer tray, she started working through the information Dianne Cody had left with her.

She started going down the list of Meredith's friends. The results of her phone census were pretty much what she'd expected: No one had seen Meredith, no one had any useful information. Oddly enough, some of the parents of Meredith's friends were unaware that the girl was missing.

That didn't make sense. The first step in finding a missing child was to contact her friends. Why would Mrs. Cody make such a detailed list and not contact the parents herself? For that matter, why hadn't the police followed up?

Gwen took a Rhode Island map out of her files and started checking addresses against responses. The parents who were aware of Meredith's disappearance all lived in the Codys' neighborhood. Those who did not were scattered over the city and into suburbs and nearby towns.

The most likely explanation was that the uninformed were parents of Meredith's school friends. The elite private academy drew students from all over the state. But why would Dianne Cody collect the phone numbers of Meredith's school friends and not make the calls?

It would be interesting to get the school's take on the situation. Gwen made a note to call the office in the morning.

She glanced at the wall clock. It was well past ten, too late to be calling on polite society. She dialed the number of one of her own contacts.

Gwen idly counted the rings. Usually it took her friend at least seven or eight to hunt down her cell phone. Tonight Gwen counted a baker's dozen.

"Sister Tamar. Who the hell is this?"

An involuntary smile curved Gwen's lips. The older's woman's voice was a scratchy growl, the legacy of decades of chain-smoking and a fairly accurate reflection of her personality.

"Real nice, sister. You take communion with that mouth?"

"Oh, it's you. Figures. Everyone else who's got my private number knows how to tell time."

Affection rang through the gruff words. The two women shared a common cause and a history that went back to Gwen's childhood. Sister Tamar's unorthodox choice of vocational name said a lot about the aging nun. It was a biblical name, taken from an Old Testament tale of a girl who was raped by her brother and then cast out in disgrace. Sister Tamar took things like that very personally. She ran a home for runaway girls, most of them victims of some sort of sexual crime. Despite her vocation, she was hooked into informational channels that most social workers didn't know existed. According to Sister Tamar, this kept her weekly confessions interesting.

"I'm wondering if a runaway girl might have come across your radar."

"Far too many of them," the nun observed. "What's your girl's name?"

"Meredith. She's fourteen. Pretty, blond, athletic."

No sense giving a last name, since Tamar wouldn't have known it anyway. She never asked. Her concern was offering her girls privacy, safety, and confidentiality. As a result, people came to her who were afraid to go anywhere else.

"No one here right now fits that description. But send me a picture, and I'll make inquiries."

"Thanks. Is there anything I can do for you?"

There was a long moment of silence. "As a matter of fact, there might be," Tamar said softly. "There's a new house in North Providence."

Gwen didn't have to ask what Sister Tamar meant. Some of the runaways at St. Agnes had escaped from prostitution. Not streetwalkers, but children held prisoner in private homes in quiet neighborhoods. These sex houses were small operations running four or five girls, often sent from other countries to live out short, miserable lives defined by isolation, terror, and sexual slavery. Gwen had helped take down two of these houses in the last five years.

"You know I'm not on the force anymore," she reminded the nun.

"All the better," Tamar said crisply. "You know the story of Judith, don't you?"

Gwen rolled her eyes. This was another grim Old Testament tale, this one about a heroine who lured an enemy general into her tent, made damn sure he was tired and happy, and cut off his head while he slept.

"A little bloodthirsty for a nun, aren't you?"

"If I were ten years younger, I'd do it myself," Tamar said savagely. "One of my girls came from that house. She got to the Polish-speaking church a few blocks away. They sent her to me."

"A Polish girl?" Most of the girls came from Mexico or South America, but there was also an influx of European girls lured with the promise of a glamorous life in the States.

"Russian. The languages are close enough that they could communicate. Here's a thought." A sly note entered the nun's voice. "Sophie said there were three other girls in the house, all of them fair-haired. You might want to look into it, see if your Meredith might have landed there."

It wasn't likely, and they both knew it. These girls were kept isolated by the fear bred of brutal treatment, but the language barrier was another highly effective safeguard. The odds of finding a local runaway in one of the sex houses were slim to none.

"If one girl went missing, they move the others," Gwen pointed out. "How long has Sophie been away?"

"She came to me this afternoon. It took me three hours just to get the address from her. You know how intimidated these girls are. Fortunately, I know a little Polish, so we could communicate. And she's Catholic," Tamar added glumly, "with an old-fashioned respect for a proper sister."

Despite the gravity of the situation, Gwen grinned. "Don't tell me you pulled the old black-and-white out of mothballs."

"We all do what we have to. And some of us, not one damn bit more than we have to."

Her meaning was unmistakable. "Tamar, you know I'd love to help, but the girl I'm looking for has been missing for four days."

"Nice family? Middle-class home, maybe a little better?"

"Yes, but—"

"Then her people called the police. You know what happens when I'm forced to do likewise."

Gwen knew. The girls went into the system, which had to be hard on them. Eventually most were sent home, which was worse. For many, there was nothing waiting for them but disgrace. Not infrequently they were "resold" by their families into a situation similar to that which they'd escaped.

She took a deep breath and yielded to the inevitable. "Okay, fine. Just give me the freaking address."

CHAPTER

Five

Several hours later, Gwen crouched behind an untrimmed forsythia, a sprawling fountain of spring-yellow flowers that filled half the small front yard. More flowers bloomed along the walk—a few daffodils, planted by kinder hands in better times. There was nothing about the place, however, to indicate that the residents were not law-abiding, flower-planting citizens.

The address Sister Tamar had given her was a small clapboard house, set in a working-class neighborhood and looking not a bit out of place.

Later on, once word got out, the neighbors would probably express surprise. Yes, they'd seen the owner from time to time. He seemed a pleasant sort, but he was quiet, kept to himself, yadda yadda. But now that you mentioned it, yes, there did seem to be a lot of cars coming and going. Gwen figured she should be used to this by now, but every now and then she wondered what people *did* pay attention to.

An old Chevy Nova pulled into the driveway. A man got out and went to the front door. He waited for several minutes, then hurried back to his car and drove away.

Gwen stayed where she was for a while, watching to see if

the would-be customer stirred any activity inside the house. The lights were on in one of the upstairs rooms, but no shadows played against the drawn shades. None of the cars parked along the street had moved since she'd arrived, about an hour before. No one had come in or out of the house.

Most likely the occupants had fled, but Gwen had to be sure. She slipped out of her hiding place and moved through the shadows to the back of the house.

The lock on the back door was a joke. She popped it easily and slowly opened the door.

The house was quiet, but Gwen would bet that it had been a hive of activity earlier in the evening. She moved from room to room, marking the evidence of a hasty departure. Dirty dishes cluttered the kitchen counters. A plate with a half-eaten sandwich sat on the small table. None of the beds in the upstairs bedrooms had been made. Closet doors were thrown open. Empty dresser drawers gaped. A few articles of clothing were scattered on the floor, either unwanted or overlooked in the apparent haste of departure.

She headed back downstairs for a closer look. One of the downstairs rooms had been made into a bedroom. Probably the pimp's. It, too, had been emptied of anything that might prove useful.

Gwen was turning to leave when she caught sight of a paper lying half under the bed. She stooped and picked it up. It was letter-size, photo weight, glossy. Probably a digital photo. She turned it over.

Her heart leaped, then thudded painfully back into place. A young girl stared out of the photo, not looking at the photographer but Somewhere Else. She couldn't have been more than thirteen, but she had the dead, flat eyes of someone whose spirit had long ago fled.

The girl was posed leaning over a table, arms spread to both sides and small hands clutching the edges. Her blond hair was caught up in two pigtails to emphasize her youth. A faceless man stood behind her, his hands gripping her hips. It was an ugly, explicit shot.

Gwen folded the page carefully, stifling the urge to crumple the vile thing. Sister Tamar would want to crop the girl's face from the photo and circulate it. Sooner or later, one of the nun's contacts would have information that would lead to the girl. It would take a lot more work to find the men who did this to her, but nothing worth doing came easy.

She went out to her car and slipped the photo into an envelope, which she addressed to Tamar at St. Agnes. Instead of a return address, she simply wrote, "Call me. Judith."

Tamar would understand, and approve.

The night sky was fading to silver as Gwen pulled into Sylvia Black's driveway. She took another quick shower, threw on some clean jeans and a T-shirt. For once she didn't bother with makeup, other than the usual liquid makeup to make her too-white skin less noticeable.

She headed for Riverside, a middle-class suburb to the south of Providence. The sun was peering over the trees when she pulled up in front of a small bungalow, a one-story affair that was probably built seventy or eighty years ago as a summer cottage. Frank Cross had purchased it right after his forced retirement.

And from the looks of the place, he hadn't done much to it since then.

The pale yellow paint was peeling, and one window was missing a shutter. The small front yard was a patchwork quilt of grass, weeds, and bare dirt. To call it a "lawn" erred on the side of charity. There was a tiny boathouse out back, a structure that was even more decrepit than the house. Beyond, a small dock.

The property was right on the water, though, and Frank was lucky to have bought it when he did, before real-estate prices leaped into the stratosphere. Gwen suspected that he was having a tough enough time as it was.

Frank opened the door while she was still coming up the walk. At six-foot-four and closing in on three hundred pounds, he was a big bear of a man. His welcoming grin made his square, weathered face almost handsome. He was on the slippery side of fifty, and his short hair was more gray than blond. But if it came to a fight, Gwen wouldn't give even odds to a man half his age.

"Hey, kid." His usual greeting, unchanged after fifteen years. From him, Gwen didn't mind.

"How's it going, Frank?"

He lifted one shoulder, indicating so-so. "Good weather for quahogs. I'm having a late start. You want to come with?"

A few hours on Frank's battered little boat, gathering clams. It was tempting.

"I'd love to, but I'm working on a case. In fact, I came to ask for some help."

Gwen noted, with a pang very close to grief, how the man's eyes lit up at the prospect. Harvesting quahogs had been a life-long hobby, and she suspected it now doubled as an additional means of support. But whatever else Frank Cross might do with his time, he would always be a cop.

She followed him into the bungalow. It was better kept than the exterior suggested, severely organized and devoid of dust and clutter. The decor, however, was utilitarian at best. The only furniture in the living room was a large green plaid sofa and a television, which sat on an old wooden lobster trap. The room that most people would have used for a dining room was dominated by a desk, a clunky old monstrosity buried beneath layers of multicolored paint. The various hues were rendered visible by the dings and scrapes the desk had accumulated in its long life. The computer equipment on the desk, however, was new and first-rate.

It was easy to see where a good chunk of Frank's pension went. He'd spent a lot of time over the last few years learning how to use the computer—taking classes, working out little tricks of his own.

"I need you to Google some information for me," she said, nodding at the infernal machine.

He lifted one brow. "What, you forgot to pay your Internet bill?"

"Hey, that's a thought. If enough of us tried that, maybe the Internet would go out of business."

"Cute, real cute," he told her. "Usually it's the old farts who are scared of technology."

She shoved her hands into the pockets of her jeans. "I'm not scared of it. I just don't like computers."

"If you say so." He winked, teasing her. But he went behind the desk and opened the cover of his notebook. After a few moments of key clicking, he looked up expectantly.

"I need to know everything you can tell me about Ryan Cody. He works for Simmons, Fletcher, and Rye. Criminal lawyers, mostly."

Frank Cross grimaced. He shared Gwen's distaste for lawyers who specialized in undoing cops' work. "This could take a while."

"I'll make coffee."

She headed into the small kitchen and took coffee fixings and a couple of mugs from the cupboard. While the coffee was brewing, she went to the fridge to get out milk. Frank always drank his black, but to Gwen's way of thinking, coffee was like chocolate: it needed milk and sugar in order to reach its true potential. Hell, no one stirred unsweetened cocoa into hot water and considered the job done. Why should coffee be expected to go solo?

The refrigerator was neat and far from full. A few condiments lined one of the door shelves, sliced deli meats and a bag of premixed salad greens half filled the cooler. There was a small carton of milk, another of juice, and a white box of takeout Chinese. The usual stuff, except for a small, half-eaten bakery cake.

That surprised Gwen into taking a closer look. Frank had never been much for sweets, and this stuff didn't even look palatable. The cake was iced in that too-white frosting that tasted like sugar, grease, and chemicals. It had some yellow trim on the edges, and the squashed remainders of what might have been sugary flowers. Gwen flicked off a bit of frosting with one finger. In her mind's eye, she caught a glimpse of a gleeful little boy, sitting in a high chair. His face, hands, and clothes were liberally smeared with chocolate birthday cake.

She closed the door quickly, not understanding what she'd

seen but pretty damn certain she'd intruded on something deeply private.

When the coffee was ready, she poured two mugs, left them both black—no sense advertising that she'd walked in on Frank's memories—and took them into the office.

She set one down on the desk. Frank reached for it without looking up, took a sip.

"There's a lot to know about this guy," he said. "The first layer is about what you'd expect. Went to decent schools, makes a good living, has a house in a nice neighborhood. One wife, three kids in private schools."

"What about the second layer?"

Frank sent her a sidelong glance and a smug grin. "Amazing, what you can find online. He's got some bills, but they're within his income, and his investments are doing okay. There's nothing too unusual about his bank accounts and credit cards."

"You can get into that stuff?" she demanded, genuinely appalled. Not that she actually had bank accounts and credit cards.

"It's not as hard as they'd like you to think. But what was really interesting is this entry right here."

Gwen bent down and read the line he indicated. "It's his name on a membership list. What's the group?"

"Underhill. A gentlemen's club, or so they like to call it." Frank sniffed derisively, took a long pull at his coffee mug.

"Yeah, I'm familiar with it. They've been investigated more than once on reports of employing underaged dancers. I wasn't in on it myself, but I've heard talk. They say some of the girls look like they should be in middle school, but their paperwork is always good. The place seems to be legal."

"Still, you've got to admit it's an interesting after-hours activity."

Especially for a man whose fourteen-year-old daughter had disappeared, Gwen thought. Aloud she suggested, "Maybe he takes clients there. You know—giving them what they want, setting them at ease, that sort of thing."

Frank sent her a look. "It's not like you to give a lawyer the benefit of the doubt. Get a grip."

"Sorry. Must be lack of sleep."

"Here's something that's sure to get a rise out of you." He paged through several screens and pointed to another list. "According to this, Ryan Cody belongs to the same tennis club as your ex." He glanced at her, gauged her reaction. "You don't look surprised."

She shrugged. "Stephen sent Dianne Cody my way, so I already knew he had some sort of contact with them. Plus, it's the sort of thing that happens in Rhode Island all the time. Seems like everybody you meet knows someone you already know."

He nodded, agreeing with her assessment. "Like the Station nightclub fire. One hundred people die, which is a big fucking tragedy any way you look at it, but I'll bet there's not twenty people in Rhode Island who don't know someone there, or someone who knew someone there."

"Two degrees of separation, tops," Gwen agreed.

"Seems like any time shit hits the fan, damn near everyone in the state gets splattered." Frank paused, grimaced. "And speaking of shit, you should probably call Weiss. He might be worth a lead."

"That's a little harsh," she commented. "Stephen has

his faults, but I never figured what you had against him."

"What's to figure? He wanted you to quit the force, settle down behind some white picket fence. That's not you."

She thought of the image she'd gotten of the little boy with the chocolate birthday cake. "It's not for everyone."

"Damn straight. Some people are better off on their own, and we're two of them."

"Yeah, probably." Gwen rose to leave, took the sheaf of papers Frank handed her.

"One more thing." He opened a desk drawer and took out a small metal device, thumb-size and thumb-shaped.

"What the hell is this?" she demanded.

"I thought you said you knew about computers," he taunted her. "It's a flash drive," he said. He rolled it between his fingers like a man about to savor a fine cigar, then placed it on the papers Gwen was holding. "Great little device. You'll love it."

"What's it do?"

"Plug it in the USB port—that's a little rectangular hole in the back of a computer—and it'll download the files. You never know when something like this will come in handy."

She rolled her eyes, but she put the gadget in her jacket pocket without further comment. Not that she wanted it, but arguing with Frank Cross stood very high on her list of Things Not Worth Doing.

Which is why she didn't bother to tell him that talking to Stephen Weiss wasn't next on her agenda. There were less painful ways of getting information. Even if those thong underwear that dancers wore were as uncomfortable as they looked, she figured she'd still come out ahead.

CHAPTER

Six

Gwen studied herself in the antique oval mirror that stood in the corner of her bedroom. Her skirt was black and short enough to show off almost the entire length of her legs, which were clad in spiderweb stockings and her high-heeled ankle boots. Her black push-up bra was clearly visible through the black mesh of her cropped shirt. A spray-in hair color lent her the solid, light-eating black favored by Goth chicks and Vampyre wannabes. Her skin was naturally pale, so for once she left it alone. False lashes and mascara rimmed her eyes. Artfully applied shadow made them look enormous, and Halloween-quality cosmetic lenses made the irises a solid, unfathomable black. The only color anywhere was her lips, which were painted the precise hue of fresh blood.

Gwen nodded, satisfied. In this getup she looked about fifteen years old, especially once she added a sullen pout. The outfit would definitely get her noticed, and it had a sort of teen-slut appeal that the club's clientele would probably find appealing.

She ran down the stairs and out to her car. Her landlady was in the garden, studying the spring growth twining its way up a rose trellis. Gwen raised a hand in greeting.

The woman's gaze sharpened. "Where have you been keeping yourself, Gwenevere? I haven't seen you for days."

Stifling a sigh, Gwen walked over to the garden to play catch-up. Although she valued the woman's advice and enjoyed her company, the newspaper ad in her pocket was very precise about the audition hours for would-be dancers.

Sylvia Black would never see seventy again, but she was still beautiful in an aristocratic fashion that was part attitude, part architecture. She had gorgeous cheekbones, and the lines of her jaw and neck were still drawn with clean, dramatic sweeps. Her white hair was full and glossy, gathered back in artfully informal coils. Even for a quiet day at home, she dressed with old-money elegance: tasteful touches of gold at her throat and ears, low-heeled Italian shoes, a two-piece slim-skirted red dress that looked as if it belonged on Park Avenue. Or possibly Nancy Reagan.

The older woman looked Gwen up and down, then lifted one carefully penciled eyebrow. "Since you've obviously become gainfully employed in a time-honored profession, perhaps I should raise your rent," she said dryly.

Gwen grimaced. "You're not far off. I'm applying for a job at Underhill, a club—"

"I know of it," Sylvia broke in. "The owner and I had common business interests some years back. Ian Forest. Lovely man."

"A client?" she asked, surprised. If that was the case, the club owner would be pretty long in the tooth. Sylvia Black hadn't worked as a professional companion for nearly three decades.

The woman sent her a sidelong glance. "Young lady, you know I don't discuss business secrets. I didn't earn a small fortune by being indiscreet."

"Oh yeah? I thought they used to call it 'an indiscretion' back in the day."

"Only if 'it,' to borrow your charming turn of phrase, ceased to be discreet and entered the public knowledge. But back to the matter at hand. Can you dance?"

Gwen shrugged. "Sort of."

"Sort of," Sylvia repeated. She sighed and shook her head in a gesture of what's-this-world-coming-to resignation. "In my day, dancing was considered an accomplishment. Ladies had ballroom dancing, of course, and often several years of ballet."

"Good for flexibility," Gwen murmured.

"Quite," the old woman readily agreed. She looked Gwen up and down again. "Your outfit is very . . . striking. But I think a touch of lipstick would improve matters considerably."

"I'm wearing some. Lots of it, in fact."

"On your lips, yes."

"Then what—"

"Please." Again Sylvia hoisted that expressive eyebrow. "You did mention that there would be dancing involved? At the Underhill club?"

"Oh. Right." Gwen gave herself a mental slap on the forehead. By now she should be used to Sylvia's habit of addressing tawdry things in ladylike terms and a forthright manner. It was better, she supposed, than coming right out and saying, "If you're going to dance topless, do something to draw the eye to those little boobs of yours, something that doesn't make your prospective employers and clients think about cup size. A little judiciously applied red paint ought to do it."

"That's a good color for you," Sylvia said, studying Gwen's face. "Very dramatic. The color contrast provides a strong focal point. Or two, as the case may be. Do you have the lipstick with you?"

"Um . . ."

"Well, run along and fetch it. You can touch up before your performance."

Gwen managed to keep a straight face until she got into the apartment. Nudity had never bothered her—she'd never understood why people put so much importance on what was and wasn't covered. But the image of herself prancing around stage with red-tipped boobs put a grin on her face. Why stop there? Why not add a few concentric circles and provide the audience with a pair of targets? For a price, the freaks could rent those little handheld Nerf crossbows with foam arrows and try their aim.

She grabbed the lipstick from the dresser—no doubt Sylvia would demand to see it—and started back out.

But she faltered as she passed the mirror. After all, it was seldom smart to disregard an expert's advice. Sylvia might look as if she came from old money, but her house and portfolio were gifts from her last gentleman friend. Obviously she knew what worked.

Gwen shrugged and peeled off her top. Her bra was so low cut that she didn't have to remove it—she could easily tug the fabric down under her breasts.

She was uncapping the lipstick when she heard footsteps on the stairs. Sylvia sometimes came up unannounced when she knew Gwen was home and alone.

"Come to supervise?" she called out.

An appreciative masculine chuckle came from the open doorway. "Only if there's nothing I can do to help," said a too-familiar voice.

Gwen whirled, hands on her hips. Stephen Weiss, her former boyfriend, leaned against the doorpost, arms folded. He was smiling, but his brown eyes glittered with something darker than amusement.

She had to admit he looked good—too damn good for her peace of mind. He'd let his wavy dark hair grow longer than usual, and his cream-colored sweater clung to his lean, athletic form. He wasn't a tall man, just two or three inches taller than Gwen. The words "perfect fit" came vividly to mind. Very vividly. It was a great image, but not one she had time to entertain.

"What the hell are you doing here?" she snarled.

He gave her his most charming smile. "Fantasizing?"

She sniffed and reached for her shirt. Stephen crossed the room and took it from her hand. "Great idea, but won't that smear?" he asked, nodding to the tube in her hand.

"It's supposed to be kiss-proof," she informed him.

This intelligence brought a wicked grin to his face. "Well, in that case . . ."

Gwen slapped the palm of her free hand to his chest and pushed him off to arm's length. "Forget it."

"Hard to do. I have an excellent memory."

"Then you'll probably recall that we're not dating anymore. Even if we were, I don't have the time for this right now."

"Whatever you say," he said softly. But he ran one hand up her outstretched arm, then moved his fingers lightly across her shoulder to trace her collarbone.

A delicious shiver followed his touch like a shadow. Gwen didn't have many modesty issues, but there was something weirdly erotic about being in her bedroom with her former lover. She was half psyched for the audition ahead and wearing a bad-girl costume. It was all so . . . convenient, maybe. After all, here they were. Gwen's libido was singing, and it was easy, so very easy, to fall into old patterns, to welcome familiar sensations.

But Gwen never trusted anything that came too easily.

She flung her arm out in a wide circle, tossing Stephen's hand aside. His confident grin proclaimed that he was all too aware of her growing response.

It was hard not to be. To Gwen, arousal was like a scent perceived with the skin rather than the nose, an almost tangible presence in the air around her that brought to mind woodsmoke and night-blooming flowers and dark green places. No man had ever described it in quite those terms—or anything close, for that matter—but they seemed to sense it. Jeffrey, Marcy's cute assistant, had said something about pheromones. That seemed as good an explanation as any for what was happening here: a chemical bypass of the heart and brain.

Stephen stepped in closer. He captured both of her hands in his and brought them to his shoulders.

Gwen didn't resist. She let the lipstick tube fall to the floor and splayed her hands against his chest. But when he leaned in for a kiss, she hooked one foot behind his ankle and shoved, hard. He tumbled to the floor with a mumbled oath.

She spun and stalked from the room. Stephen lunged after her and seized one stiletto heel. The unexpected stop sent her sprawling to the floor, facedown. An unexpected chuckle burst from her. Despite her annoyance, this was starting to be fun.

"Nice move," she congratulated him. Before he could respond, she rolled onto her back and kicked out, hard. Her foot met air—he'd already moved aside. He made a quick grab and his hand closed around her ankle.

She started to struggle, then remembered what she was wearing. "If I get a run in these stockings, you're dead," she promised him.

"Take them off," he suggested with a grin.

As much as she hated to admit it, the idea held more than a little appeal.

"You first," she purred.

Stephen sent her a wary look, but he was not a man to lightly abandon any opportunity to get naked. He released her ankle and rose to his feet, watching her as if he thought she'd disappear if he so much as blinked. He peeled off the sweater quickly, waited for her reaction. Gwen nodded encouragement. With a shrug, he undid his belt.

She waited until his pants were well south of his knees before she launched herself off the floor and into a flying lunge.

But this was not the first time they'd wrestled, and Stephen had learned a few of her tricks. His arms closed around her and brought her down with him. They tumbled to the floor together, laughing.

Stephen rolled her underneath him, pinning her firmly. He propped himself up on his elbows and smiled down at her. "I thought you'd come around to my way of thinking."

Her breathing was a little faster than the mock struggle could justify. "You always assume that," she informed him. "Have I ever told you that you're an insufferable bastard?"

"It does sound familiar." Stephen brushed his cheek against hers, moving her face slightly to the side so he could nip at the tip of her ear.

Lust shimmered through her like golden light. "If you don't let me up, I'll kick your ass." Eventually.

Stephen lifted his head. "You're a black belt," he said, smiling. "If you'd wanted to, you could have handed me my ass by now, twice over."

She seemed to remember that it was a very nice ass. Her hands slid down his back and refreshed her memory. "You never know. I might yet."

"Yeah, right," he murmured. "Seems to me you're exactly where you want to be."

"Maybe."

He slowly lowered his face to hers until their lips were barely touching. "Old time's sake?" he murmured, punctuating the question with a little nip at her lower lip.

Gwen's sigh of surrender came from some deep and primal place. "I've heard worse reasons."

His kiss deepened, and his hands tangled in her hair. She met him eagerly, turning the kiss into a fierce duel. Her legs came up to wrap around his waist, and her body curved in a feline arc that lifted them both from the floor.

Then she twisted, flipping them over. In one fluid movement she was on her feet and dancing out of reach.

Stephen propped himself on one elbow and sent her a dazed and puzzled frown. "What the hell's gotten into you? I could have sworn you were right with me."

"And then some," she said truthfully. Her body was screaming at her for ending the fun, but she turned to the mirror and started adjusting her clothes. "I've got an appointment, and these things take more time than I have right now. But thanks for the warm-up."

He sat up abruptly. "Warm up for what? What kind of appointment?" he demanded.

Gwen shot a quelling glance over her shoulder. "I'm working a case. By the way, I suppose I should thank you for the referral. Is that why you stopped over?"

"Partly." He rose and started to collect his scattered clothes, then came to stand behind her so their eyes met in the mirror. "I came to tell you that I've been offered a job in Boston. It's a good opportunity. I'll probably take it."

The smile she sent his reflection was quick and genuine. "Congratulations. You've been dying to get back to a real city. Your words, not mine."

"You'd like Boston. Why don't you come with me, give it a try," he suggested.

This, she hadn't expected. She spun to face him. "You're not serious."

He considered. "You know, I think I might be. Why not? It wouldn't be the first time I asked you to marry me."

Gwen sniffed. "Forget it. You only proposed because you knew I'd just laugh at the whole white-picket-fence scenario you had going. What's changed since then?"

"Well, for starters, my mother's nagging me to settle down with a nice Jewish girl."

"Hello?" She spread her arms wide and invited his inspection. "Are you blind, or are you trying to give your mother a stroke? Besides, who says I'm Jewish?"

"With a name like Gellman, you're sure not Italian," he pointed out. "And when it comes right down to it, you really don't know what you are."

That stung more than it should have. "Oh yeah," she sneered. "Gwenevere Gellman, the Jewish-Arthurian princess. Camelot by way of Long Island. Oy, it's the grail! Sure, your mother would buy that."

He took a step toward her. "It's worth a shot."

"Is it?" she countered. "Half the appeal our relationship held for you is that you knew damn well it wouldn't go anywhere. It didn't, but I have to. I'm running late—do me a favor and lock the doors when you leave."

She pushed past him and strode out of the room before he could launch a rebuttal. Sex with Stephen tended to take up a considerable amount of time and energy, but once he started arguing, the lustiest marathon was, in comparison, a stand-up quickie.

Fortunately, Sylvia was nowhere in sight. Stephen had parked behind Gwen's car, but not so close that she couldn't cut a tight circle onto the grass and go around. Gravel spun under her tires as she hurtled down the drive, silently cursing herself for wasting so much time. If she hurried, she might just make the audition.

The drive to the club took about fifteen minutes. Underhill was amazingly close to the business district, discreetly tucked into the second floor of a sedate brick building.

Gwen took a long breath, steadying herself for the task

ahead. Unfortunately, the effects of her unsettling encounter with Stephen lingered, as if he had left fingerprints on her every nerve ending. It was, she thought glumly, a hell of a way to audition for a strip club. At this rate, she'd leave the place feeling happier than the customers.

She swung out of the car and sashayed to the club, feeling as if she were moving to the pulse of inaudible music that was as sultry as jazz but far more tension-filled and edgy.

She presented the newspaper ad to the bored young woman sitting at the reception area and was waved into the club.

The place was a model of discreet decadence. Open doorways on both sides of the reception area led up stairways to the mezzanine encircling the main room. The center of the room was open with a high ceiling, but a ring of booths, privacy ensured by dark glass, encircled the club. Tables were scattered throughout the room for those less concerned about privacy than proximity. It was hard to slip bills under a G-string when there was smoked glass between you and the dancer.

Several girls, none of whom looked a day over sixteen, stood on the stage, listening intently to a middle-aged woman with an oversize clipboard and overprocessed blond hair. Some of the girls were smiling, others waiting with expressions so intense Gwen assumed they were actively willing the woman to speak their names. Three girls, faces slack with disappointment and bruised pride, were already gathering up their things.

Even though Gwen should have been focusing on the stage, her gaze was pulled to a man standing at the far side of the room, just beyond the range of the soft lighting. Though he was little more than a silhouette, Gwen instinctively knew that he was staring at her. There was a force to his scrutiny that formed an almost tangible connection between them. An image of glittering motes dancing in a sunbeam came to mind, and she could almost feel the warm, bright shaft of sun on her skin. The warmth spread through her, and the scent of woodsmoke and wildflowers became almost overpowering.

Gwen snatched her gaze away. Heart pounding, she catwalked toward the stage.

The clipboard woman noticed her, and a pinched expression crossed her face. "Auditions are over."

She stopped, silently cursing Stephen for distracting her from the job at hand, and herself for allowing the distraction.

"One moment, Althea," suggested the man in the shadows.

His voice had the same disconcerting effect as his gaze. It was deep and warm, with a touch of some indefinable accent. He moved into the light, and Gwen's mouth actually watered. The man was tall and lean, with black hair and eyes nearly as blue as her own. His face brought to mind fallen angels.

The blond woman frowned at him. "All the openings have been filled."

"Make another."

She made an exasperated sound. "We haven't even seen her dance!"

"Haven't we?" He turned toward Gwen. "Walk to the stage, if you please."

She walked, feeling as if she were moving through a haze of sunlight and woodsmoke. With each step the sensual pull between her and this man became more intense.

The dancers seemed to sense that something unusual was

taking place. Their eyes followed Gwen as she came to the foot of the stairs. She glanced up at one girl and was startled to see the hunger in her eyes.

"You see, Althea?" the man concluded. "That's what she can do by simply walking across the room."

His eyes met Gwen's, and the expression in them was strangely intimate, knowing. "Choreography can be learned, but not chemistry. Young lady, welcome to Underhill."

With that, he turned and disappeared into a darkened doorway. Althea waved the other girls on their way and came over to Gwen.

"Name?" she demanded.

"GiGi Silver," Gwen said, giving the name on her fake ID.

"All right, GiGi, you start tomorrow. We rehearse from noon to five. When I think you're ready, we'll schedule performances." She peeled a sheet off the clipboard. "Fill this out and bring it with you."

Gwen glanced at the forms. "Age, Social Security number, birth certificate." She gave the recital a rising inflection that turned the recital into a question.

"We can help you get your paperwork together," Althea said. "Bring whatever you have with you tomorrow."

"I've got it now." She gave the woman a rueful smile. "In case, you know, age was a problem. Most people think I'm a lot younger than I really am."

She handed over a driver's license that gave her name as Gwen G. Silver and her age as nineteen. It was a good forgery, but Althea's lips twitched as she studied it.

"I've seen better," she said flatly as she handed back the card. "See you tomorrow. And lose the contact lenses. The rest of the look is okay, but the black eyes are just creepy."

"You got it."

Gwen sauntered out, making no effect to hide her smirk of triumph. There was no way Althea could know it was inspired by visions of a soon-to-come police raid. If all went well, Underhill's ass would be hers.

Well, not exactly hers. At best, she might find something at the club that Quaid could use to finish the job.

Gwen's bright mood dimmed, and she reminded herself of her reason for being here. Meredith Cody was missing, and the Underhill club was one of the few leads Gwen had.

And come to think of it, there was no earthly reason for her to be so eager to hand Quaid a career-boosting bust.

In a back office of the club Underhill, Ian Forest perched one hip on the corner the gleaming teak desk and sent a complacent smile down at the slim, silver-haired man seated behind it. "I've just hired a rather remarkable new dancer."

"Yes, I know." The older man scowled. "You don't need to tell me the nature of the audition. The essence of it still clings to you."

Ian Forest inspected his fingernails. "Would it interest you to know that I never touched the girl? Never even came close to her?"

The aggrieved expression faded from the man's face. "Go on."

"The wheel of the year turns toward Beltane. The girl senses and responds to it, even if she doesn't know what it is she feels."

The older man rose slowly to his feet, his keen blue eyes intent on Ian Forest's face. "You're implying that she's a member of the Gentry?"

"I sensed Quality the moment she entered the club. Before, if truth must be told."

He shook his head in disbelief. "How is this possible? How could she not know? How could *we* not know of *her*?"

"Obviously the girl was placed among humans secretly, without consent of the council. But the wheel turns, drawing the lost child home. April is nearly past. In a few days it will be Beltane eve, the time of the changeling. What better time to reclaim one of our own?"

"That holds great risks," the man cautioned.

"And an equally great potential for reward," Ian countered. "As we both know, there are those who might consider such rewards worth any risk."

They sat in silence for a long time, each with his own thoughts.

"Bring her in," the older man said at last. "But first, find out who she is. And more importantly, find out *what* she is."

As to that, Ian Forest already had a good idea, but he wasn't ready to share his thoughts.

"Who and what," he said lightly. "If the bloodlines run true, aren't those things one and the same?"

Seven

Gwen dunked a pair of french fries in ketchup and popped them into her mouth. She and Marcy were seated at a corner table of a chain fast-food restaurant, indulging their shared passion for food in which the principle ingredients were salt and grease.

The story of her day's adventure hadn't taken long to tell, but then, she'd left out most of the juicier bits. "I start work tomorrow," she concluded.

Marcy shook her head in disbelief. "You actually applied for a job in a strip club. A gentleman's club," she corrected herself, putting a heavy dose of irony into it.

"If I want to find Meredith, I can't get squeamish about one of the few leads available to me."

"I wouldn't exactly call it a lead," Marcy observed.

"Okay, then how about a coincidence?" countered Gwen. "The father pays big bucks to gawk at jailbait. His club membership lapses, and a few days later, his fourteen-year-old daughter disappears."

"Could be she had reason to run."

"Yeah, and that could be part of the whole Cody-likes-little-girls thing. I'm looking into that angle, too. But I'm telling you, Marcy, there's something else going on at that club."

"Do you have evidence, or is this instinct talking?"

Gwen hesitated. "I'll let you know when I've got something you can use."

"Deal." A sly smile edged onto Marcy's face. "Can I come and watch you dance?"

"In a gentleman's club, a drooling dyke might stand out in the crowd," Gwen told her.

Marcy chuckled. "Heaven forbid I should offend their delicate sensibilities."

"Yeah, the irony did not escape me. Scandalizing perverts might be a worthwhile way to kill a Friday night, but what would Trudy say?"

The blond woman winced, then grinned. "Yeah, there's always that."

They subsided into comfortable silence, devoting their attention to decimating the small haystack of fries heaped between them.

Why, Gwen wondered, couldn't men switch gears as easily as Marcy did? A few years back, she'd helped Marcy get rid of the abusive son of a bitch she'd married. It hadn't been easy or pretty, and when the dust finally settled and the therapy started to kick in, Marcy realized that she was seriously attracted to women in general, and Gwen in particular. But that wasn't Gwen's style, and eventually Marcy had moved past it. They'd stayed friends. No problems. *Stephen,* on the other hand? Problem.

Marcy picked up a wad of napkins and began to wipe the evidence of chicken nuggets off her fingers. "So, what's next?"

Gwen pulled her thoughts back to business. "I'll make some calls tonight to people who deal with runaways."

"Most of them on our side of the law, I hope."

"Some of them," she said casually. "And first thing tomorrow morning, I'm going to Cody's office."

Her friend regarded her in silence for a long moment. Gwen resignedly prepared herself for another lecture about caution.

"You're not going to wear that outfit, are you?"

This wasn't what Gwen had expected to hear, and it brought a grin to her face. Yeah, a short black skirt and spiderweb stockings might raise some eyebrows at Simmons, Fletcher, and Rye.

"I'll wear something the current Queen Elizabeth could consider dowdy," she promised. She nodded to their shared tray. "You finished with that?"

Marcy picked up one of the few remaining fries and took an experimental nibble. Her nose wrinkled in distaste. Gwen understood completely. The peculiar alchemy that changed potatoes into french fries was short-lived. After the first few minutes, they underwent a second transformation into something resembling salty cardboard.

They disposed of the tray and walked out of the restaurant. The only other person in the parking lot was a young Black man, who leaned against a car as if waiting for someone. When they walked past, he pushed himself off the car and started toward them.

Gwen turned to face the kid. Without making it too obvious, she set herself into defensive position—weight on the balls of her feet, arms loose but ready.

"Yeah?" she inquired.

He gave her an appreciative sweep of eyes. "Looking good, girl."

Marcy's hand clutched convulsively at her arm. Gwen shook her off, a little impatient. Her friend might be a tough litigator and dyed-in-DNA dyke, but to Gwen's way of thinking she could sometimes get a little too girlie, not to mention whiter than Wonder Bread. Gwen's outlook was more politically correct: she expected the worst from everyone.

A car started up in the next parking lot, and the headlights cut a swath into the darkness. The young man lowered the hood of his sweatshirt and stepped into the light.

"I've seen you around," Gwen realized. This realization did not prompt her to relax her stance. "You were with Quaid the other day. His new partner?"

"That's right." He tipped his head toward the restaurant. "You got some time?"

Whatever he had on his mind, it was something he was willing to discuss in a public place. She shrugged. "Why not? I could eat."

Marcy's expression of suburban angst gave way to disbelief. "Again?" she demanded.

Gwen slid her a look. "Jealous?"

"Hell, yes. I'm going to have to spend an extra hour in the gym for every one of those chicken nuggets, and you're going back for seconds without even a pang of guilt. I'll bet you get extra fries again, too," she said wistfully.

"Why not? He's buying."

Marcy still looked uncertain. "Call me tomorrow?"

"Absolutely." Gwen all but shoved her friend into her car.

She waved good-bye and then held out a hand to the young policeman. "Gwen Gellman."

He took her hand in a firm grip. "Damian O'Riley."

"You're kidding."

"Afraid not. You gonna make the usual joke about the 'black Irish?'"

"It hadn't occurred to me."

He smiled. "In that case, I *will* buy you those extra fries."

They got their food and settled down at the table Gwen and Marcy had recently vacated. Gwen unwrapped her sandwich with genuine interest, but Damian pushed his tray aside. He took a stack of photos from the front pocket of his sweatshirt and put a picture on the table, a head shot of a twentysomething blond.

"Angela Travers," he said. "She filed a sexual assault report from the hospital. The guy cut her up some, nothing too serious." He looked at Gwen as if waiting for comment.

She took a big bite of her fish-and-mayonnaise sandwich and nodded for him to continue. He fanned four more pictures out on the table, three women and one man. "All three of these women reported a purse snatch. This guy here was mugged in the parking lot of his health club. The weird thing is, they took his gym bag but not his wallet."

"Maybe they thought his wallet would be in the bag. A lot of workout clothes don't have pockets," Gwen observed. She dumped a package of salt on her fries. "Where is this going?"

"Stay with me," he urged. He placed down another picture, a young woman with shoulder-length brown hair. "Just last week, this woman filed an assault report. She was at the movies. A couple of guys behind her were talking, making all kinds of noise.

She tells them to shut the hell up, they get pissed. One of them grabs her by the hair and yanks hard enough to tear out a good-size chunk."

Gwen winced. "That'd hurt like a bitch."

"Uh-huh. She runs out of the theater, rounds up the manager. By then, the assholes were long gone."

Damian dealt a picture of a round-faced man. "Dude meets this pretty lady down at the comedy club, one thing leads to another—that story. They're in the hotel room, her boyfriend comes roaring in. Hits our man over the head, takes his shit: money, watch, jacket. Left the car, though."

"Badger game," Gwen concluded.

"You'd think. But here's the thing: the boyfriend come in *after* they do the dirty deed."

"That is different," she agreed. "Usually the man storms in before things heat up. Saves time, not to mention wear and tear. I've got a question."

One side of his mouth lifted, forming a wry smile. "Just one?"

"Hey, I've got to start somewhere. How come you have these pictures? Since when has the PD been taking mug shots of the victims?"

"We'll get to that. This very fine lady is not what some folk might call a victim. She was picked up for soliciting." He put two photos of an attractive Black teenager on top of the pile. One was obviously a mug shot, the other resembled the rest of the photos.

"Holy shit," Gwen muttered. "That's Jackie Teal, one of Tiger Leone's girls." She looked up at Damian. "Jackie was at Winston's the night of the raid."

"They all were."

She stared at the cop, not quite taking this in. He tapped the scattered photos. "A lot of weird shit been happening to these people. Small stuff, lots of variety. No pattern to it."

"So how did you put it together?"

"There was a camera in the entrance hall of the club. Every damn person came in the front door got his picture took. Makes you wanna know why."

"You got that right," she muttered. Why the hell hadn't this come up during the investigation? Internal Affairs should have been all over this.

"So I started looking around, asking around, seeing what else these party people been up to. I've just been at it for a couple of days, but I found some familiar faces. Like you said, we don't take pictures of the vics, so it's hard to know how many of the people who were at the club that night reported crimes over the past year or so."

"These people are just the recent victims," Gwen repeated.

"That's right. Be real interesting to know what stories the rest of them might tell—you know, the people who didn't file a report or commit a crime since the bust. I don't wanna *think* about how long it would take to track all them down."

He paused, shaking his head at the enormity of it, sighing over the futility. "Fingerprints, that's one thing, but pictures? Even if there was a way to do a computer search on a picture, there's no database for civilian mugs."

"That's not entirely true," Gwen said slowly. "What about the DMV?"

"Motor vehicles?" he said incredulously. "Girl, how many

people you know look like their driver's license? Shoot, those cameras could make Halle Berry look like a fat old homeless man on a bad-hair day."

"I'm not saying it would be easy, but on the other hand, I'm not sure it's impossible. Computers can do damn near anything. This friend of mine told me you can buy a dog collar that will analyze your dog's bark and tell you what mood he's in."

That brought a grin to his face. "Yeah? How's that work?"

"You program in your dog's breed. There's a tiny computer screen on the collar. The dog barks, up pops one of those smiley-face things the kids use online. That tells you if the dog's happy, anxious, scared, philosophical. Democrat or Republican. Whatever."

"No shit," he marveled. "People can't think of no better way to spend their money?"

She lifted her paper coffee cup. "That's what coffee's all about. The good stuff runs about three bucks a cup, which can make a dent pretty fast. So, why are you coming to me with this? Are you working vice, or IA?"

A look of genuine insult crossed his face. "This got nothing to do with the rat squad," he said firmly. "This is all me. It's not even a case, not officially. I'm doing it on my own time."

"Oh, Quaid would love that."

He leaned to one side, hooked an arm over the back of his chair, and sent her a considering look. "Fact is, he suggested it."

This surprised a burst of short, disbelieving laughter from her. "Did he also suggest that you talk to me?"

"That didn't come up in the discussion," he said.

Gwen noted his careful choice of words, the studiously

neutral expression on his face. Interesting. "So? Why are you here?"

Damian studied her in silence for a long moment. "What you said the other day, about the room numbers and the missing women? It got me thinking, you putting things together like that. I asked Quaid about it. You could tell he didn't like talking about it, but he told me about your hunch. Said he should have listened. Even told me you had the best instincts of any cop he knew. Picked things right out of the damn air."

Gwen's eyebrows flew up. "Yeah, he used to lavish me with compliments just like that."

"He's not all that bad. Once he saw I wasn't going to let go of the Winston thing, he suggested I look around on my own time, keep it off the books."

"You wouldn't do your career any favor asking questions around the station that no one wants to hear," she agreed.

"There's still some talk about what went down that night. Some of it makes sense, some doesn't. I thought maybe you could help me sort it out."

"Don't you think that if I could have done that, I would have already?"

"Not while you were on the job," he stated. "There was some bad juju going on there. It binds things up, clouds the Eye." His tone made it very plain there was a capital "E" involved.

She raised one eyebrow into a skeptical arc. "And you think I'm some sort of voodoo priestess?"

"No, not that," he said seriously. "You don't have the right feel. My grandmother was vaudun, and you're something different. Psychic, witch, shaman—I don't know. Whatever you are, it's something I've never seen. And that's saying something. Growing up in my family, I've seen shit shoulda turned me whiter than you."

Because he was so matter-of-fact about this, Gwen admitted, "Sometimes I sense things, usually from handling objects or going to places where things happened. But not all the time. It comes and goes."

"Yeah, but you got a good head on you to make up for the days the magic don't work. I would never have thought of the DMV as a photo data bank."

"I'm not saying that's what's going on. Shit, what I know about computers could be painlessly carved on my thumbnail. The DMV thing just seems like something a computer geek would think up."

"Yeah." He leaned forward suddenly, folding his forearms on the table. "Talk to me," he urged. "What do you think this bullshit little crime wave is about?"

"First off, it tells me the department was wrong about Tiger Leone. He was not his own boss."

Damian nodded slowly. "Yeah, I see what you're saying. Someone besides us got the pictures from that night—probably the camera had some sort of webcam hookup. Someone knows who was there that night and how to find them."

Gwen noted that he included her in "us." Since she wasn't sure how to feel about that, she ignored it.

"The question is, who's the someone on the other end of the webcam."

"Uh-huh." Again he tapped the photos. "And the very next question is, what the fuck?"

"Who and why," Gwen paraphrased. "Think about it: What's the common thread here?"

He raised his hands and spread them, palms up. "You tell me."

"One woman loses a chunk of her hair. Three purses get snatched. Women always carry a comb or brush in their purses. It's like, I don't know, a law or something. And a guy would be more likely to have a comb in his gym bag than his wallet."

He sniffed. "Sounds like some crime-lab geeks collecting samples."

"Exactly," she told him. "Some of the people bled. I'll bet their attackers took off with a blood sample. That could also explain why the badger game went into overtime. If you're looking for variety, a used condom is a good source of DNA. Bet they didn't find one at the scene."

"I'd have to check the report, but you're probably right."

"Seems to me someone doesn't want a pattern to emerge, so they're collecting DNA in a variety of ways: hair, blood, tissue samples."

The cop's face suddenly went slack.

"What?" Gwen demanded.

"You ever meet Kate, the woman Quaid was seeing?"

Gwen noted the past tense but didn't comment on it. "No. Quaid and I didn't chat much. I heard people on the squad mention her once or twice, that's all."

"She dumped him this week. I was sort of there," he admitted. "Not really *there*, you understand—"

"But close enough to hear."

"Yeah. Anyway, she works for the medical examiner. When Quaid mentioned the raid at Winston's, she pitches a fit. Way she was talking, it sounded like she'd been keeping it bottled up for too damn long. It's too hard to get involved with a cop, she never knows when or if he's coming home, there's no telling who's getting pissed off at him and what they might do about it—that story."

Gwen nodded. "I've heard it told."

"Anyway, she goes on like this for a while, really gets rolling. Probably didn't mean to let half of it spill."

"Cut to the bottom line," Gwen advised him.

"The cops who died that night? Someone broke into the lab, cut the bodies up pretty bad."

Bile rose in Gwen's throat. "I never heard."

"I guess folks tried pretty hard to keep it quiet. Out of respect, I thought. Kate's read on this was that the raid on Winston's didn't take down all the bad guys, and they were sending a signal to the rest of us. Could be she was wrong, and someone was collecting tissue samples, like you said. Whatever, it scared the shit out of her, and when Quaid mentioned Winston's and said someone should take a closer look, she lost it."

"Someone should take a closer look," she repeated. "Quaid said that."

"Yeah." Damian blew out a long breath and gathered up the photos. "So if someone is taking DNA from everybody who was at the club that night, what they think they gonna find?"

"It's a good question."

"It's a damn good question, seeing that you're one of those people. So, you going to help find the answer?"

Gwen didn't even have to think about it. "Oh, yeah."

"What, no arguments?" he said, feigning surprise. "Not what I'm used to getting from my partners *or* my women."

His teasing, good-natured though it was, touched a sore spot. It had been a long day, filled with frustrating near misses.

Still, the day wasn't quite over.

"You've already got a partner, and one's probably all you can handle," Gwen observed. She sent him a slow, feline smile. "But I'll bet you can't say the same thing about women."

His face fell slack with momentary astonishment. An intrigued light sparked his dark eyes, and he raised his soft drink cup in salute. "You see how it is? I *knew* you were psychic."

CHAPTER

Eight

೭ Shortly before nine o'clock the next morning, Gwen walked into the offices of Simmons, Fletcher, and Rye. Apparently the law firm was a thriving concern. The reception area was spacious, and the furnishings were either good antiques or excellent reproductions. There were fresh flowers on the reception desk, behind which sat a woman with steel-gray hair and an I-don't-take-shit-from-anyone expression. Men and women in blue or gray suits strode briskly here and there. Self-importance wafted from them like expensive cologne.

Gwen hadn't even tried to look as if she belonged there, but she wore a disguise all the same: trendy, thick-soled shoes with clunky heels, jeans, and a jacket from her collection of high-school and college wear culled from various lost-and-found closets. This one had the name and logo of the school Meredith Cody attended.

She sent the receptionist an uncertain smile. "I really need to talk to Mr. Cody? I'm, like, a friend of Meredith's? You know—his daughter?"

The woman smiled reassurance. "Sit down, dear, and I'll give him a call. What's your name?"

"Fiona Warwick," she said, supplying one of the names on the list Dianne Cody had so carefully compiled.

As Gwen settled down on one of the chairs, her eyes went to the front door. There was no sound, no movement, nothing to draw her attention. All the same, she knew without doubt that there would be something of importance to see.

After a moment a man walked in, moving with the quiet assurance of someone who was very familiar with his surroundings. Unlike Gwen, he looked as if he belonged in the office. He wore a beautifully cut suit in a gray so dark it was nearly black. His tie was a subdued shade of burgundy, perfectly knotted, and his dark hair boasted an expensive haircut and subtle touches of gray at the temples. He wore a watch of some pale metal, either silver or white gold, on his right wrist, and a ring of similar metal on the middle finger of his left hand. His face was extremely lean, with pronounced hollows beneath each cheekbone, and his lips were a thin, straight line. Dark brows shadowed deeply set, hooded brown eyes. His gaze touched Gwen's and moved away without seeming to make contact.

But in that brief moment, she felt the power of his presence like a fist in her gut.

It wasn't sexual, not in the same way her strange encounter with the man in the club had been, but disturbing none the less. Her gaze followed him down a carpeted hall.

"Fiona?"

Gwen jumped and looked up. A nice-looking blond guy in his early forties was smiling down at her. She noted that the smile didn't quite reach his eyes. In fact, he looked more than a little anxious and none too happy to see her.

"Are you Meredith's father?" she asked.

"Yes." He sent a furtive glance around the reception area.

"Why don't you come into my office? We can talk there."

She followed him down the same hall the dark man had taken, into a spacious suite of rooms. In the outer office, a very blond woman in a pale gray designer suit was fussing with a large silver tray. On it was a coffee urn, a pair of mugs, and a plate of fancy breakfast pastries: standard breakfast-meeting fare. Her bright, good-morning smile turned brittle when she noted Gwen at Cody's side.

"Shall I tell Mr. Edmonson you'll be with him shortly?" she asked, disapproval chilling her voice.

Cody appeared to take this in stride. Small wonder—apparently he had more icy blonds in his life than you could find in a Hitchcock film festival.

"Give us a few moments, Ashley," he said, smiling as he ushered Gwen into his office.

Once inside, he shut the door and settled down behind his desk. He gestured to the leather chairs on the other side of the desk.

Gwen shook her head. Once Ryan Cody heard what she had to say, she'd most likely have to get right back up again.

"Thank you for seeing me, Mr. Cody," she said briskly. "I am here about Meredith, but I'm not one of her school friends. My name is Gwen Gellman, and I'm a private investigator. I apologize for the deception, but I thought you might prefer to keep this meeting confidential."

He leaned back and regarded her with narrowed eyes. "You're assuming a great deal, starting with the notion that I might want to talk to you, confidentially or otherwise."

"I know that your daughter has been missing for the better part of a week."

"So you came here hoping I'd hire you to find her?" He let out a short, bitter laugh. "And they call lawyers ambulance chasers!"

"I'm already on retainer, Mr. Cody. We have a mutual friend in Stephen Weiss."

Both of these pieces of information were true, if unrelated. Ryan Cody's eyes widened as he made the desired connection, then narrowed in sharp irritation. The progress of emotions was fleeting—Gwen might not have caught them if she hadn't been studying his reaction so closely. He quickly arranged his features in a warm, almost grateful smile.

"Stephen's a great guy, but I never expected this. Please, sit down. Tell me what you've done so far, and what I can do to help."

It was a good act, Gwen noted. Earnest, convincing, enough charm to make you inclined to like him, but not enough to bring images of snake oil to mind. Oh yeah, he'd be great in a courtroom.

She took the chair he indicated. "You reported Meredith's disappearance to the police?"

"At once," he agreed. He folded his hands on the desk. "Of course, we didn't know she was missing until morning. She might have been gone for several hours by then."

"Do you have any idea why she might have wanted to leave? Any problems at school? Anything out of the ordinary going on at home?"

He gave a helpless shrug. "The usual thing, I suppose. She's a typical fourteen-year-old girl."

Obviously he thought this should mean something to her. Gwen had no idea what "the usual thing" was for a typical fourteen-year-old girl. She'd spent that year, and the ones just before and after it, in juvenile detention.

"Can you be more specific?" she requested.

He sighed heavily. "To tell you the truth, she and her mother haven't been getting along. Nothing serious, I guess, though there are several days each month when I'm tempted to check into a hotel, preferably one in another state. They argue about everything. I'm told it's a very common stage for mothers and daughters."

He gave that comment a rising inflection that invited Gwen's confirmation. She murmured something noncommittal.

"So you've had no contact with your daughter, or anyone who might have seen her, since her disappearance? Nothing to add to the information you gave the police?"

"Yes, that's right. May I ask what your plans are, and what steps you've taken so far?"

Gwen shook her head in feigned regret as she rose to leave. "That would take more time than I have right now, but I did want to touch base with you. Perhaps we'll speak again?"

He stood with her. "Looking forward to it. Can you see yourself out?"

"No problem. Thanks for your time."

Her next stop was the Cody home, which turned out to be a lovely white colonial with a view of the bay. Dianne Cody answered the bell. Her eyes widened, then filled with a mixture of hope and dread.

"No news yet," Gwen hastened to tell her. "I'm just wondering if I could ask you a few more questions, maybe take a look in Meredith's room."

Gwen didn't have much hope that going through the girl's room would help. The extreme sensitivity of the past few days was fading, but there was always a chance she might still get a useful impression from one of Meredith's belongings.

"Of course." Dianne moved aside to let Gwen pass. "Can I get you something to drink? Some tea or coffee?"

"I'll probably hate myself in an hour for turning down caffeine, but I can't stay long." She turned to face the woman squarely. "You should probably know that I went to your husband's office. I implied that Stephen Weiss hired me. Even if Stephen backs me up, it probably won't take Mr. Cody very long to figure out I'm working for you."

Dianne Cody accepted this with a cool nod and no discernible change of expression in her ice-blue eyes. "I suppose you had to talk to him."

"He didn't have much to say. One thing I found interesting, though, was that he made of point of telling me that you and Meredith don't get along. Maybe he already figured you hired me and was sufficiently pissed off to take a shot at you?"

"That's possible, but he's right about Meredith and me," the woman said candidly.

"What's the problem?"

Dianne Cody sighed and touched one hand to her hair, lightly smoothing the already perfect lines. "Nothing serious, you understand. It's just the usual thing."

Again, with the "usual thing." "What do you mean by that?"

"I can show you her room and let you draw your own conclusions," she offered.

Gwen shrugged her acceptance. She followed Dianne through a spotless living room to a broad, curved sweep of stairs. The upstairs hall led past two bedrooms, one of which had the overly coordinated, no-personality look of a guest room, the other obviously belonging to a pair of young boys. Both rooms were neat and orderly. The third door was closed. Dianne opened it and stepped aside.

"Meredith's room has been left exactly as it was," she said.

Gwen moved to the doorway. "Damn," she muttered.

The girl's bedroom was a disaster area, all the more jarring when compared with the immaculate order of the rest of the house. Dianne negotiated a path over to the stereo and hit the On button. Raucous music at high volume blared into the room. She quickly turned it off and sent a telling look at Gwen.

"That's how she likes to play her music," Dianne said. "It's a matter of dispute between us, as is her wardrobe." She pointed to several skimpy garments tossed onto the floor, things that wouldn't look out of place in Gwen's closet. "We also argue about how she keeps her room, how much time she spends on the phone and the computer. Fortunately, she has the discipline to keep up her grades and her music practice, or we'd argue about that, as well."

"Got it. The usual thing," Gwen said.

She studied the chaotic mess, noting the tumble of schoolbooks on the desk, the unmade bed with its scattered heap of stuffed animals, the collection of whimsically painted porcelain cows on a glass curio shelf. Meredith appeared to have enough clothes, jewelry, electronic equipment, CDs, and other pricey crap to keep any three teenagers happy.

"This might be a stupid question, but can you tell if anything was taken?"

"Her backpack is still here, and her suitcase. The money her grandmother gave her for her birthday is still in her drawer."

All of which would be high on a runaway's priority list. Gwen picked her way around the room, opening a few drawers, picking up an occasional discarded item. Nothing gave her any sense of Meredith or any impression of what might have happened the night she disappeared.

Finally she headed back downstairs. Dianne Cody was standing in the family room, staring idly out the glass doors that led to the patio. She turned toward Gwen, a question in her eyes.

"Nothing," she said succinctly. "I thought I'd head over to the school next. Are they likely to have problems with me talking to Meredith's friends?"

"Under the circumstances, I doubt it," Mrs. Cody said. "Ask for Gina Kazlowski, the guidance counselor. She was an enormous help last fall, when our family was under siege."

A missing piece fell into place. "Did you ask Ms. Kazlowski to contact the parents of Meredith's school friends?"

Dianne blinked. "Not personally, no. Ryan called the school. Is there a problem?"

"Just covering all the bases," Gwen told her.

She went back to her car and dialed the number of Meredith's school. The school secretary asked her to hold. Gwen started her car and pulled out of the Cody's driveway while she waited for the guidance counselor to pick up.

"Gina Kazlowski," chirped a bright female voice. Young and cheerful, a smile built into the tone. If the visual matched, she'd have shiny brown hair and a lot of pastel sweater twins. Central casting's idea of the perfect second-grade teacher.

"My name is Gwen Gellman. I'm working for Dianne Cody, and calling about her daughter, Meredith."

"Yes! How is Meredith? We were all so sorry to hear about her cousin."

"Her cousin," Gwen repeated.

"Julia, isn't it? The poor girl. We miss Meredith, of course, but she's doing a very brave thing, spending time with her cousin. It's difficult for anyone, much less a teenaged girl, to watch a loved one go through a terminal illness."

So *that* was how Ryan Cody explained his daughter's absence from school. Jesus, the man had an active imagination! Or a morbid streak.

On the other hand, perhaps the guidance counselor knew more than she was letting on.

"There seems to be a misunderstanding," Gwen said. "I'm a private investigator. Mrs. Cody hired me to look into her daughter's disappearance."

"Oh, no!"

The young woman's response was a shocked whisper, and it came hard on the heels of Gwen's announcement. Her reaction had come from the gut, with no time to invent, prevaricate, or retrench.

She didn't know. Gwen was willing to bet good money on that.

"What happened?" Gina Kazlowski demanded. "Is this connected to last fall's incident?"

"I'm not drawing any conclusions just yet," Gwen said. "And perhaps I shouldn't discuss this any further. I was under the impression the Codys had confided in you. May I assume you'll keep this information confidential?"

"Of course! And I understand completely. Last fall, there was a lot of talk and speculation. It was hard on Meredith—kids her age hate being the focus of so much attention. Of course her parents would want to protect Meredith, especially if . . ."

Her voice trailed off, unwilling to put words to the grim possibilities.

"I'll bring her home," Gwen promised, "and you'll help her make her way back from wherever she's been."

"Yes."

Just that one word, spoken with such certainty and purpose that Gwen found she could forgive the perkiness. She promised Gina Kazlowski to fill her in when she could, and rang off.

On impulse, she dialed the police station and asked for Captain Walsh. The desk officer who answered the phone had a familiar voice, and his manner cooled considerably when she left her name.

Gwen gritted her teeth and waited for the call to go through. "Captain's office," announced a female voice. A faint accent indicated that Portuguese was her first language.

"Mary, it's Gwen Gellman. Don't put me through to the chief—I'm actually calling to speak to you."

There was a long moment of silence. "It was thoughtful of

you not to ask for me," she said, her voice soft and slightly embarrassed. "There's some people here, if they knew—"

"Got it," Gwen said, cutting the explanation short for both their sakes. "Listen, I need to call in a favor. Can you check for a missing-persons report? Meredith Cody, age fourteen. It would have been filed on Thursday."

"Sure. You want to hold?"

"As long as Walsh isn't likely to pick up while you're looking."

"No problem there. He's off somewhere. Hang on."

The connection muted to the flat silence peculiar to on-hold calls. Mary was back on in moments.

"There's nothing on Meredith Cody. Is she is Providence?"

"Suburbs."

"I don't suppose it would matter. I did a statewide check. Nada. Since she's a kid, I looked in the Amber Alerts, too. Nothing there, either."

That fit into the emerging pattern. After a moment, Gwen said, "Thanks, Mary."

"You don't sound too surprised."

"Truth be told," Gwen said wryly, "I'm a hell of a lot more surprised than I should have been."

CHAPTER

Nine

The aged wall clock in Gwen's apartment wheezed loudly, then gave off a single dispirited gong. Only eleven o'clock, Gwen noted, and she was already set for her first day as a teenage stripper.

Her Goth-chick persona was firmly in place, with a bit more red worked in. She'd twisted bits of foil onto the tips of her hair before spraying it with the black temporary color, then used a cotton swab to dab scarlet on the protected ends. A liberal application of gel had turned her short mop into medusalike spikes. As usual, she'd been careful to smooth some of her hair over her ears—her one hard-and-fast rule when it came to grooming. They were, to put it mildly, not her best feature.

The black-and-red theme continued: her high-heeled ankle boots with black stockings, a short black skirt, and a very brief lace-up shirt with a layer of sheer black spiderweb over red satin. She finished off the look with a choker made from a broad scarlet ribbon and fastened with a cameo—a white skull carved in profile, toothy grin livid against a flat black oval.

Her office phone started ringing when she was halfway down the stairs. She picked it up on the fourth ring.

"Stay away from my family," demanded a woman's low,

furious voice, speaking before Gwen could even say hello. "You're fired. Stop looking. Stop everything. Just . . . leave us alone."

It took Gwen a moment to catch up. "Mrs. Cody? What's going on?"

"I changed my mind. Just leave it at that."

"Something has happened to upset you," Gwen said evenly. "You don't strike me as a person who's easily thrown off stride, so it must be something significant. Since that something concerns me, I need to know what's going on."

There was a short silence. "All right, but it would be easier to show you than tell you. Meet me at the Waterfront, near Brewed Awakenings. Do you know it?"

"Yeah."

The line went dead. Gwen shrugged. The coffee shop was easy walking distance from Underhill. As long as Meredith's mother wasn't too long-winded, Gwen wouldn't have any problem making both appointments.

Dianne Cody was waiting for her on the stone plaza outside the shop. Her cream slacks and pale blue sweater said ice princess, but the look she gave Gwen was one of scalding fury.

Her lip curled as she took in Gwen's outfit. "And you wonder why I don't want you working for me?"

"I was making inquiries into Meredith's disappearance," Gwen told her. "Where I'm going, your pretty pastels would look as out of place as my getup would be at an East Greenwich PTA meeting."

"At least today you're wearing *something*," she snapped.

She threw a large manila envelope at Gwen. She caught the envelope, but photos spilled out onto the stone plaza.

Gwen stooped to gather them. All of them were images of her, printed from digital files. And, as Dianne Cody had pointed out, all of them were nude shots. Some were more than a little explicit.

The photos made her feel profoundly uncomfortable, violated. Oddly enough, it was not so much the subject and style of the pictures that disturbed her, but the fact that photos of her existed at all. *Any* photos.

She calmly gathered them and returned them to the envelope, then rose to face the furious woman. "I was a vice cop for over ten years," she explained. "These pictures were taken a couple of years ago, while I was investigating an Internet porn operation featuring underage girls. Without these pictures, it would have been difficult to convince the people involved that I was one of them, and willing to play."

Some of the steam seemed to seep out of the angry woman. "There's more," she said, tapping the envelope in Gwen's hands. "There's a report from the child-welfare services. Apparently you were in and out of foster homes for much of your childhood. You were difficult—running away, getting in fights."

Gwen shrugged. "You hired a PI, not a babysitter."

"But I still bear some responsibility for what you might do in my employ. In one of your foster families, a teenage boy died. Violently."

Even now, with nearly a quarter of a century between her and those dark months, the memory turned Gwen's blood to ice. She kept her face carefully devoid of expression.

"And you're assuming that I was somehow responsible for this?"

Suddenly Dianne looked uncertain, uncomfortable. "After his death, two other girls who'd stayed with that family came forward with allegations of abuse."

It was the sort of statement that came with a built-in question; not, however, a question Gwen was prepared to answer.

"Yes, I heard about that," she said evenly. "But I didn't know those girls and couldn't offer you anything more substantial than rumor. I was ten years old at the time, very small for my age, and was never a suspect in that boy's death."

"You were in juvenile detention," Dianne pointed out.

"Twice," Gwen confirmed, "but not for that. So tell me: How is any of this relevant to Meredith's disappearance?"

Dianne Cody waved one hand as if dispelling a puff of foul smoke. "I don't want scandal of any sort touching my family."

"Your daughter is missing. If I can find her, do the skeletons in my closet really matter?"

Dianne Cody's pale blue eyes focused on her with laserlike intensity. "There are pornographic photos of you on the Internet," she said distinctly.

"True, but that doesn't necessarily spell scandal. Most of the pictures were on a private site. The others were custom jobs— taken for some client's specific request. My pictures aren't easy to find online."

The implications of this hit her. "Actually, that makes it worse," Gwen said slowly.

The woman confirmed this opinion with a grim nod. She took the envelope from Gwen and removed some stapled pages. "Whoever sent this knows a great deal about you. This is a report from your former precinct. You were under review for conduct unbecoming an officer, and you were implicated in the deaths of two policemen."

Gwen snatched the papers from the woman's hands. It appeared to be a photocopy of the actual report.

"Someone really doesn't want me looking into your daughter's disappearance," she murmured.

"Yes, and that person would be me," retorted Dianne.

"That too, but what I meant was that someone doesn't want *anyone* looking too closely. This someone has enough contacts in the legal community to put his hands on police records, as well as documents that should have been sealed. Whoever got hold of my juvenile record is no stranger to the law. More importantly, he knows how to get around it."

Angry red dots appeared on Dianne Cody's cheeks. "If you're implying that my husband is involved—"

"Who reported Meredith's disappearance to the police?" Gwen demanded.

"Ryan did, but I don't see what—"

"He never made the report."

The color slowly drained from the woman's face. "That's not possible," she whispered.

"I checked. There's no missing-persons file on Meredith Cody, not in Providence, not anywhere in the state."

Dianne stared at her with unseeing eyes. Gwen pushed the dazed woman down on a bench—better to sit than fall.

"There's more," she said. "Your husband didn't alert the school counselor, either, except with some story about Meredith visiting a sick cousin. No one contacted any of the parents of her school friends."

"Why would Ryan do that?" Dianne asked helplessly. "Why wouldn't he want anyone looking for Meredith?"

Gwen sat down beside her. "Two reasons come to mind. Either he knows where she is, or he knows why she ran."

"If he knows where she is, why wouldn't he—"

She broke off as understanding came, then shook her head decisively. The vehement movement—or perhaps the return of one certainty in a situation so uncharacteristically beyond her control—brought some of the color back to her face.

"No, that's simply not possible. He couldn't have hurt Meredith. He couldn't have done any of the things you're implying. Ryan's not . . . he's not that way."

Gwen never enjoyed shattering illusions, but it was time to put a few unpleasant truths on the table. "Are you aware, Mrs. Cody, that your husband had a membership in Underhill? A gentlemen's club?"

The euphemism didn't register on the woman's face. "He belongs to a number of social organizations."

"This is a private nightclub with a reputation for employing underage dancers. Exotic dancers," Gwen specified.

Dianne looked dubious. "That's just . . . There has to be some explanation."

"I agree, and I plan to find it. In fact, that's why I'm dressed like this. I'm on my way to the club to start work as a dancer."

"In a nightclub," the woman repeated.

"That's right. I'll keep the job just long enough to poke around. If there's any connection between your husband's membership at the club and Meredith's disappearance, I'll find it."

She shook her head helplessly. "What connection could there possibly be?"

"Your husband's membership lapsed shortly before Meredith disappeared. The membership fees, by the way, are very steep. Maybe steep enough to be some sort of payoff. I'm looking into that. Even if I'm right about a payoff, it could be completely unrelated to Meredith's disappearance. But I'm not ready to make that assumption."

Dianne looked at the envelope containing the photos. "If it was my husband who warned you off, that means he's familiar with . . ."

"My previous work?" Gwen finished for her. "Possibly. Pornography built the Internet. I'm guessing most people have taken a peek at things they wouldn't browse through in a bookstore."

"The idea of Ryan looking at little girls . . ." Her voice trailed off again.

"It's possible that he had one of his investigators check me out," Gwen told her. "Someone who knows how to dig up any dirt worth finding. How did you get these pictures?"

The woman grimaced. "With my morning e-mail. One of the pictures was part of the actual message."

Gwen nodded. Before she'd given up on e-mail, she'd had her share of spam that filled her unsuspecting computer screen with someone's permanent vertical smile.

"Naturally, the e-mail caught my interest enough to prompt me to download the attached files."

"You didn't delete the message, did you?"

"Of course not. I thought it might be possible for someone to trace it back to the source. I'll get you a copy of the message."

Gwen made a mental note to get Frank started on that right away. "So I take it I'm not fired."

The woman smiled faintly. "Not yet, anyway." Her gaze turned searching. "This case you were working on—did you find the people who were selling those pictures?"

"Some of them, yes."

"Where are they now?"

A vivid image came to Gwen's mind: Tiger Leone's face as she had last seen it, made hideous by a bare-toothed grimace and more hate than any human eyes should have been able to hold.

"If my friend Sister Tamar is right about such things, they're shoveling coal in hell."

An expression of fierce approval flashed into the woman's eyes. "I didn't bring your fee with me."

"Stick it in the mail," Gwen said dismissively. "Now, about your husband. Can I speak to him again, or should I proceed with the assumption that he doesn't know I'm still on the case?"

The spark in Dianne Cody's eyes leaped into a blaze. "Oh, he'll know," she said succinctly.

Ten

ᘓ The insistent pulse of dance music greeted Gwen as she walked into Underhill. It wasn't yet noon, but a local band had already set up and was deep in rehearsal. Two of the new girls were onstage, moving tentatively through the steps of a loosely choreographed dance. Althea stood by, hands on hips, watching as critically as a drill sergeant inspecting recruits. She didn't have her clipboard today, but the lack of it did little to detract from the overall impression.

A slinky brunette minced over to Gwen on painfully high heels. "You're one of the new girls, right? Has anyone shown you around yet?" she asked, all but shouting over the music.

Gwen shook her head and gave the girl a grateful smile. She followed her through the club to a door marked NO ENTRANCE. EMPLOYEES ONLY.

The decibel level dropped considerably when the door shut behind them. Her guide leaned against it with a sigh of relief. "Not exactly the Philharmonic, are they?"

"No, but I don't suppose people come here to see *Swan Lake*," Gwen pointed out.

The girl gave a rueful chuckle. "Too true. I'm Sarah. This your first gig?"

Gwen shrugged. "I thought I'd try something different. This has to be better than waiting tables."

"It pays better, that's for damn sure. This is how I'm paying for college. Pre med." She thrust out one foot and scowled at the arch-killing shoe. "Maybe I'll specialize in podiatry. How ironic would that be?"

"Not quite as bad as dancing your way through divinity school, I guess."

Sarah groaned. "Don't let Althea hear you say that. Her mind starts going in that direction, she'll start thinking that maybe wings and halos would make us look more innocent. She's an okay dance instructor, but subtle? The dancers here are supposed to project a fresh-young-thing look, but it's all Ian can do to keep her from putting us in pigtails and little plaid skirts."

"Ian Forest, right? What's he like?"

Sarah considered this. "Old school," she decided.

"There's an old school for strip clubs?"

The girl laughed. "Sorry, that was a little vague. I was thinking in terms of manners, way of speaking. More European than American, maybe."

"Okay."

Sarah pushed away from the door and teetered down the hall. "There's the dressing room," she said, pointing into an open door on the right. "Go ahead and claim any locker that's open. Bring a lock with you tomorrow, if you don't want people borrowing."

"What's down there?" Gwen asked, pointing to the door at the end of the hall.

"Back office. You'll need to drop off your paperwork, if you haven't already. Most likely no one will be there right now, but there's an in-box on the desk."

"Thanks."

"Althea will talk to you about wardrobe, but you might want to poke through the dressing-room closet to see what's there. I'd help, but I need to go practice falling off these damn shoes."

Gwen nodded. "I'll be okay. Thanks."

Sarah picked her way back toward the club floor. Gwen took out the form Althea had given her and walked to the office. She opened the door a crack and peered in. As Sarah had predicted, no one was in.

Gwen slipped inside. She dropped the form into the in-box and went to the low wooden file cabinet beside the desk. Inside was a row of hanging folders, color-coded and neatly labeled. She quickly got the lay of the land and found the folder marked "Expired" in the Membership section.

She opened the folder and took out a computer printout dated the first of the month. Ryan Cody's name was on the list of lapsed memberships. Following the Name column was one marked "Action taken." The form indicated that in each case notice had been sent.

That sounded ominous, until you considered that Cody's name was one of half a dozen. Gwen doubted that each of the members had been pressured by a kidnapping. She jotted down the names and addresses anyway. Might be worth checking.

She replaced the folder and walked into the hall. Althea strode toward her, scowling.

Gwen gestured to the door behind her. "Sarah told me to leave my paperwork on the desk. That's okay, isn't it?"

"Yes, but it's probably worthless," the woman said. "The address on your old ID doesn't exist. The street is legit, but the numbers on that street only go up to forty-four. You listed your address as forty-six."

"Oops," Gwen murmured.

The woman pushed past her into the office. She removed a file from the cabinet and took from it a laminated card.

"This is a nondriver's ID. Less common than a driver's license, and harder to spot."

Gwen examined the card, noting the address in nearby Cranston. "So this is an actual place?"

"A woman's shelter. Quiet, good reputation."

"Nice. But what happens if someone checks into this, like you did with my old ID?"

"The director will back you up. I've already sent your info to her. She'll have a file on you, in case anyone asks. There's not much info in it, but no one will be expecting much. Confidentiality issues."

"A woman's shelter," Gwen repeated. "What kinds of people stay there?"

Althea's lips twisted in annoyance. "Why do you care? You won't actually be living with them."

"But if someone asks, I should probably know something about the place."

The woman conceded this with an impatient shrug. "Battered wives, abused kids."

"Don't I sort of fall between those two categories, age-wise?"

"Don't worry about it. They take in teenagers."

"Just trying to get my story straight," Gwen said.

Althea's eyes narrowed. "Your best bet is to skip the story-telling altogether. I need you onstage in five minutes. Ian wants you performing by this weekend, and unless I'm very mistaken, we've got a lot of work to do."

Three hours later, Gwen hobbled away from the club and its grimly satisfied taskmistress. She kept up the pained limp all the way to the car, even though the heels on her favorite boots were every bit as high as the fuck-me pumps she'd worn onstage. There was no point in ruining Althea's fun, and a few feigned blisters would give her an excuse to skip practice if she needed to.

A quick postrehearsal shower at the club had washed the two-toned color from her hair, and she'd dialed down the face paint a few notches. Waiting for her in the car was her leather jacket and a pair of low-heeled shoes. Without the stiletto heels, with her jacket zipped to conceal her skimpy shirt, she looked reasonably respectable.

She drove over to East Providence and found Sal's Garage tucked into the back of a strip mall. The old frame building looked slightly out of place among the chain stores and car dealerships. It was a remnant of an earlier time, stubbornly holding its ground while the new grew up around it.

The waiting room was empty, and the cracked vinyl on the chairs and the scattering of old magazines on the scarred coffee table gave the place an abandoned air. But an older man sat smoking behind the desk, and the faint whir and clatter in the garage behind him suggested that real work was still being done.

"Help you?" he asked in a manner that suggested no discernible interest in doing so.

"Maybe. How well do you know Sal Almeida?"

Something flickered behind his eyes. He sucked at his cigarette, blew a malodorous cloud in her direction. "Sal don't work here. Hasn't for a long time."

"I'm not looking to get my car fixed," she told him. "I'm a private detective, working for someone who's had business dealings with Mr. Almeida. Obviously I can't discuss the case in detail, but I'm looking into the possibility that someone other than Mr. Almeida might have been responsible for Joe Perotti's death. Perhaps one of his friends or family might want to answer a few questions, maybe help him out?"

The old man eyed her thoughtfully. "You should probably talk to his boy. Jimmy. Works over at the cable company."

Gwen thanked him and headed over, calling for directions as she drove. She pulled into the lot, following a white van with the company logo. The van parked near the cable building, close to several similar vehicles.

A tall, sandy-haired woman wearing the cable-company uniform got out of the truck. Gwen pulled up alongside and rolled down her window. "Do you know where I can find Jimmy Almeida?"

The woman pointed to a solitary van on the far side of the parking lot. "Pretty sure that's him over there."

A dark-haired man sat in the driver's seat and seemed in no hurry to leave. His head was down, his shoulders hunched. His left hand cupped his ear. Talking on a cell phone, Gwen surmised, and not about something he wanted advertised.

She nodded her thanks and started over. When she got close enough to get a better look, she pegged Jimmy Almeida for about forty. Whoever was on the other end of the phone was doing most of the talking, and Almeida didn't seem particularly happy about whatever was being said. His thick black mustache and dark sunglasses made his face hard to read, but the iron-trap set of his jaw—and the resulting twitch of muscle in one cheek—suggested his frame of mind.

Gwen tapped on the window. He sent a frown her way and held up a finger to indicate she should wait. He ended the conversation with a few muttered syllables and swung out of the van.

"You the detective?" he demanded.

"I didn't expect that guy from Sal's Garage to call ahead," she said. "Saves time."

"Yeah? The way I see it, you're wasting your time and everyone else's. Sal Almeida fixed the brakes on Perotti's car. He went to jail for it. End of story."

Gwen lifted one eyebrow. "Somehow I doubt that's the story your father wanted you to tell me."

The man folded his arms and leaned against the van. "You want his story, you talk to him."

"I might. Since I'm here, though, maybe you could tell me yours."

The jaw clenched again. He started to take off the dark glasses, changed his mind. His shoulders rose and fell with the resignation of one about to repeat an oft-told tale.

"There is no story," he said wearily. "I put in a day's work, go home to the family. Weekends, I coach kids' soccer and go to Mass. The TV's always on when the Pats play, and every fall the Sox break my heart. There's ten guys just like me on every street."

"You say that like you don't expect me to believe it," Gwen observed.

He indicated the van with a tip of his head. "That's what I do. It pays less than being a mechanic, but some people didn't trust my work. Others wanted me to pick up where my old man left off."

"And that's not something you'd consider."

"That's right." He sneered. "Sorry if that don't fit into your plans."

The surlier he got, the more Gwen was inclined to like him. The apologetic smile she sent him was almost entirely genuine. "I can understand why you don't like talking about this. Believe it or don't, but I wouldn't be here if it wasn't really important."

She paused, letting him decide. After a moment, he nodded for her to continue.

"You remember Perotti's lawyer, the guy he threatened after he made parole? His little girl is missing."

The annoyance seeped out of Almeida's eyes, to be replaced with real concern. "And you think there's some connection?"

"I have to look into it. When a kid disappears, you can't afford to leave any stone unturned."

The guy who coached kids' soccer on the weekends nodded. "What do you want to know?"

"For starters, what all was Joe Perotti into?"

He let out a derisive sniff. "You want to narrow that down some?"

"Okay. Did he run girls?"

"Not that I heard. Gambling and drugs on the side, but mostly he was in construction. He did a lot of work in the area, up by Worcester. Around."

"He was an older man, been around for a while. It's odd that 've never heard his name in connection with the New England nob."

"Perotti was good at keeping his head down. There's talk he got set up back in Ray Patriarca's time. Couldn't stand Junior Patriarca—I guess not many could—but he got on with Bianco. Around then, I stopped paying attention."

Gwen nodded. "So you don't know who your father might have been working for."

"Lady, I don't *want* to know. He says the man who paid for Joe Perotti's brake job would make old Ray Patriarca look like a neutered tabby cat."

"That's a grim thought."

"Yeah. Yeah it is." He lifted one eyebrow. "You sure you want to be in the middle of this?"

"I want to find the kid. I'll go where that takes me."

He studied her for a long moment, his eyes unreadable behind the dark lenses. Then he took a gold chain off his neck, held it out to her. A small charm dangled from it, a twisted horn made from red coral.

"Take this," he said. "Where you're going, you're gonna need it."

Gwen looked at the charm. "Isn't this a ward against the evil eye?"

Jimmy looked as if he were about to say something, then he shook his head. "Just take it," he muttered and stalked off.

She watched him go, then shrugged and put the charm in her pocket. Back in her car, she dialed Sister Tamar's number. One of the girls answered and went to fetch the nun.

"Any luck with your runaway?" asked Tamar, getting right into the heart of things.

"Still looking. There's a shelter in Cranston I want to check out." She gave the address.

"Yes, I know that place, and I don't trust the woman who runs it. Shelter residents tend to come and go, but quite a few of her kids have run off. Since they were runaways to start with, this hasn't raised a lot of eyebrows, but I have my suspicions."

"What's her name?"

"Sherry Fenton."

Gwen let out a long, low whistle. "You've got good instincts."

"You know this woman?"

A vivid memory flashed into mind—an image of a tall, whip-thin teenager, sharp-nosed and sleek as a ferret, crouched on the white-tiled floor of the girls' bathroom. She straddled a new girl: Tashia, part Vietnamese, part African-American, turned thirteen the day before she landed in juvenile. A tough little bitch with a smart mouth. Sherry had ripped off Tashia's towel and was about to administer one of her trademark lessons in respect. In her hand was a large tube of toothpaste—the weapon of choice for a sadistic female rapist. Three other girls huddled against the wall, their eyes rounded with fear and fascination.

Gwen had launched herself at Sherry in a flying tackle, knocking her off the younger girl. Tashia had grabbed her towel and run off, sobbing.

They'd rolled and kicked some, exchanged a few short-arm punches. Gwen couldn't get the upper hand. Sherry was fresh out of the shower, her skin baby-oil slick. She'd bellowed to the other girls, who promptly came to her assistance. The three of them had dragged Gwen off Sherry, slammed her into a wall mirror hard enough to shatter it. Gwen had come up with a shard in her hand just as the matron and her assistants charged through the door. When the dust settled, Gwen's hand had needed eight stitches. Sherry's arm, twenty-two.

All of the girls had named Gwen as instigator, Tashia included. Gwen didn't hold it against her. It wouldn't be the last time gratitude would lose out to scared shitless.

"Yeah, I knew Sherry Fenton," Gwen said softly. "She was in juvenile the same time I was."

"Road to Damascus?" asked Tamar.

Gwen had to think a minute before she made the connection: a biblical reference to some hard-ass prosecutor who changed sides after he found his road blocked by an avenging angel. She wondered, briefly, if Marcy would have budged under similar circumstances. Probably not, and just as well—she couldn't see her friend fitting in with the other apostles.

"I doubt Sherry has changed that drastically," Gwen told the nun, "but she's probably good at making people *think* she has. After she got caught, she figured out how to play the game. She was a real overachiever: good grades, good behavior—at least as long as any of the adults were watching."

"And when they weren't?"

"She was a sadistic, manipulative bitch."

A moment passed as the nun gave her time to elaborate, something Gwen had no intention of doing.

"Any news on Sophie's friends?" she asked. "The other girls from that house in North Providence?"

"Not yet," Tamar said grimly. "But when I find them, you

owe me the head of one heathen general in a hemp sack, or the modern equivalent thereof."

"Those were the good old days."

"Amen," the nun said fervently. She hung up, and the dial tone sang the prayer response.

Gwen clicked off the phone and leaned back into the driver's seat. "Sherry Fenton," she murmured, and for a moment she felt again the long, cold shadow of fear that had followed her through the tough months after that fight.

She shook off the chill and reached into her jacket pocket and took out the coral pendant—the talisman against evil that Jimmy Almeida had given her. A wry smile lifted one corner of her lips.

Would he be surprised, she wondered, to find out how right he'd been?

Eleven

◈ Her cell phone rang as she pulled out of the cable-company parking lot. She palmed the seat for it and picked it up on the third ring.

"Yeah?"

"Is this Gwen Gellman?"

The voice sounded familiar, but the connection wasn't good enough for Gwen to place it. "That's right."

"This is Ian Forest calling."

Her heart suddenly felt like a bungee jumper diving toward the pit of her stomach. It rebounded before it could hit bottom, bounced around a while.

Shit. She was definitely busted.

"Could you come by my office at your earliest convenience? Not the club, but my private office." He gave the address of an office suite not far from where she was.

Gwen considered her options. She'd have to deal with this new development sooner or later, and perhaps if she moved fast she could do some damage control.

"When?"

"Now, if that's possible."

She glanced at the dashboard clock. "I can be there in ten, fif-teen minutes."

"I look forward to it."

She found the office in the allotted time and tried the door on the office suite he'd indicated. It was locked. She tapped at it.

It swung open immediately, and Gwen found herself staring up into a disturbingly familiar face. It was the man at the club, the one who had told Althea to hire her.

From what Sylvia had told her, Gwen had expected a much older man. This guy looked to be in his late thirties. The only service Sylvia could have offered him back in her heyday would have been babysitting.

"You're Ian Forest?" she demanded.

He looked faintly amused. "An interesting question, consid-ering you're the one who auditioned under an assumed name. You were expecting someone different?"

"Someone older," she said, adding hastily, "you seem kind of young to manage a nightclub."

"The same might be said of you and your profession. Few teenage girls take up work as private investigators, or can claim fourteen years on the police force."

He had her there. "If you wanted to warn me away from your club, you could have done it on the phone," she observed.

"Yes, but I'm curious to know what brought you to Under-hill. Please, come in."

There didn't seem to be anyone else in the office, so Gwen followed him into the office and sat down. He pulled up a seat across from her.

"So, how can I help you?" he inquired.

He was being surprisingly reasonable about this, Gwen observed. "You checked me out, you know what I do for a living."

"That is an evasion, Ms. Gellman, not an answer. Perhaps you're looking into that old charge concerning underage dancers?"

She shrugged. It made sense to let him keep thinking that way.

He leaned back in his chair and sent her an easy smile. "By all means, ask your questions. You'll be able to assure your employer that his or her suspicions are groundless."

Before he makes that claim again, he should have a talk with Althea, Gwen thought. "If that's true, then why am I here?" she asked. "You could have kept quiet, let me poke around."

"True, but it so happens that I have a matter of my own that requires such services as you provide. I wish to find the heir to a family fortune."

"Two questions: why you, and why me?"

"As to the first, I'm an old friend of the family. I have long assumed that every member of the family was killed in an accident, but it seems that a child might have survived. I'm asking you rather than another detective simply because you happened to cross my path."

"You've got the wrong girl," Gwen said flatly. "I handle family problems, runaways—that sort of thing. And as it turns out, I'm busy. There are lots of other PIs who can give you what you're looking for."

"That may be so, but since you're here, perhaps you'd take a look at the file? If you decide not to take the case, I'll look elsewhere."

"I don't have the time to look at it right this moment."

He smiled at her. "I never supposed that you would. You're welcome to take the file with you. Get back to me at your convenience."

To her surprise, Gwen actually found herself considering his request. "How can I work for you, if I'm already on an investigation that includes your club?" she wondered aloud.

"The matter is one of considerable interest to me, but no real urgency. Once you've completed your scrutiny of the nightclub, you can proceed without conflict."

Ian rose and walked over to a long, narrow table fashioned from some shining dark wood. On it was a single large envelope. He picked it up and walked toward Gwen.

Their eyes met, and she felt a tug of the strange compulsion that had marked their first meeting.

She leaped from the chair and snatched the envelope from his hand. "I'll take a look at it, but I'm not promising anything," she said as she backed toward the door.

A strange, knowing glint kindled in his blue eyes. "You seem very eager to leave."

"I have an appointment."

His gently chiding smile politely called her a liar. "In that case, we'll speak again soon. And not by telephone, I hope. It allows so few . . . conversational nuances to come through."

He took several steps toward her and extended his hand. Gwen started to reach for it out of habit. She was still several inches short of a handshake when she felt a bubble of energy, as tangible as the heat rising from a stove burner. Power sparked under her fingertips and began to dance through her veins.

She snatched her tingling hand back and fought the urge to scrub it against her thigh. "I'll call you," she said shortly.

His soft, knowing chuckle followed her as she fled.

❦ The past twenty years had either been very cruel to Sherry Fenton, or far too kind. Gwen remembered her as a force, a malevolent crackle of energy that danced even when the girl herself held still. The woman who greeted her at the front door of the oversize Victorian looked like a certain type of suburban mom, softened by resignation and inactivity, bloated by dreams swallowed so long ago they were all but forgotten.

Sherry Fenton was well past plump. Her chin-length brown hair emphasized the perfect roundness of her face. Her shapeless body strained the seams of a fuzzy sweater, cotton-candy pink. There was no recognition in her eyes, but Gwen caught the quick flash of calculation as she decided what the newcomer might be worth to her.

"Can I help you, honey?"

"I hope so," Gwen said tentatively, digging into her pocket for a wallet-size print of Meredith's picture. "My friend ran away from home. Someone told me she might have come here."

She held the picture up at eye level. The woman studied the picture, then her eyes moved slightly to the left—evidence that she was preparing a creative response, not accessing a memory.

A warm smile spread over her face. "It's a good thing you came to me. Which one of my friends sent you?"

Not bad, Gwen thought, but good old Sherry had always been good with a nonanswer. She handed over her new ID.

The woman gave it a moment's study, then lifted her gaze to Gwen's. The suburban softness was gone, and the calculation in her eyes was back in full.

"So you're one of our new phantom residents."

Gwen smiled and nodded. "That's what made me think about coming here. Althea said you got public funding, so I figured that some of your girls are probably runaways for real."

"That's true, but you realize this information is strictly confidential."

"I figured that, but 'confidential' usually means the information is expensive, not unavailable."

Sherry tugged at her earlobe, something she used to do when she was genuinely amused. She moved back and let Gwen into the hall. She did not speak again until they were in the small office just off the entrance hall. She shut the door and leaned against it. Cutting off access—another familiar habit.

"Underhill pays very well. We could set up a weekly payment."

"Too slow," Gwen insisted. She added a note of desperation to her voice. "I need to find Meredith now. I'd do *anything* to find her!"

The woman's assessing gaze slid over Gwen. "There are quicker ways to make money. I know some people who might be able to help you find extra work. Maybe we can work something out."

"Maybe we can," Gwen agreed softly. She lunged forward and grabbed the woman's wrist, twisting it so that her palm was facing up. With her other hand she pushed up the fuzzy pink sleeve.

On Sherry's arm was a long pale scar, a reminder of the fight that had earned Gwen another six months in juvenile.

The woman's eyes went from the scar to Gwen's face. Recognition came then, and with it a jolt of shock. *"Gellman?"*

"You know me," Gwen said softly, "so you also know I mean exactly what I said. There's not much I won't do to find Meredith Cody. If you have any information, it'd be a real good idea to tell me now. Not after I've handed over half of my next six paychecks, not after I've met your friend the pimp. Now."

"This is impossible," Sherry muttered. "You're . . . you're my age!"

Gwen shrugged. "Amazing what clean living and a clear conscience can do for you. What about Meredith?" She punctuated the question by giving Sherry's arm an extra little twist.

The woman winced but didn't try to fight back. "The girl was never here, but I could find out if she's in the system somewhere else."

"You do that. I'll be expecting your call." Gwen took a business card from her pocket and slapped it into the woman's palm. She released Sherry with the same feeling of relief she might have felt upon relinquishing a grip on a snake. Sherry slunk away from the door.

Gwen opened it, then glanced back. "By the way, if you're thinking of calling the people at Underhill, I suggest you ask for Ian Forest. He knows I'm asking around. Althea doesn't. There's always a possibility he'd like to keep it that way."

The former terror of juvenile hall turned paled. "I understand."

Gwen gave the woman a curt nod, glad that one of them did.

She puzzled over this as she drove back through Providence. The prospect of confronting Ian Forest terrified Sherry, and unless the woman had changed even more than her appearance suggested, she didn't scare easily.

The question was, what did Sherry know about Ian Forest that Gwen didn't?

CHAPTER

Twelve

Later that evening, Gwen went to Frank's house for what he called their weekly chowder festival. After the day she'd had, a bowl of quahog soup and some little crackers sounded pretty damn festive.

The scent of sizzling bacon led her into the kitchen. Frank was stirring the bottom of a soup pot with a wooden spoon. "Hand me those onions," he said without looking up.

She passed him a small dish of chopped onions and went to the fridge for the cream. The clams had already been steamed open and chopped in generous bits, and the reserved broth was simmering in another pan. Two long, slender bay leaves floated on the surface.

Frank turned the heat down under the pot, then deftly fished out the bacon strips and dumped them on some folded paper towels. He added the onions to the bacon drippings, stepping back to avoid the burst of fragrant but eye-watering steam. He stirred for a moment, then ladled in some of the broth.

Gwen got bowls from the cupboard and set the two-person kitchen table, then got a pot of coffee going. They worked together in comfortable silence, with the ease of long practice.

Finally they settled down with steaming bowls. Frank waited

until she took the first sip, then handed her the salt shaker, his face a study of resignation. It was a compromise, one they'd reached after years of him nagging her to taste before adding salt.

They ate the first bowl in silence. Seconds were for conversation. It was another familiar pattern, one that suited them both.

"I have a case for you, if you have the time," she said.

His eyes lit up with something much like longing. "I can probably fit something in. Might need to rearrange a few appointments—I've been helping out some at the ten-o'clock meetings at St. Brendan's."

"You're still going to AA?" Gwen asked, surprised.

"It's not like antibiotics, kid. You're not cured after ten days. Hey, don't look so worried. I figured it was time for me to give something back, be a sponsor for someone who's just starting the program. You know the guy. Street person, used to be an informer. He got clean, found a job and an apartment." Frank's face shone with pride in these accomplishments.

"Good for him. And good for you, too."

He dumped a handful of oyster crackers into his soup. "So tell me about this case."

"A missing heir. Some family friend wants to go on an Anastasia hunt. That's all I know, but I brought the file with me. I threw it on your desk on the way in."

"I'll take a look at it later. Any luck with the Cody girl?"

Gwen reached for the pepper mill, ignoring her friend's pained expression. "There weren't many leads to start with, and Ryan Cody's Underhill membership didn't add much to the picture."

"Did you talk to Weiss?"

"Yeah. But I didn't have time to get much information about Ryan Cody. We got sidetracked."

A strange expression crossed Frank's face. He reached for his coffee cup and took a sip.

"He got a job offer in Boston and asked me to come with him."

"To Boston?"

"I turned him down," she assured him.

He studied her over the edge of his coffee mug. "You sure that's what you want?"

Gwen stared at him in astonishment. "This *is* Frank Cross that I'm talking to, isn't it? I thought you couldn't stand the guy."

He shrugged. "My opinion of Weiss doesn't matter. It's how you feel about him that counts." He leaned back in his chair, waiting her response.

"Okay," she said slowly, "I think he's a decent enough guy who doesn't want to settle down with one woman. He was looking around while we were dating."

Anger flashed in Frank's eyes. "That's why you broke up."

She shook her head. "Not really. That is, it wasn't the reason, but it was related to the reason."

"Works for me all on its own," Frank muttered. "You deserve more than a guy who keeps a little something on the side."

"As much as I hate to disillusion you, I *was* the side dish. Or one of them. It turns out Stephen was sort of engaged to a perfectly nice pediatrician. She was the perfect woman for him—professional, attractive, athletic, the sort of girl he could bring home to mama. We found out about each other, and we both dumped him. Me and the doctor, that is," she qualified. "As far as I know, the mother's still in the picture."

"Good for you."

She pushed aside her empty bowl. "I knew he was seeing other people. That didn't bother me. What *did* bother me was his reason for dating me. He called me and the other two side dishes his 'shiksa goddesses.' You know what that means?"

Frank's brow furrowed. "Sounds like some Japanese thing."

Gwen chuckled. "Not even close. 'Shiksa' is a Yiddish word for women who aren't Jewish. The quintessential shiksa is probably a leggy blond, but there's also a semantic undertone of a woman who's unattainable, and therefore desirable."

He lifted one eyebrow. "Been reading the dictionary, have we?"

"I looked it up. I didn't particularly like the idea that Stephen was interested in me because I was unsuitable."

"Can't blame you for that."

"There's also the fiancée to consider. Maybe I didn't expect him to play the monogamy game, but someone else did. I don't like cheaters."

"Goes without saying. So, how did you two get from there to a proposal?"

She shrugged. "That, I still haven't figured out. At the time, he already had a fiancée. Maybe he was comparison shopping. Who knows?"

"One thing I will say for him, he stood by you while everyone in the department was walking around you like dog shit on a sidewalk."

"There's that," she agreed. "What's this sudden fascination with my social life?"

Frank stabbed his spoon at a floating cracker, pushing it

under. Stalling. "You saw the cake in the fridge the other day."

"Yeah."

"I've been getting one every April sixteenth for the past twenty years. That's my kid's birthday."

Surprise jolted through her. "I didn't know you had a kid."

"His mother and I divorced years before you joined the force. I haven't seen my son for over twenty years. His mother moved to Florida and remarried. She thought it would be too confusing for Jason to have two fathers."

"And you were okay with that?"

"Seemed like the best thing to do. As his mother pointed out, I barely knew the boy. I wasn't home enough. You know the job—long hours, late nights, odd shifts. I'd leave before he woke up, and come home after he was in bed. Sometimes weeks went by when I didn't see him at all."

He sighed heavily. "And now the *years* have gone by. Twenty-five of the fuckers. As of last Sunday, my boy has been in this world for a quarter of a century. Put all the hours I spent with him end to end, and you'd have, what? A couple of weeks? Maybe a month?"

Gwen could think of nothing to say. A few years back, this would have been the sort of conversation they might have had at a corner table of a dark bar, with a bottle of Jamison's between them. Not knowing what else to do, Gwen poured them both another cup of coffee. Frank's ironic smile acknowledged the reference. He slurped a little and set the mug aside.

"Maybe Weiss isn't the right guy for you. But forget what I've been telling you all these years. Family's important. Don't be too late in finding that out."

"You can't miss what you never had."

"Are you sure about that?" he persisted. "If you've never had something, how can you know you don't need it?"

"There's a problem with the logic," she said dryly, "but it's so circular I'm not sure where to start."

He shrugged, conceding. "Do you know much about your family?"

She'd told him years ago that she'd been raised in the system, but they'd never gone into any detail. Since he seemed to need to talk about this, Gwen obliged.

"There wasn't much to find out. My parents surprised a burglar in the middle of the night. They were both killed. I went to the state."

"Do you look like one of your folks?"

That struck her as an odd question, but she figured it had something to do with his own situation.

"Hard to say. I've never seen a picture of them. What about your kid?"

"Takes after his mother. She's nearly half Wampanoag, so the boy was darker than me. Probably ended up smaller, too. Donna was a little thing."

Frank shook himself and reached for his coffee. He took a sip. "But it's getting late, and you've got better things to do than listen to an old man go on."

"You're not old, but you're right about the time." She rose. "Maybe you should call your son."

He looked up. There was hesitation in his eyes, and a faint shadow of fear. Gwen had never seen either in his face before this moment.

"I doubt he'd want to hear from me, after all this time."

"But wouldn't it be better to know, one way or another?"

"Yeah," he conceded.

"So?"

"So maybe I'll look him up."

"Don't try to tell me you don't have his number," Gwen persisted. "A man who remembers to buy a birthday cake every April sixteenth tends to keep track of things."

Frank looked a little sheepish. "Maybe."

"Call him," she repeated. She finished her coffee, then carried her bowl and mug over to the sink.

"This missing heir case—how high a priority?"

She turned to face him, leaning back against the counter. "The client isn't looking for a quick resolution. So take your time, enjoy hacking into various databases."

"What's the budget?"

Gwen suppressed a grimace. She'd been so eager to leave Ian Forest's office that she hadn't talked about the fee. "Standard rate. Just keep track of hours and expenses. Soon as I cash the check, I'll bring the money over."

"No hurry. You concentrate on finding the Cody girl."

"Yeah. I'm heading straight to Underhill from here."

He gave her a look. "I thought you said that wasn't panning out."

"True, but I wanted to give it one more look before I move on. Maybe one of the girls knows something about Meredith."

"How likely is that? Let's say Underhill people are involved. They wouldn't keep the girl anywhere near the club."

"Tiger Leone used to move his people around a lot. If the

owners of this club play the same game, one of the girls might have seen her."

"Guess it's worth a shot. Call me if you need anything."

"Thanks, partner." On her way past, she dropped a hand on his shoulder. He reached up, covered her hand with one of his. Gwen waited for him to speak his mind, but after a moment he gave her hand a little pat and released her.

"Later, kid."

Their conversation played and replayed in Gwen's mind as she drove to Underhill. Frank was probably the best friend she had in the world, and what did that say for her? Fifteen years she'd known him, and never once had he talked to her about his son. Of course, she hadn't exactly been forthcoming about her early life, either.

And what about Stephen? Guys came and went—sometimes, almost literally—but he'd stuck around through some tough times. In fact, he was probably the closest thing she'd ever had to a serious relationship. That was pretty pathetic, considering that the guy was engaged to another woman at the time. And she'd had her own secrets; Stephen knew nothing about her psychic moments. In fact, she'd made a point of avoiding him whenever Freak Week rolled around.

By the time she rolled into the club's parking lot, Gwen had concluded that something was seriously fucking wrong with her. Probably that came from growing up in the system: not enough space, not enough privacy, not enough of anything good. You learned to need less and built walls around the little that was yours. The more people you had around, the more you needed to hide, and the deeper the isolation.

Not that unusual, she told herself sternly. Deal with it—everyone else does.

She rejected that thought even as it formed. Thanks to her random little jaunts through other people's memories, she had a pretty good idea what "alone" felt like to other people. The only person she'd encountered whose sense of otherness and isolation rivaled hers was an elderly street woman who gossiped with fire hydrants.

It was a relief to put these thoughts aside in favor of the job. She entered Underhill by the side door and went directly to the dressing room.

Sarah smiled and waved her over. "You working tonight, GiGi?"

"This weekend," Gwen said. "But I wanted to get your opinion on something. I was talking to a friend of mine. She's definitely got the sweet young thing going on, and she can dance. But she's really nervous about the auditions, so I told her I'd bring her picture in, pass it around. I think she'd be hired here, but since we're friends she thinks I'm biased."

Sarah took the picture and let out a whistle. "How old is this girl?"

"Just turned eighteen. I used to date her older brother."

"She's pretty enough."

"My only concern is that she's sort of a type—you know, blond cheerleader, girl next door."

Sarah passed the picture to a well-upholstered Latina. "What do you think?"

The girl glanced at the photo. "Too skinny," was her only reaction.

"That's not possible," disagreed another dancer. She looked at the photo and decreed, "Needs more makeup."

In five minutes, Gwen had gotten opinions from most of the dancers. More important, she had collected impressions. Judging from their reactions, none of them had seen Meredith before.

She hadn't really expected anything different. She'd seen nothing to suggest that there was any connection between Ryan Cody's idea of a good time and his daughter's disappearance, yet all her instincts told her not to cross Underhill and its manager off her list.

Ian Forest had been so certain there would be no problem with the girls' paperwork, even though Althea had blatantly handed Gwen a false ID. But if he had one government employee in his pocket, probably there were others.

Yes, Gwen concluded, it might be very interesting to take a long, hard look at Ian Forest.

She went out the back door into the parking lot. A shadow shifted, and Ian stepped into her path, appearing so suddenly that Gwen got the disturbing sensation that she'd conjured him with her thoughts.

"I meant to tell you earlier today that you look much better without those black contact lenses," he observed. "Women seldom try to camouflage their beauty, but you do it at every turn."

"Yeah, whatever. Listen, I won't be returning to the club. Like you said, you're clean."

"Except for the identification card Althea gave you," he said.

Her eyebrows flew up. "You're very forthright about forgery."

"Why not? It was a deliberate ploy. I assumed you would check out the address."

"You talked to Sherry Fenton?"

He smiled. "You sound surprised."

"I got the impression she'd rather wrestle an alligator than deal with you. She's scared shitless of you."

"I find that saves a considerable amount of time. When I ask questions, she tends to answer. As for the ID, I assumed your curiosity would be piqued. It was a quick way to find out what you were really up to."

Gwen had to admire his strategy. Even if he were lying through his teeth, it would explain—not only to her, but to anyone else who might have reason to ask—why one of his employees had given her a false ID. No doubt Sherry Fenton, if pressed, would agree to anything Ian wanted her to say.

"What did Sherry Fenton tell you?"

"You're looking for a missing girl, a teenager named Meredith Cody. Is she by any chance related to Ryan Cody, one of our members?"

"You know all of your clients by name?"

"We have a very distinguished clientele," Ian said carefully.

"Rich scum," Gwen observed.

"That's an oversimplification. True, some of our members are rather unsavory. In today's business world, perhaps that's to be expected. But our membership includes government officials, business leaders, and quite a few attorneys. What happens at Underhill stays at Underhill. They know the value of that. In fact, many of our clients are invested in the club."

"How about Cody? Is he a part owner?"

"As of several months ago, yes."

"So that's why he let his membership lapse," she mused.

"Did you know that his account was flagged for collection?"

Ian looked mildly annoyed. "A bookkeeping error. Mostly likely the notice was sent on the renewal anniversary as a matter of course."

"You and Ryan Cody are business partners, and you didn't know his daughter was missing?"

"Not until today, no."

"So it's just a quirk of fate that your business partner's daughter—who by the way, would not look out of place on your stage—goes missing?"

His lips firmed. "That's a rather large leap of logic, Ms. Gellman. I own a nightclub. That does not make me a kidnapper or a pedophile."

"But you cater to perverts."

His blue eyes went steely. "I earn a great deal of money from Underhill, but if there is any exploitation in what I do, it is not at the dancers' expense. They are as well aware of the clients' weaknesses as I, and are not above exploiting pathetic fantasies."

"You don't seem to like your clients very much."

"I loath them," he said candidly. "As much as you do. Possibly more. But you and I must make our way among the human slime as best we can."

"Yeah, but that doesn't mean you have to join them."

A strange smile lit his face. "I'm glad to hear you say that. We'll speak again soon, I'm sure."

Gwen was starting to feel more than a little unnerved. "Don't count on it."

"So you've decided not to take my case?"

Oh, yeah. That. She was tempted to tell him what to do with

his missing heir, but the memory of Frank's face when she'd handed over the case stopped her.

"I'll find your guy."

He tsked. "You haven't read the file yet, have you? The heir is a woman."

"Oh. Shouldn't that be heiress, then?"

"Not since the early twentieth century," he said dryly. "The feminine ending seems to have come into considerable disfavor with many women."

"Must be nice to have nothing better to worry about," Gwen said. "I'll take the case, but finding Meredith Cody comes first."

"Understood. Then we have a deal."

She nodded and moved to leave. He stepped into her path and lifted one hand, palm toward her. Without thinking, she laid her palm against his.

Again she felt the strange crackle of energy. It sparked under her hand and spilled down her arm, spreading thought her with golden light. She had a sudden, vivid image of Ian experiencing her in much the same way: a cool blue glow, as intoxicating as starlight.

She dropped her hands, clenched them at her side. "What the fuck was that?" she demanded.

"A pact," he said simply. "An exchange. A handshake, if you will."

She let out a shaky, incredulous laugh. "If that's a handshake, God only knows what you could do with a kiss."

He chuckled, and Gwen realized that she had spoken the words aloud. She bit her lip, mortified.

"Actually, it's not such a closely held secret," he murmured, leaning toward her. "If you like, I would be very happy to enlighten you."

Gwen backed away. "Thanks, but I prefer to be 'enlightened' after dinner and dancing."

He lifted one ebony brow. "How about tomorrow night?"

"*What?*"

"Tomorrow night. Dinner and dancing, and whatever enlightenment might come of it."

"You're asking me for a date?" she demanded.

"It was your idea," he reminded her.

"I was making a smart-ass remark, not extending an invitation," she said firmly. "Besides, I was talking about kissing, not dating."

He smiled. "As you wish."

His arms went around her, surprisingly strong. More from instinct than outrage, Gwen made a half-hearted stab at his foot with one stiletto heel. She missed and stumbled forward against his chest, her arms pinned between them. Before she could pull away, his lips found hers.

All thoughts of retreat slid from Gwen's mind. She'd expected heat and light; instead, Ian's kiss flowed through her like cool ocean waves. Sensation began to build, taking the rhythm of the surf it resembled.

A small voice in the back of Gwen's mind, barely audible in the storm, asked her if she knew what she was doing. She didn't have a good answer.

Everyday logic returned with a rush. She shoved away from him.

"Don't ever do that again," she told him, stabbing a finger into his chest.

"As you wish," he repeated. "I won't kiss you again until you ask me to. Again."

He was so arrogant, so certain of himself. Certain of *her*. She sneered. "Not in this century, buddy."

Ian Forest merely smiled, "If you can wait, so can I."

The comment was so outrageous that it stole any response Gwen might have made. She shook her head and walked away. Ian Forest's laugh followed her like a fading shadow.

CHAPTER

Thirteen

First thing next morning, Gwen went back to Ryan Cody's office. She got past the receptionist without mishap, but the Prada-suited dragon guarding Cody's office was another matter. When Gwen came to the door, the secretary actually got up from her desk and took up position in front of her boss's door.

"Mr. Cody does not want to see you, Ms. Gellman," she said coolly.

"Ask him again."

"There's no need for that."

"Then ask him if he'd like to hear what Sal Almeida had to say about the Perotti murder."

The woman glared at her for a moment, then spun and tapped on the door. She went into Cody's office, firmly shutting the door behind her.

Gwen quickly moved behind the desk and slipped the flash drive into the port in the back of the secretary's computer. The nasty little device downloaded the files more quickly than she would have thought possible.

The sound of footsteps in the hall outside had her lunging to take a seat, the electronic thief clenched in her hand.

The dark man she'd noticed during her first visit entered and disappeared into Cody's office. After a few minutes the secretary returned to her post.

"Mr. Cody can see you in fifteen minutes. Would you like to wait, or will you come back?"

"I'll wait."

About twenty minutes later, a heavyset man rolled into the office. With a jolt of astonishment Gwen recognized Dennis Walsh, the police captain and her former boss. He gave Gwen a fulminating glare.

The secretary nodded politely to him and picked up the phone. After a few murmured comments, she hung up. Ryan Cody opened the door to his office.

"Please come in, Captain Walsh. Ms. Gellman."

She followed them into the office. "This is my attorney, Wallace Edmonson," Cody said, nodding toward the dark man.

Edmonson stepped forward and shook hands with the captain, then nodded to Gwen. "May I take your jacket?"

She stripped off the battered leather garment and handed it to him. He draped it carefully on the coat tree and took a seat at the small conference table.

Once they were settled, Cody cleared his throat. "Ms. Gellman, you have been making some serious accusations. I agreed to this meeting because I want to make it very clear that I will not tolerate you telling lies to my wife."

"What lies would those be?"

"Captain Walsh denies your allegation that no report was made of my daughter's disappearance. In fact, he brought a copy of the report."

"May I see it?"

Walsh looked to Cody, who nodded. He handed it over. Gwen studied the report. It looked legit, but Mary had said she couldn't find any record of Meredith, and Gwen trusted her word over Walsh's.

"Can I keep this?"

"There's no reason why you should," Walsh told her.

"Is there a reason why I shouldn't?"

"That's not the point," Cody said. "You have no further need for it."

Gwen gave him a cool smile. "Dianne Cody hired me to find her daughter. Until I do, or until she says otherwise, I keep looking. Unless, of course, any of you gentleman can give me a legal reason why I shouldn't?"

Her question was met with sullen silence. She gave them a moment, then stood up. "In that case, I should get back to work."

Edmonson rose with her. He retrieved her coat and held it out for her. Gwen took it from his hands rather than allowing him to help her on with it. For some reason, she was reluctant to touch the man.

She called Frank on the way over and asked him to meet her at his house. She walked in without knocking and found him already at his computer.

"Here's your little thief," she said, handing him the flash drive. "Think you can make him empty his pockets?"

He gave her a smug little smile. "Told you it would come in handy. What do you have here?"

"The desktop files, Cody's secretary."

His smile faded. "That was a hell of a risk. What are you looking for?"

"I'm not sure, but Cody's looking more interesting by the hour. Pull up his calendar. I want to know where he's going, who he's talking to. I don't know what's going on yet, but I'm pretty damn sure he's in it up to his ass."

Frank inserted the drive and busily clicked the computer keys. His printer began to hum. "You can take a copy of the calendar with you. I'll browse the other files later and see if anything else pops."

"Thanks. You're at work early," she commented. "Usually you're still on the boat."

"Yeah. I got a start on that missing-person case last night. You're gonna be sorry you didn't keep this one for yourself."

"Why's that?" she said absently.

"Here's the situation: a young couple and their baby girl were killed in a car accident. I spent most of the night digging for information, but there's no record of them. Nada. Zilch. Zip."

Gwen started to get interested. "A car crash, you said. Was one of the parents driving?"

"The mother. And yes, she had a driver's license. Problem is, it was a fake. There were no credit cards registered to these people. No bank accounts, no Social Security numbers."

"Dental records turn up anything?"

"Now, that's where things really start to get interesting. The night of the accident, someone broke into the morgue. Four bodies went missing. Our little family were among them."

Gwen let out a whistle of astonishment. "That must have been a huge scandal."

"You'd think," he agreed. "The strange thing is, I was on the job at the time, and I don't remember hearing about it. It's not easy to keep that sort of thing quiet."

She knew what he meant. A macabre story like that would be a hot topic around the coffeepot and a focus for the black humor that cops frequently deployed as a defense mechanism.

"Reminds me of something I heard this week. You know Quaid, my last partner?"

"You've mentioned him."

"He's working with a rookie, Damian O'Riley. The kid came to talk to me, told me something he overheard. Apparently the bodies of the two cops who were killed in the raid on Winston's were mutilated while they were in the morgue. I was on the job for several months after that, and never heard a word."

Frank shook his head in disbelief. "Sounds like someone over there's burying more than stiffs."

"Quaid's ex-girlfriend works for the coroner. Maybe we should get together for a little girl talk."

"That doesn't sound too likely, but if Quaid's new partner is talking to you, maybe the girlfriend will, too." Frank looked at her keenly. "Or maybe it's Quaid who's got something to say to you, and he's working himself up to it."

Her phone rang before she could think of a reasonable response to that. Frank gestured for her to get it.

"Hey there," Stephen said, his voice reeking good cheer and testosterone. "How about dinner tonight?"

Gwen sighed. "I can't, Stephen. The middle of a case isn't the best time for a trip down memory lane."

"But you have to eat, right? A quick meal, nothing fancy." He named a small restaurant downtown, one of Gwen's favorites. They made incredible fish and chips, and brought vinegar to the table for the chips without you having to ask for it.

Come to think of it, she noted, she hadn't had time to talk to him about Ryan Cody. "Seven o'clock?"

"Sounds good," he said.

She clicked off the phone. Frank nodded approval. "Nice to see you taking my advice for once."

"I've always taken your advice," she told him in a sour tone. "But up to now, it's always been good."

CHAPTER

Fourteen

◦ The restaurant Stephen had chosen was on State Street in a tall, narrow brick building that seemed to have more corners and angles than was strictly necessary. Stephen was already seated when Gwen walked in. His face lit up, and he rose to meet her.

"You look great," he said, taking in her outfit: black jeans, a black sweater, low-heeled black dress boots, a silver Celtic triskel ion pendant. It was, for her at least, incredibly conservative.

"I feel like a freaking schoolteacher," she muttered.

Stephen sent her a wolfish grin. "If any of teachers had looked like you, I wouldn't have cut classes."

"You never cut classes," she said flatly. "I'd bet good money on that."

His grin faded, then reshaped into a rueful smile. "Sadly you're right."

When he bent to kiss her, Gwen turned her cheek toward him. "Oh, that's cold," he murmured against her skin. "Where's the hot-blooded Goth chick from the other day? We have some unfinished business."

"Maybe, but do you think this is the place to start that particular business transaction?"

"After dinner, then?"

She hesitated, honestly tempted. "I'm short on time right now."

He chuckled and pulled her chair out for her. "In that case, it's a good thing I took the liberty of ordering for us. Fish and chips, plus whatever fried appetizer seemed most likely to absorb grease. That sound about right?"

"Good man," Gwen commended him. She settled down and folded her hands on the table. "So. Tell me what you know about the Cody situation."

His eyebrows rose. "Something tells me I should have ordered the oysters."

"Spare me the sarcasm, Stephen. It's hard to get serious about flirting when you've got a missing kid on your mind."

"Fair enough," he allowed. He reached for his wineglass and rolled the stem between his fingers. "There's not much to tell you. I was supposed to go running with Ryan Cody that morning. We meet maybe two, three times a week. I got to the house and found the whole family in a panic about Meredith."

"And you told Dianne Cody to contact me?"

"Not at the time. I told Ryan that I was dating a private investigator."

"Among other people," she murmured.

A faint, wry smile touched his lips. "Oddly enough, Ryan said much the same thing. Only he wasn't smiling at the time."

Gwen leaned back in her chair and cocked her head to one side. "Just for the record, are you currently engaged to anyone?"

He pretended to wince. "I suppose I deserved that."

"Hey, I wasn't taking a shot." She sent him a demure smile and a sidelong glance. "Just a census."

"Oh. Good one," he said, lifting his wineglass in mock salute. "Are we going to talk about your case, or are you going to bust my chops?"

"A little of both sounds good to me," Gwen said. "My job has so few other perks."

"Go ahead and smirk," he told her. "Amusement is good. I've noticed that when women are smiling, they're less likely to throw things."

"Ah. I take it Julia didn't do a lot of smiling when she found out about your shiksa goddesses?"

"Not until she drew blood," he grumbled. "That seemed to cheer her up."

Gwen nodded. "That's always a mood-brightener for me, too."

He eyed her suspiciously. "I was indulging in hyperbole. And you?"

She gave him an enigmatic smile.

Just then the waiter came by with a large white platter heaped with what appeared to be vegetables, batter-dipped and fried, resting on an enormous bed of onion rings.

Stephen regarded the fragrant mound with dismay. "What did broccoli ever do to deserve a fate like that?"

"It didn't have to *do* anything. Broccoli is innately evil. I think it has something to do with original sin."

"More of Sister Tamar's theology?"

Gwen pushed the green stuff aside to get at the onion rings. "What can I say. The woman's a philosopher. But let's get back to the Cody family. What can you tell me about Meredith?"

"Very little. She's a pretty teenage girl, lots of friends, always on the go."

"I heard that she and her mother don't get along very well."

He shrugged. "Can't help you there. I don't spend much time around the family."

"So how did you and Dianne hook up?"

"She called me at work and asked for information on the PI I'd mentioned."

"Did that surprise you?"

"A little. Ryan seemed adamantly against the idea. Of course, emotions were running very high that morning. He was barking at everyone."

"Do you know Ryan Cody well?"

He considered that. "We know each other from the club. We've been playing tennis and running together for maybe five, six years."

"But you wouldn't know much about other aspects of his life?"

"Such as?"

Gwen wiped her shiny fingers on her napkin and reached for her water glass. "He had a membership at Underhill. It's a gentleman's club, exotic dancers. Very young exotic dancers. Did you ever go there with him?"

"Who, me? No!" he said indignantly. He leaned in closer. "Does this have anything to do with Meredith?"

"It might."

He glanced around the small, crowded room. "This isn't exactly private. Maybe we should wait until after dinner to get into details."

Gwen nodded agreement and let him pour her a glass of wine from the bottle he'd ordered. Their dinner came shortly thereafter, and they ate in near silence.

They stepped out into a perfect spring evening. A few streaks of rose and gold gleamed against the deepening sapphire of the sky and reflected in the silvery waters of the canal. A small stream of people flowed toward the Waterfront. Haunting music rose from the water, along with the scent of woodsmoke.

"Apparently there's a Waterfire tonight," Stephen said, eyeing the food vendors and street performers setting up on a nearby corner. "Do you want to walk for a while?"

Since they still had matters to discuss, Gwen nodded. They made their way down to the canal, joining the people strolling along the walkways. Fires burned in dozens of large, round iron braziers in the middle of the canals. The rise and fall of Gregorian plainsong lent an otherworldly air that seemed not at all incongruent to the crowd's festive tone.

The music shifted as they walked: a soaring Italian aria, a plaintive Turkish folk song accompanied by the soft plinking of an oud. All of it was beautiful and evocative, a powerful counterpoint to the visual impact of fire against night-dark water.

They stopped on the bridge overlooking the circular basin at the Waterfront's end. Fires blazed in a ring of braziers, and the flames leaped and swayed like ancient dancers in some pagan circle.

Stephen leaned his elbows on the rail and stared into the ring of flame. "That really threw me, what you said about Ryan Cody and that club. It's . . . I don't know . . . distasteful. There's something wrong with grown men who like teenage girls."

"I've noticed that," she said glumly. "One of the problems with looking about seventeen years old is being a magnet for assholes."

He looked at her sharply. "Are you including me in that group?"

"I don't know. Should I?"

Stephen turned his gaze back to the water. "Don't get me wrong—I love the way you look. But for me, it's not that you look young. It's more . . ." He floundered for words, hands milling as if that might help draw forth the right explanation.

Finally he swept one hand wide, in a gesture that encompassed the urban block party. "Waterfire is about primal forces in a pretty, accessible package. It's fun, but it's also very powerful."

Gwen smiled faintly. "So what you're saying is that I'm your idea of a walk on the wild side."

He blew out a long breath. "It doesn't sound very flattering when you put it that way, but yeah, I guess so." He pushed away from the rail and began to walk. Gwen fell into step, and they walked for several paces in silence.

"What you said about me never cutting class," he said suddenly. "That really bugged me."

Gwen thought about that for a moment. "Sorry?" she said experimentally.

"No need to apologize," he said morosely. "You were just pointing out the problem. I follow the rules better than most Boy Scouts."

It didn't seem the time to point out certain notable exceptions. "Lots of people do," she said. "More or less."

"And look where it's gotten us. Life has gotten so freaking tame," Stephen retorted. "You go to the right schools, get the right job, marry the right woman, have kids that will repeat the cycle. Where's the surprise? Where's the adventure?"

"Face facts, Stephen. This was fun, but we both know I don't fit into the rule book."

"Who cares? I'm tired of following the plan, coloring inside the lines."

She slanted a look at him. "Yeah, but a steady diet of wild side isn't exactly your speed, either."

"Maybe it could be." He stopped suddenly and looked down at her with something like panic in his eyes. "Marry me, Gwen."

Gwen shook her head, more in disbelief than denial. Didn't he hear the irony in his "proposal"?

Stephen was no more interested in commitment than she was. Something else was at work here, and Gwen thought he'd put his finger on it pretty well. For some reason these public bonfire parties—a local Providence phenomenon that had evolved from a piece of performance art—seemed to evoke ancient memories, primal rites. Gwen could feel the power of it rising in her like woodsmoke. It was difficult to dismiss Stephen's offer entirely.

There was no place for her in Stephen's future, and frankly, that was part of the appeal. Two social workers and several ex-boyfriends had suggested that her background had left her wary of commitments. Maybe that was why Stephen suddenly seemed more attractive now that she knew he'd be leaving. Whatever happened this night was about now, not about family or future. That suited her just fine—she'd never had the first and didn't count on the second.

She seized the front of Stephen's shirt and drew him closer. "Is your place pretty much packed up?"

He nodded, and his eyes kindled. A rare moment of perfect understanding passed between them. "Yours, then."

"I'll drive."

Fifteen minutes later, they sprinted up the stairs to Gwen's apartment. Halfway up the flight, Stephen caught her arm and spun her to face him.

She sank down to sit on the stairs, pulling him with her. He knelt on the step below her and moved between her knees. They leaned into a kiss, hands tangling in each other's hair as the kiss deepened. Gwen wrapped her legs around him, pulling him closer.

Stephen broke away from the kiss, leaning back enough to allow him to reach for the hem of her sweater. She batted his hand away and pulled the sweater over her head in one quick, impatient movement. Her bra followed with scant ceremony.

A breathless chuckle escaped him. He cupped her in his palms, his thumbs tracing teasing little circles. Gwen set to work on his shirt buttons, and in moments he shrugged off the shirt and tossed it heedlessly aside.

A sharp, insistent ringing cut through the sensual haze. They both jumped. Gwen grimaced and reached for the small cell phone hooked to her belt.

"It could be important," she told Stephen, who was regarding her with an incredulous stare. She clicked it on.

"Gellman, I've got some info on that missing heir case. Trust me, you're going to want to see it right away."

It took Gwen a moment to recognize Frank Cross's voice, though it was as familiar to her as her own. In her hypersensitive state, he sounded different, as if a sea of emotions seethed beneath the surface of his words.

"Is this good news or bad?"

"Interesting," he said with careful emphasis.

"So, tell me." Gwen gestured Stephen's protests into silence, then pointed up to her apartment. He sighed and trudged up the stairs.

"Not over the phone," Frank insisted.

She took this in. "Is the information that sensitive?"

"Let's just say that you have to see it to get the full impact. I'll scan some of this stuff and e-mail it to you."

"I'd really prefer to see the file."

"Jesus, Gellman—I know you don't like computers, but when are you going to join the twenty-first century?"

"First thing tomorrow, I'll put up a fucking Web page," she told him. "Listen, is this something that can wait until tomorrow morning?"

There was a moment of silence on the end of the line. "Sounds like dinner with Weiss went into extra innings. Nice to know you're taking my advice."

She glanced up the stairs. "And adding some embellishments of my own."

"Got it." Frank's approving grin was audible in his voice. "I'll send the file over to your office first thing tomorrow."

"No, I'll come over there—"

The dial tone announced that the connection was dead. Gwen shrugged. If she went over first thing, she could catch him before he sent a messenger.

She rose and climbed the stairs. The door was open, and Stephen stood with his back to her. He'd already shed his clothes, and for several moment Gwen was content to enjoy the view.

Then she noticed that he was holding a sheaf of papers,

shuffling them with quick, sharp movements. Shock and disapproval radiated from him in waves. The stiffness of his stance and the tension apparent in the way he held his shoulders left no doubt in Gwen's mind as to what he was holding.

"There's nothing there you haven't seen before," Gwen said, keeping her tone as neutral as possible.

Stephen spun to face her. He waved the sheaf of photos Dianne Cody had given her. "These are pictures of you. Nude pictures."

"You know I worked vice. Those pictures helped me get close to a man who sold this shit over the Internet."

He stared at her as if he hadn't heard a word she'd just said. As if he'd never seen her before. Apparently she'd just colored outside of the lines, and he didn't seem to like the resulting picture.

Gwen huffed with exasperation and strode over to him. She took the papers from his hand and started to place them back on the kitchen counter.

The vision struck her without warning, stopping her in midstride. She saw a long, wide street, one she drove several times a month, and across from a flower shop, a blue frame house. She'd seen that house, could find it easily if she wanted to. The question was, why would she want to?

A faint, strangled oath drew her eyes to Stephen. His glazed stare was fixed upon the colored shadows that played against the old white formica of her counter.

With difficulty, Gwen focused on the shifting colors. To her astonishment she made out the faint outlines of the blue frame house, the neon sign on the florist shop, and the multicolored swish of cars passing between. It was her vision, playing out for all to see like some ghostly hologram.

The colors shifted over Stephen's naked body, vivid against his too-pale face. His breathing was too shallow and quick.

"Stephen!" she said sharply.

The strange vision disappeared like a popped soap bubble, and Stephen's eyes flashed to her face. They held horror and the beginnings of shock.

"What in God's name was that?" he whispered.

"I wish I could tell you." An unfamiliar need for comfort—both giving and getting—filled Gwen. She took a step toward him. To her surprise, he retreated. Her throat constricted with the sure knowledge of what was to come.

"What's the matter, Stephen?" she said softly. "You were the one who wanted to color outside the lines."

He shook himself like someone awakening from a nightmare and began reaching for his clothes. "Some lines shouldn't be crossed. Maybe I could have dealt with the idea of you doing pornography, but the other thing? No way. Call it a quirk, but I like to keep anchored in reality."

"What happened was real. We both saw it—whatever 'it' was."

Stephen paused, shoes in hand. There was a touch of regret in his eyes, like a small footnote at story's end.

"Sorry, Gwen, but this is a little wilder than I can handle."

She stood silently and watched him dress, knowing there was nothing she could say that would make him want to stay, and not blaming him in the slightest for wanting to go. Hell, if she were in his position, she'd run, too.

He stopped at the door, turned back to face her. Gwen lifted her chin and raised an eyebrow in silent inquiry. But there was nothing to add, and they both knew it.

After a moment he shook his head and turned away. The sound of quick footsteps rattled down the stairs without pause. He didn't even stop to put on his shirt. Gwen had a mental image of him fleeing down the drive, struggling into the shirt as he ran. The thought was too painful to be amusing.

Gwen sank down onto the sofa and dropped her head into her hands, envying Stephen his ability to turn tail and run. She'd spent most of her life wondering who she was, *what* she was. Pretending she was a normal kid, pretending she didn't care that she wasn't normal.

She'd known people who wanted what she had. They read trendy books about modern witchcraft, tried to develop their psychic potential through meditation or ritual or drug-induced trance. Desperately wanting the magic to work.

Gwen suspected that most of them, if they ever got their wish, would melt down their pentacles, recast them into silver bullets, and shoot themselves.

Or maybe they'd do what she did: keep going, keep quiet. Never tell anyone that her life was about outrunning whatever it was that haunted her.

If tonight's events were any indication, her private demons seemed to be gaining on her.

Fifteen

An hour later, Gwen walked down the street she'd seen in her vision, dressed in high-school casual. The florist shop was long closed, but the convenience store next to it provided a good place to lurk and watch.

There were no lights on in the blue house, no car in the drive. The post holding the mailbox had been knocked over, and the metal box lay crushed and rusting on the grass. It was hard to tell whether or not the house was occupied. Spring had been late in coming this year, and the newly green grass had yet to require trimming.

Gwen stayed in the store as long as she could without awakening suspicion. When she figured she was nearing the end of her reasonable lurking time, she went to the register with one of the magazines she'd been pretending to browse, grabbing a bag of chips and a couple of candy bars on the way. An extremely thin young man with a bad mullet cut and worse acne rang up the sale.

"Do you live in this neighborhood?" she asked.

He looked startled by the question, as if he was unaccustomed to being an object of interest.

"Yeah?" His wary tone anticipated some humiliation to come.

She shrugged. "My parents are thinking about buying a house near here. I hate my old neighborhood, and was hoping this one was a little safer."

The kid relaxed visibly, and his head bobbed confirmation. "Shit happens, but not much that's really bad."

"Mostly tagging, vandalism, that sort of thing?"

"Yeah."

Gwen's lips curved in a relieved smile. "Hey, did you see the job someone just did on that mailbox across the street?"

He waved a hand in airy dismissal. "That was months ago."

"Oh. No one lives there?"

"Yeah, I've seen a guy come and go. Maybe he doesn't get much mail. Or maybe leaving it down is his way of ducking junk mail." He sent her a tentative grin.

She rewarded him with an appreciative chuckle. "Spam is a pain in the ass, but at least it doesn't kill trees. So, are you still in high school?"

"Junior year," he confirmed.

"Me, too! Maybe I'll see you there."

A deep blush suffused his face at this prospect. She gathered up her purchases and gave him a wink.

Frustration sped her steps as she stalked back to her car. No mail meant that she couldn't identify the occupant—not from outside the house, at any rate.

She took a small locksmith kit from the glove compartment and selected a single tool from it. One was usually enough; she'd learned at an early age that very few locks could hold her in or out. Hideously illegal, of course, but she hadn't been caught at it since she was eleven.

Gwen cut through a couple of yards and climbed over the low chain-link fence surrounding the small backyard. There was no sign of life in the house, but from this vantage she saw evidence that the occupant might have been there this morning. Two metal trash cans had been emptied and tossed back into the yard, obscured from street view by an untrimmed hedge. Along the street were a few other cans, indicating that trash pickup had been this morning.

She went to the back door and let herself in. A quick check of the house confirmed that she was alone.

Gwen went from room to room, not sure what she was looking for, only that it had something to do with the photos someone had sent Dianne Cody.

The most obvious connection would be to the photographer. But there was no photo lab in the house, no darkroom. No rolls of film scattered about.

On second thought, that wasn't particularly surprising. Most Internet pictures started out digital.

"Oh, shit," she muttered, realizing where the evidence was likely to be.

She found the computer in an upstairs bedroom and reluctantly turned it on. Frank's words from earlier that evening came back to her. Maybe he was right. Maybe she should do something about her aversion to the damn things. Although, when she stopped to think about it, it wasn't the computer itself that bothered her, but the idea that records of her passing could be kept and traced on the electronic highways. The thought was profoundly disturbing, for no reason that she could understand.

She brushed aside her discomfort and sat down at the

keyboard. As luck would have it, the computer was password protected. She flicked off the machine and started to search the room for anything photographic.

There was nothing to find. No files, no backup disks or CDs. No discarded prints in the wastebasket. A shredder stood beside the computer desk, but the receiving basket was empty. Since the trash had been picked up that morning, there was no hope of finding anything in the outside bin.

In short, there was nothing in this house to suggest that her disturbing vision had reflected reality.

On impulse, she went to the main bedroom and opened the closet. The clothes hanging there were unremarkable, with one exception: a row of oxford shirts in rosy pastels: pink, salmon, peach. There was not a single blue or white shirt in sight.

A grim smile thinned Gwen's lips. Tad Zimmer had worn a pink shirt the day he'd taken the pictures that had shocked Stephen. She'd seen Zimmer several times since, and come to think of it, every time he'd worn some shade of pink.

Just to make sure, she retraced her steps to the office. She pulled a plastic bag from her pocket and used it to pick up a pencil from the holder on the computer desk. Tad Zimmer had been fingerprinted, if little else.

The photographer had slipped through the net after Winston's. She hadn't even been able to bring charges against him. Since Gwen was not a minor, he hadn't actually done anything illegal.

Nor was there any reason to believe that he had anything to add to her current search. Most likely this latest vision was like so many in the past: random images whose only apparent purpose was to frustrate her and make her feel alien and alone.

And now, that old torment was not enough. Now she had to live with the knowledge that at any time something could trigger a light show like the one that had scared off Stephen.

"No loss," she muttered as she carefully relocked the back door.

Maybe not, said a small voice in her mind, but what about the others?

Gwen ran down the list of people she trusted: Tamar, an aging bride of Christ, fierce as the Old Testament. Sylvia, a classy hooker who'd floated into retirement on a golden parachute some CEOs might enjoy. Marcy, an ambitious lawyer who didn't give a damn what people thought about her choice of friends and lovers. Most of all Frank, who over the years had moved from partner to friend to family. Despite those years, she had no idea how he might react if she started spilling Technicolor nightmares all over his nice, neat kitchen.

The thought of confronting Stephen's horror in Frank's eyes was too painful to bear. She instinctively squeezed her eyes shut, trying to block out the disturbing image.

A blaring horn brought her back into the moment, and she swerved to avoid the oncoming car. She backhanded tears from her eyes and focused grimly on the road.

Sylvia's house was dark by the time Gwen got home. She parked the car and plodded up the stairs. Her black bra still hung from the railing, where it had landed earlier that night. She gave it a quick yank. Delicate straps gave way with a snap. Fuck it. She'd intended to throw the damn thing away, anyway. The fewer reminders she had of this night, the happier she'd be.

She tossed the ruined garment into the trash and fell face-first onto her bed. Tears threatened to well up, but the demand of sleep was stronger still.

As Gwen sank into the darkness, she noted with rueful gratitude that whatever dreams might await could trouble no one but her.

CHAPTER

Sixteen

∾ The morning sunlight was still fresh and new when Gwen pulled up in front of Frank's house. She tapped on the door. No one answered, but his old black Chevy was in the driveway and the lights were on in the study. Gwen tapped again, then tried the door. Since it was unlocked, she walked in. Recently Frank had taken to wearing earphones at the computer. Maybe he'd cranked up the music so loud he couldn't hear the door.

But there was no one at the computer, and no voice answered her hail. Puzzled, Gwen walked through the kitchen into the living room. There was a glass on the coffee table, one of the squat, thick-bottomed tumblers Frank used for his morning grapefruit juice. Beside the glass stood a half-empty bottle of scotch.

Gwen's heart plummeted. Sobriety had been a long, hard struggle for Frank, but he'd stayed on the wagon for more than five years. What could have happened to make him turn his back on all his hard work?

Maybe Frank had called his son last night after he'd spoken to her. He'd already been mourning the years lost. If the call had gone badly . . .

Gwen shook her head. No, that didn't ring true. When

something went wrong, Frank took to the bay, not the bottle. She walked around back to see if his boat was gone. The rowboat was still tied to the ramshackle dock, but Frank's small fishing boat was out in the river, seemingly adrift.

She made a quick call to the police, then untied the rowboat and headed for Frank's boat with long, hurried strokes.

No one answered her call. Gwen pulled the rowboat up alongside and crawled onto the larger boat.

Frank was not asleep in the small hold, as she'd hoped. There was no sign that he'd been on the boat at all. His fishing equipment was still secured in the locked rack, the nets neatly folded. The ropes that had secured the boat to its mooring had been untied, not cut. If setting the boat adrift had been a prank, the asshole who did it had taken his time.

She looked for the key, thinking to bring in the boat with the rowboat in tow. When her search came up empty, she threw out the anchor to keep the boat from drifting.

When she'd done all she could, she climbed back into the rowboat and headed back for the dock.

Her oar struck something hard where only water should have been. Gwen twisted in the seat to see what she'd hit.

For a long moment her mind refused to process what her eyes saw. Then a cry burst from her and caught in her throat, a scream cut short into a strangled sob.

A large, dark form floated in the water. Even face down, there could be no mistaking Frank Cross's body. Few men were that big, that broad.

Gwen fell to her knees in the bottom of the boat and reached for him. She drew him to her as best she could, tried to maneuver him into the boat. It soon became apparent that she would capsize before she could accomplish that goal.

Finally she took a rope and tied it around his chest, under his arms. Tears fell freely down her face as she rowed toward shore. It wasn't right, towing him like this, but she could think of no other way.

The town police were there by the time she pulled up at the dock. She told them briefly what she'd found, then stood helplessly on the shore while the three men brought Frank's body from the water.

One of them, a young man with a long, rather horsey face, led her into the house. She sat down at the kitchen table and pretended to drink the water he poured for her.

The officer sat down across from her. In Frank's place.

An irrational wave of resentment hit her, so powerful that it bordered on hatred. She covered her eyes with both hands as if holding back a sudden rush of tears.

"I know this is hard for you, but I need you to tell me what you can."

His voice said that he hadn't seen her reaction. Gwen got a grip, lowered her hands. "As I told you outside, the man was Frank Cross, a retired Providence cop. He was my first partner."

"You're on the job?" he said, surprised.

"Not anymore," she said, her tone closing the door on that topic. "Frank and I have been friends for years. I came over this morning. The door was unlocked, so I came in."

"This is your usual pattern?"

"Yeah."

"Did you find anything unusual?"

She nodded toward the living room. "A bottle of Scotch and a glass. Frank doesn't drink."

The young cop rose and walked over to the coffee table. He picked up the bottle, and his eyebrows lifted when he noted how much was gone. He set it down and reached for the glass.

"Don't touch that," Gwen said sharply. Jesus, what did they teach these townies?

He looked at her, his face quizzical and a little resentful. "Is there a problem?"

"I want that checked for fingerprints."

A supercilious expression crossed his face. "Ms. Gellman, it looks like your friend drank too much, decided taking his boat out was a good idea, and fell into the water."

"That's not what happened."

For the first time, a flicker of suspicion crossed the young cop's face. "And you know this why?"

She rose and walked into the room. "Frank was a recovering alcoholic. He hadn't had a drink in over five years."

"People fall off the wagon," he suggested. "Maybe something happened that pushed him over the edge."

Again she thought of Frank's son, Jason, who'd spent most of the last quarter century without his father.

"I don't think so," she said slowly. "In fact, he called me last night, very exited about a project he'd been working on."

"So maybe he wanted to celebrate."

"Not with that stuff," she said, nodding toward the bottle of Scotch. "When he used to drink, it was Jamison's or nothing. He always said the Scots couldn't *spell* whiskey, much less make it."

The officer smiled faintly. "My grandfather used to say something like that. What was the project Mr. Cross called to discuss?"

"I don't know much about it," she hedged. "Something to do with renovating his house, I think. We were going to talk about it today. That's why I came over."

He nodded, accepting that. "Do you know his next of kin?"

"He has a son, Jason Cross. He lives in Florida."

"Do you know how to get hold of him?"

"I can find out." Until she had a better handle on what was going on, Gwen didn't want the town cops poking through Frank's files.

She watched as the coroner came and pronounced, and Frank's body was taken away. The town cops left, taking the glass to check for fingerprints. Gwen had the distinct impression that they only did so to humor her.

When she was alone, she went to the office to look up Frank's son. She stopped dead at the entrance to the room. The desk was empty except for a box of tissues and an old coffee mug holding an assortment of pens. Frank's notebook computer was gone.

"It's a portable computer," she muttered. "Maybe he took it with him on the boat."

Even as she spoke, she knew this wasn't the right explanation. As far as she knew, Frank had never taken his computer out on the water. He liked to live in the moment, to be where he was. Frank was one of the few people she knew who shared her dislike for cameras. It puzzled them both, all those people recording their days rather than experiencing them.

No, Frank went out on the water to fish or quahog, not to do paperwork. That's what the office was for, and Frank had always been one for keeping everything in its place. Something was very wrong here.

All of which put Gwen in a quandary. If she pushed the police to look more closely at Frank's death, she'd have to tell them about the case Frank was working on.

The case.

A shiver of apprehension radiated upward from the pit of Gwen's stomach. Hands shaking, she yanked open the largest desk drawer and rifled through the neat row of files hanging there. The case Ian Forest had given her was not among them.

She sank down in Frank's chair, forcing her mind to examine the situation methodically. The first thing to do was to eliminate the obvious reason Frank might have had for falling off the wagon. She picked up his phone and called the last number dialed.

After a moment, her cell phone began to ring. That undermined the possibility of a disturbing conversation with his son after he'd spoken to her.

She tried to decide whether this was good news or bad. She didn't want Frank's death to be a stupid, senseless accident, but the alternative was even more difficult to face.

The police didn't seem inclined to regard his death as a homicide. Unless she could come up with an argument compelling enough to prompt an investigation, they were likely to dismiss Frank as a used-up drunk.

It wouldn't, she noted bitterly, be the first time.

No, this was her task, the last thing she could do for him. But Frank was dead, and Meredith Cody, as far as Gwen knew, was not. She couldn't handle both investigations, at least, not alone.

After a moment of hesitation, Gwen picked up her cell phone and dialed.

"Quaid here."

He pronounced it "hee-yuh," making two syllables of the word. Like many Rhode Island natives, he'd go to considerable lengths to avoid pronouncing an "r," reserving that letter for places where none existed in nature. At the end of "Donna," for example.

Gwen shook off her mild annoyance. She seldom noticed the various local accents, but everything about this man irritated her. Like the saying went, if you liked someone, you wouldn't mind if he dumped a bowl of soup in your lap, but if you disliked someone, the way he held his fork could make you furious. Garry Quaid pissed her off just by breathing, which made this phone call even more difficult.

"It's Gellman," she said reluctantly, "and I need your help."

Seventeen

There was a long moment of silence at the end of the line. Finally Quaid said, "I'm listening."

Gwen took a long breath. "Frank Cross died last night."

"Your first partner?"

"That's right. I pulled him out of the bay."

"Drowned?"

"Looks like." Some might have found his terse, matter-of-fact comments cold, but at the moment Gwen appreciated it. Right now, the last thing she needed was a show of sympathy, real or feigned. If Quaid offered her a shoulder to cry on, her first impulse would have been to put a bullet through it.

"The coroner said Frank was alive when he went into the water," she said. "His boat was adrift, and there's a half-empty bottle of Scotch in his house. The responding officers seem pretty convinced that he drank too much and fell in."

"But you don't buy that."

"Damn right."

"Gellman, I hate to bring this up, but wasn't he pushed into early retirement because he hit the bottle kind of heavy?"

"Among other reasons, yeah. But he hadn't had a drink in five years. He never kept any alcohol in the house."

"So he went out and picked some up."

"If he was going to go to the trouble to buy booze, he wouldn't have come home with Scotch," she persisted. "Back in the day, he wouldn't touch the stuff. Irish whiskey only. It was a matter of ethnic pride, or some fool thing."

"Do you have anything else, or are you working on one of your hunches?"

If there'd been the faintest note of sarcasm in his voice, she would have hung up. "His notebook computer is missing."

"What about backup files?"

It was a good point, and one she should have picked up on. "I haven't checked," she admitted.

"A notebook computer. Pretty fancy for an ex-cop," he mused. "What did Frank Cross do after he retired?"

"He had a license to harvest quahogs. He sold them to a market down in Warren."

"And for that he needed a computer?"

"No, but he actually liked the infernal devices. He called himself the world's oldest geek. He did stuff on the Internet, went into political chat rooms, that sort of thing. A hobby."

"Uh-huh. So, is there any particular reason why someone would want to kill him for whatever was on his computer?"

It was an obvious question, one Gwen shouldn't have missed. It wasn't like her to talk herself into a corner.

"Frank Cross was the closest thing to a father I've ever had," she said, taking refuge in the truth. "I'm pretty shaken up, and probably not making sense."

"Understandable," he said, his tone neutral. "What do you want me to do?"

"I heard that Kate Myers works for the coroner's office. Any chance you could ask her to talk to me? Off the record, if possible?"

He didn't answer right away. "I can ask," he said cautiously, "but she's going to want to know what's going on. For that matter, so do I."

"If Frank was murdered, I'm not going to let it be covered up. And don't try to tell me the department will take care of its own."

She heard the faint hiss of an exasperated sigh. "Look, I can understand why you might think along those lines, but that's not the way things are done."

"Yeah, right. Tell me: Are case numbers assigned chronologically?"

There was a moment of silence as he tried to connect the apparently unrelated lines of thought. "You know they are. Why?"

"Find out where 87665 falls into the time line, then get back to me."

She hung up and opened Frank's desk drawer, the one where he'd kept his flash drive. The little device was gone. So was the neat stack of backup discs. His address book, fortunately, was still there.

Despite his affection for computers, Frank kept an old-fashioned, paper-and-ink address book, the kind that came in one of the miniature fake-leather day planners. Probably it was a remnant from his days on the force, when notes were jotted down on a pad rather than keyed into a file. He'd been talking about getting one of those little hand computers that reminded Gwen of Game Boys.

She opened the book and paged to the alphabetically logical spot. Jason Cross's name had been added recently in Frank's neat block printing. There had been three phone numbers, but the first two were neatly inked out. It had probably taken Frank a couple of tries to get the most recent number.

Gwen dialed the number. After three rings, someone picked up.

"This is Jason."

The faint background crackle suggested that she'd gotten his cell phone. That wasn't good: this was the sort of news best received when there were no other distractions.

"My name is Gwen Gellman, and I'm calling from East Providence, Rhode Island. This is about Frank Cross, a retired policeman."

"My father?"

The surprise in his voice gave her a definitive answer to one of her questions: Frank hadn't called his son last night, not on the desk phone or any other.

"I believe so. He was found dead this morning of an apparent drowning. I'm very sorry."

Jason Cross was silent for a long moment. "So am I. I'd always wanted to get to know him."

"So why didn't you?"

Gwen winced at the sound of her own words. She hadn't meant to browbeat Frank's son—the words sort of slipped out on their own.

"You're very blunt," he observed. "From what little I've heard about my father, I'm guessing he appreciated that trait."

"Yeah, he did."

"Did you know him well?"

"We were partners. He trained me."

"Were you very close?"

"I wasn't sleeping with him, if that's what you're asking," she snapped.

"No. The thing is, before I answer a personal question, I like to know who's asking and what stake they have in the answer."

"Oh." The response struck her as oddly reasonable. "All right, then. Frank was the best friend I had. The closest thing to family I've known."

"I see," he said quietly. "In that case, I didn't contact him because he made a choice, and I thought it was important to respect that."

"Sounds like there was more than enough respect in the Cross family to go around," Gwen said. "Frank wanted to contact you, but your mother thought it might be too confusing for you, and he respected her wishes."

"He talked about me?"

"A little." Because he'd sounded so wistful, she added, "He might not have talked about you much, but I know he thought about you often. He bought a birthday cake last week. He said he bought one every April sixteenth."

"Really." There was another long silence as he absorbed this. "I'd like to talk to you about him, if you don't mind."

She hesitated. Frank's loss was like an open wound, and she wasn't sure she could stand to talk about him to anyone, much less someone who was a stranger to them both. But how would she feel, if she met someone who could tell her about her parents?

"Sure," she decided. "I'll give you my number."

"I meant in person. I'll be there by tonight. Can you give me the address?"

She gave him the information and hung up, feeling both comforted and saddened. Jason Cross seemed like a nice guy. He should have been in Frank's life. All Frank had was her, and what had she done for him? Brought him a case that had probably gotten him killed.

The full realization of that slammed into her like a freight train. Her legs gave way and she sank to the floor, numbed by the terrible possibility, unable to move, barely able to breathe. All the world had narrowed to this single, terrible thought:

She had brought him the case, and it had killed him.

CHAPTER

Eighteen

◯◯ Gwen's cell phone rang, shattering the terrible inertia that gripped her. She snatched it up. "What?"

"It's Quaid. I checked out the case number you gave me. It was filled out early yesterday morning. If you don't mind me asking, why is the timing so important?"

Gwen sucked in a long, shuddering breath. Frank was dead, but she might still be able to do something to help Meredith.

"Yesterday morning, Walsh showed me a missing person's report that was supposedly filed a week ago."

"Captain Walsh," he specified.

"That's right."

"You were at the station?"

"No, he met me at a civilian's office and brought the report with him."

"Wait a minute—you're saying the captain deliberately falsified a report?"

"That's what it looks like."

"Why would he do that?"

"I'm still working that out."

"I don't know, Gellman. That doesn't sound like Walsh."

"Is that right? We are talking about the same guy who claimed he never assigned me to shadow Tiger Leone? Who told people I'd asked for a personal leave? It was real convenient, the way all that paperwork disappeared."

The silence on the other line was long and heavy. Gwen could almost envision Quaid thrusting one hand through his hair in befuddlement.

She understood his predicament, and knew that at some level he probably didn't want to get his hands around this. The thing was, if you knew about corruption, you had two choices: you kept silent, which meant you became part of the situation, or you did something about it, which also meant that you became part of the situation. The choice sucked, and she honestly wasn't sure which way Quaid would go.

"Even if you're right about Walsh being crooked, he's not stupid," Quaid pointed out. "Filing a false report is a huge risk."

"Maybe he thought it would play better than trying to explain another piece of missing paperwork," Gwen suggested bitterly. "Or maybe he just didn't have time to think it through."

"Explain."

"I'm looking for a missing teenager. The father told the mother he'd made the report. Four days go by, nothing happens. The mother's getting frantic by then, and she quietly hires me. I made some calls and found out there's no official record of the kid's disappearance. That was day before yesterday. The mother was, to put it mildly, not happy to hear this."

"Damn," he muttered.

"So yesterday I go to the father's office to ask some follow-up questions. He tells me to wait. Within twenty minutes Walsh walks in with an original report. There was a lawyer there, too.

Probably the father thought that much backup would intimidate me into dropping the case."

"Who is this guy?"

"He's an attorney. Other than that, I'd rather not say."

"What the hell is going on here?" Quaid murmured, more to himself than to her.

"Whatever it is, you can be pretty sure that Walsh is either in the game or on the sidelines."

"You said the father's a lawyer. Maybe Walsh knows the guy and was just doing him a favor. That doesn't make it right, but it could mean he isn't part of whatever else is going on."

"Oh yeah—police captains and criminal attorneys are natural allies," Gwen retorted.

"Good point," he said reluctantly. "And no matter how you slice it, someone's trying to cover up the girl's disappearance and Walsh just made it easier."

He sounded troubled, which was a mark in his favor. The way he'd handled Damian O'Riley was another. Quaid cared enough about finding answers to take another look, and he was concerned enough about his young partner to steer him away from asking career-damaging questions. Still, that wasn't enough to balance the scales against Carl Jamison and the vial of drugged wine that didn't make it into evidence.

Gwen reminded herself that any dealings she had with Quaid would have to be cautious.

"So. About Kate Myers."

"I called her. She agreed to meet with you. There's a Thai place over in Riverside, on Willet Avenue. You know where the supermarket is?"

"I can find it."

"The restaurant's in that plaza, toward the back. She'll meet you at noon."

"Thanks."

He made a sound that might have been either a snort or a laugh. "Let's see if you're still thanking me after you talk to Kate."

The phone went dead. Quaid wasn't one for lengthy farewell speeches, which was fine with Gwen. She'd never had much fondness for small talk, either.

She glanced at her watch. It was closing in on noon. She just had time to check for backup files before leaving.

A careful search of the office turned up nothing: no photocopies of anything pertaining to Ian Forest's case, no backup disks. In fact, there was not a single disk of any kind. Even his music CDs were gone—the originals as well as the backup copies.

Smart, she noted. An album of vintage rock would have been a good place to hide a backup CD. Someone had given this considerable thought.

Deeply troubled, she locked up the house and drove to the restaurant. From the outside, it looked like the usual hole-in-the-wall strip-mall joint: the neon sign, the close proximity to a Laundromat and a video-rental store. The inside was pleasantly surprising. The place was scrupulously clean, the tables covered with white tablecloths. Gorgeous Thai tapestries hung on the walls, along with a few lesser but interesting pieces of art. Best of all, it smelled wonderful.

Gwen's stomach rumbled in appreciation. She'd always maintained that nothing could deter her appetite. This morning's events were definite proof.

Only three of the tables were occupied. At one of them, the table nearest the kitchen, a woman sat alone. She stood up when she saw Gwen.

Kate Myers was tall, with brown hair cut in chin-length layers. She was probably in her mid to late thirties, and she was pleasant looking, if not exactly pretty. And, Gwen noted, she did not look particularly happy to be here.

They shook hands. "Thanks for meeting me so far from work," Gwen said.

"The choice was deliberate," Kate Myers stated. "I don't want anyone to know that I'm talking to you." She grimaced. "I didn't mean that the way it sounded. But to be very frank, any suggestion of reopening the investigation into Winston's nightclub gives me nightmares."

Gwen settled down in her chair. "I can understand that."

Kate gave her a keen look. "I suppose you would. Actually being there must have been terrifying."

"There wasn't much time to think about it."

"That's where your job and mine differ. Once the case comes to me, I've got nothing but time, and I have to take a long, hard look at everything." She reached for her water glass and took a quick, nervous sip. "I've been in forensic medicine for seven years, and I thought I'd seen just about everything. But what was done to officers Yoland and Moniz was . . . simply not human."

Gwen leaned forward. "Then you'll be glad to know that's not what I wanted to talk about. Frank Cross, my first partner, died last night. I want someone I can trust to oversee the autopsy."

Kate Myers lifted one eyebrow. "And you trust me?"

"Quaid apparently does, and that says something. He's the suspicious type."

That brought a faint smile to her face. "I won't argue with that assessment. The autopsy can probably be arranged. I'm tempted to ask what you think I should be looking for, but I don't want that to skew my observations."

"Fair enough."

A slim, smiling waiter bustled over and handed them menus. Kate waved it away and asked for the vegetarian pad thai.

Gwen studied her menu. "There doesn't seem to be many fried options."

"You sound disappointed," Kate observed.

"Yeah. I never met a high-fat calorie I didn't like."

"Then try chicken panang," the waiter suggested. "It's not fried, but it's in a creamy sauce, red curry in coconut milk."

"In a pinch, creamy's good." Gwen handed the menu to the waiter. He smiled and hurried off.

Kate studied Gwen for a moment. "So you're not looking into the nightclub fiasco? Not ever?"

"Not at the moment," she specified. "I am curious, though, who's responsible for keeping such a tight lid on what happened to Yoland and Moniz."

The woman took a sip of water. "That would have to be the chief medical examiner, Sam Giles."

"Older guy," Gwen recalled. "Been there forever."

"Since before we both were born," Kate agreed. "He's going on seventy."

Something occurred to Gwen, something Frank had told her about Ian Forest's case. "It's not the first time this guy decided to play his cards close. Just the other day Frank and I were talking about a family that was killed in a car crash a while back. The bodies, three of them, disappeared from the lab."

"Disappeared?" she echoed.

"Yeah. Does that sound possible?"

Kate drained her water glass; something to do, Gwen observed, while she decided on an answer. "It's possible," she said at last. "My first year on the job, a Jane Doe went to the incinerator before the autopsy was performed. Miscommunications are rare, but they happen. When did that incident occur?"

"Frank didn't say."

"If you'd like me to look into it, let me know."

"Thanks."

The waiter returned with steaming plates. Gwen sampled hers and heaved a sigh of pure bliss. The thinly sliced chicken was tender, the sauce both creamy and spicy, the green beans and red pepper easily avoided. And it had snow peas, one of the few green things she actually enjoyed.

"On another matter," she said. "If someone—and we're talking a private citizen—wanted to have some DNA sampling done, where would they be likely to go?"

Kate put down her fork and dabbed her lips with her napkin. "Damian O'Riley asked me that same question two or three days ago. What's going on?"

"Judging from what you've told me, I don't think you want to know," Gwen said candidly.

Her eyes searched Gwen's face, seeking answers or reassurance. Unfortunately, Gwen was short on both. After a minute Kate pushed aside her plate.

"I'm scared," she admitted softly, her eyes on the table. "I know terrible things happen. I see the results of them every day. But I always felt safe, removed from it. Untouchable." She glanced up at Gwen. "You must think I'm a coward. At best, a naïve fool."

"Not really. I think most people feel the way you do," Gwen said. "Listen to the news, and when anything hits the fan in any small town or suburb, the first thing out of everyone's mouth is, 'Gee, I never thought something like this could happen around here.'"

"Now that you mention it," Kay said ruefully, "that does sound like a particularly stupid cliché."

"Yeah, but maybe it's better that way. When you walk around watching for things that could go wrong, it gets to be a habit. Then it starts to color how you look at people, how you see the world."

"I can see how it would," she said thoughtfully, as if that explained a few things she's often puzzled over. Gwen was fairly certain that Quaid was high on that list.

Kate glanced at her watch. "I have to run, but I'll be in touch with you soon."

Gwen caught the waiter's eye and gestured for the check. "I've got this. Thanks for meeting me."

"No problem." A faint smile touched the woman's lips. "You've definitely given me a lot to think about."

An hour later, Gwen strolled through the shopping mall that dominated downtown Providence. It was a huge, glitzy thing. From the highway, that's pretty much all you could see, that and the Dunkin' Donuts Civic Center. It all but hid the capital building from view, replacing it with a monument to the Providence Renaissance. In one of her more cynical moments, Marcy had suggested that a former mayor had planned it this way, out of spite for the laws prohibiting convicted felons from being state governors.

Damian O'Riley stood in the food court, giving due consideration to the list of possibilities offered by the 1950s-style burger joint.

His gaze fell on Gwen, and a smug smile edged onto his face. Anyone who looked at him would have no doubt how their last evening ended.

She strolled over. "Play poker much?"

He blinked. "How's that?"

"Never mind." She handed him the plastic bag containing the pencil she'd taken from the blue house. "I need someone to run prints on this."

His eyes lit up. "This about the Winston thing?"

"Maybe," she lied. "Can you do it?"

"No problem. Got anything else for me?"

She ignored the grin, the good-natured innuendo. "I talked to Kate Myers. She told me you were looking into DNA labs."

"Yeah." His face turned somber. "There's a lot of them, and most of them are places you can mail away to. Long distance is no way to get an inside contact."

"No local places?"

"Some. I'm still working on that."

"I'm guessing that some of this testing was done off the books. Watch for people who come in early, stay late," she suggested.

"Good idea. One thing I can tell you is this: whatever our

guy is looking for, he wants it bad. These labs want two bills to run a paternity test. That's one test. There were over two hundred people at the club that night. If this is off the books, the person running the tests will want extra to cover the risk."

He pocketed the pencil. "So, anything else been happening in your life?"

She shoved aside the wave of grief and forced a smile onto her face. "People like you and me have a life?"

"I hear that," he agreed mournfully.

Gwen's cell phone shrilled as she was getting into her car. She settled down and clicked it on. "Gwen Gellman," she said as she reached for the ignition.

"Ms. Gellman, this is Angela Harris calling from the Providence Hospital. Your name was listed as an emergency contact for Sylvia Black."

For the second time today, Gwen felt the icy touch of dread. "What happened?"

"Miss Black had a heart attack. She is alert and asking for you. Would it be possible for you to come right to the hospital? She seems very agitated, and she insists upon talking to you."

"I'm about twenty minutes away. Tell her I'm on my way."

Gwen pulled out of the parking lot and drove impatiently through the narrow residential streets. It was a relief to hit route 195, and she cranked up her speed until the old Toyota wheezed and rattled in protest.

The road ended in a sharp Y. Gwen bore left onto 95 South, then swung into another curve. The exit to the hospital was almost directly off the divide and across four lanes of highway. When the traffic was heavy, anyone determined to take the exit on the first try was taking their lives in their hands.

Gwen made it across unscathed. She negotiated the seemingly endless hospital construction and found a parking space of dubious legality.

She hurried to Sylvia's room. For a long moment she stood silent in the open doorway, stunned by the change in her friend.

The woman looked years older, so pale that her fragile skin was almost translucent. Gwen took some comfort in the familiar details: the lustrous coils of white hair, perfectly manicured nails on blue-veined hands.

"You're the only person I know who can make a hospital gown look elegant," Gwen said softly.

Sylvia's gaze flashed to the doorway, and she extended one hand. Gwen came into the room and took it in both of hers. "Damn it, Sylvia, you scared the shit out of me."

The older woman managed a faint smile. "That was, of course, my entire intention."

"Smart-ass." Gwen sat down, still holding her friend's hand. "Tell me what happened."

"Ian Forest came to the house to see you this morning. *The* Ian Forest, the man I knew more than thirty years ago. *And he hasn't changed in the slightest since I knew him*." The woman's voice shook. Her pupils were huge with remembered shock, nearly swallowing the blue of her eyes.

"Sylvia, that not possible," Gwen said gently. "Why are you so sure it's the same man? Did you talk to him?"

The old woman shook her head. "There was no time. The shock of seeing him again set me back on my heels."

"The shock knocked you on your ass," Gwen said grimly.

First Frank, now Sylvia. When she caught up to Ian Forest, he was going to have a lot to answer for.

"You've met Ian, haven't you? At the club?"

"Yes," Gwen said shortly.

"And you didn't wonder about his age? I told you he was an old acquaintance."

"I thought about it. Maybe the man you saw today was Ian Junior?

"Not possible. Ian couldn't have children. He was very emphatic about that."

Gwen figured that Sylvia would have reason to know. "It's a weird situation, I'll grant you that. But there's bound to be a good explanation. I'll go look for it."

"Thank you." Sylvia let out a long sigh, and her eyelids drifted shut. Her tense fingers relaxed in Gwen's hands. "If you don't mind, I'll try to rest now," she said, her voice slurring off toward sleep.

Gwen eased away from the old woman's grip and walked from the room. She found a hospital phone and punched in Ian Forest's number. He answered on the second ring.

"We need to talk. Can you meet me in half an hour?"

"Where?" he said without hesitation.

"My office. You know where it is." She slammed down the phone, drawing a reproachful glare from a passing nurse.

Gwen made it home with a few minutes to spare, but Ian Forest was already waiting for her. He stood outside the property, leaning on the fence beside the open driveway gate. Gwen pulled up beside him and rolled down her window a few inches.

"Meet me at the main house. There's something in there I want you to see," she told him.

He lifted one eyebrow, a gentle commentary on her hostile tone. "Perhaps we could drive up together?"

"Forget it. I don't trust you enough to let you in my car."

"But apparently you have no problem letting me into your home."

It was hard to argue with that logic. Gwen leaned over and unlocked the passenger door. He slid in and sent her a considering look.

"I hadn't expected to hear back from you quite this soon. I trust your other case was resolved?"

Gwen slammed the gear into drive and stomped on the gas. Her back wheels spun, spitting pebbles until the tires got a grip. The car took off in a sudden, neck-snapping lurch.

"This isn't about your case," she said shortly. "But we'll get to that later."

"As you wish."

She pulled to an abrupt stop next to the walk that led to Sylvia's front door, then half turned to look at him. "First, tell me why you came to see me earlier today."

"You're looking for a missing child. I came to offer my assistance."

Gwen's eyes narrowed. "Why?"

"As I told you before, her father owns a part interest in my club. It is to my advantage to resolve this matter as quickly and quietly as possible."

"That's interesting. I thought you said you didn't have anything to hide."

"Everyone has secrets, but I'm less concerned with potential legal problems than I am with the media coverage that seems to attend such things. I am a very private person, and I don't wish to have my name and image appear in the local news. Nor do most of Underhill's clients."

She swung out of the car and slammed the door. "What sort of help were you thinking about offering?"

He got out and walked around to her side of the car. "I have acquaintances in many walks of life, and resources that may augment those available to you," he said quietly. "I'm assuming you're working in conjunction with the authorities. Let me put the word out elsewhere."

It sounded so reasonable that Gwen was tempted to take him up on his offer. The problem was, she had no idea who and what "elsewhere" entailed. For all she knew, accepting Ian Forest's help might put Meredith in even greater danger.

"I'll think about it," she said curtly. "Right now there's something I want you to see."

She unlocked the door and led the way down the entrance hall and into a paneled sitting room. Over the fireplace hung a portrait of Sylvia, painted when she was in her thirties.

Even though the painting was probably done in the mid 1960s, there was something about Sylvia that reminded Gwen of movie stars from an earlier, more glamorous time. Her bone structure brought to mind a young Katharine Hepburn. Thick, glossy auburn hair spilled about her shoulders. Her dress was white, cut low enough to show off a spectacular figure. She sat on the floor, her wide skirt spread out around her. It was a contrived pose, but somehow Sylvia made it look perfectly natural.

"Do you know that woman?" Gwen demanded, pointing to the portrait.

Ian studied the picture, then turned to Gwen with a faintly quizzical expression. "It looks very much like someone I knew quite some time ago. Sylvia Black." He smiled faintly. "Her name suited her, with its connotations of woodlands at midnight. A lovely woman with a heartful of secrets and shadows."

The simple, strangely apt poetry of his response made Gwen's throat constrict. It was getting harder and harder for her to believe that Sylvia had been mistaken about this man. "When was the last time you saw her?"

He shrugged. "I'm not sure. More than a few years."

"Try forty," Gwen suggested. "Sylvia Black is my landlady, and she's seventy if she's a day. Apparently she saw you when you came here earlier today."

"I see," he said softly.

"She had a heart attack. The shock of seeing you again, looking exactly as you did forty years ago, put her in the hospital." Gwen studied his face as she spoke. It was hard to read, but she was pretty sure there was no hint of surprise. Suspicion, never far from the surface, reared its head.

"Did you know Sylvia lived here? Did you do this on purpose?"

He turned to face the portrait. "I returned to Providence four years ago, after an absence of more than thirty years."

"You're evading the question."

"No, I'm answering it. It did not seem likely to me that anyone would remember my name or my face."

"Why not? It's a very memorable face."

His eyes flashed to her face. "Under different circumstances, I would consider that a compliment."

If there had been even a hint of flirtation in his voice, Gwen would have punched him. But he sounded weary, weighed down by something almost like grief.

"You're upset about Sylvia," Gwen observed. "She meant a lot to you."

"As much as that sort of woman could." He held up one hand to forestall Gwen's angry retort. "Any deficiencies I perceived in Sylvia Black were not due to her profession, but her race."

Gwen frowned, puzzled. "Caucasian?"

"Human."

After a moment's shocked silence, she let out a burst of laughter. "And what the hell do you consider yourself?"

His blue, blue eyes focused on her with disturbing intensity. "A member of one of the Elder Races."

She stared at him for a long time. He seemed reasonably sane and perfectly serious.

"Elder Races," she repeated. "Are we talking Aryan supremacy, or Tolkien? Because, no offense, you don't look much like Legolas, and you're a little old for the whole skinhead neo-Nazi thing."

He ignored her mocking tone. "Surely history proves that few cultures remain static. You wouldn't suppose that members of the local Jewish Orthodox temple worship in quite the same manner as their nomadic forebears, slaughtering bulls and so forth. The local pipe-and-drum corps wear the kilt, which is admittedly somewhat anachronistic but far less so than going about naked and painting themselves with woad. Need I continue?"

"Please don't." Gwen raked both hands through her hair.

She searched his face, looking for some explanation that she could understand. "You can't be serious about this."

"How else can you explain why our mutual friend found me so little changed by the passage of time? My people age very slowly, and appear much younger than we truly are." He studied her closely, as if waiting for a particular reaction.

Gwen shook her head helplessly. "That's impossible. Crazy."

"No more so than the mystery you'll uncover in the file I gave you."

A fresh wave of grief tore through her, too much to contain. The room spun, swimming in her tear-blurred vision.

Dimly she was aware of him helping her to a chair. He sat down across from her. "Tell me."

Gwen wiped her eyes and considered his somber face. If this . . . lunatic knew anything about Frank's death, he was covering it well. Hell, either he was completely crazy, or he was the best actor she'd ever seen.

Then why, she wondered briefly, did she feel so strong an urge to confide in him?

"I have a friend who sometimes helps me on cases," Gwen said, picking her words carefully. "Since I was busy looking for Meredith Cody, I thought maybe he could get a start on your case."

Ian Forest went very still. "You gave the folder to someone else. That, I did not anticipate. Where is it now?"

"I don't know."

"And where is this friend of yours?"

"He's dead," Gwen said wearily. "I pulled him out of the bay myself just this morning. All the information was missing—the file, his computer, you name it."

"I see," he said slowly. "Do the police suspect foul play?"

"No, they seem pretty sure it was an accidental drowning," she said bitterly. "It was made to look as if he drank himself into a stupor and fell off his boat."

Ian nodded thoughtfully. "I suppose that's for the best."

"Is it?" she snapped. "What about his reputation? What about the people who cared about him?"

"Such as yourself?" he answered. "If you know the truth, what does it matter what others think?"

"He has a son."

"And does this man share your opinion?"

"I don't know. I've never met him."

Ian considered this. "Perhaps you should take his measure. If he seems sensible, tell him what he needs to know."

This struck Gwen as good advice. "The problem is, I don't know the truth. Not all of it, at least. Yet."

"Perhaps," Ian said softly, "it would be far better for all concerned if you let it go."

Gwen let out a soft, bitter laugh. "That would be convenient for you, wouldn't it?"

"I had nothing to do with this man's death," he said. "I will swear to it by any oath you name."

She scoffed. "Like I'd take your word for it."

"Then test me and see." He held out both hands, palms up.

"I don't read palms," she told him. "Tea leaves, either."

He smiled faintly, as a patient teacher might to humor a sulky child. "Bring an image of your friend to mind, and see if it finds any resonance in my thoughts."

Without stopping to think, Gwen placed her hands over his.

Immediately her mind was flooded with memories. They were whole and complete, not like the random images she sometimes received from handling things. They flowed through her, too fast for comprehension, like water through a fine sieve.

Finally the flow ended. There was nothing of Frank in Ian's memories, except for a faint response to her grief—an odd mixture of sympathy and impatience.

Gwen withdrew her hands and slumped in her chair, her mind spinning. She could retain none of Ian's memories, other than a certainty that he had told her the truth.

"So this is how a flash drive feels when it's downloading files," she muttered.

"That's an interesting analogy," Ian said. "I'm surprised you like computers. So few of us are comfortable around them."

The comment struck Gwen as odd, but she brushed it aside as far less important than anything else that was going on.

"What was in that file?"

"Very little," he said. "My friend James Avalon was killed in a car accident, along with his wife and daughter. I listed their names, the date of the accident, and their home address—they lived in the Alfred Drowne neighborhood in Barrington. James was a musician, his wife, Ruby, was a freelance artist. They had no regular place of employment, very little personal paperwork—at least none that I could get my hands on."

"Who could have thought that the information in that file was worth a man's life?" she demanded.

Ian looked thoughtful. "I would very much like to know the answer to that question myself."

CHAPTER

Twenty

❧ Gwen's phone rang. She picked it up and slid a pointed gaze toward Ian Forest. He rose from his chair and went over to study Sylvia's portrait—a polite fiction of privacy. She clicked the phone on.

"They contacted us! The people who have Meredith!" Dianne Cody's voice was shrill, frantic.

"Slow down, Mrs. Cody," Gwen said calmly. "What was the nature of the contact? Did they make any demands?"

"No. Nothing. It's just a . . . an e-mail."

Gwen gritted her teeth. After a brief, private struggle, she yielded to the inevitable. "Let me give you my e-mail address. I'll need you to forward that to me."

"*No!*"

She blinked, startled by the vehemence of Dianne's refusal. "Okay, print it out. I'll pick up a copy."

"I can't do that, either. You'll understand when you see it."

A sick suspicion crept over her. "Is Meredith all right?"

"She's alive," the woman said. Her voice caught on a sob. "Please come."

It was the "please," more than anything else, that conveyed to Gwen the extent of Dianne Cody's distress. "I'm on my way."

She clicked off the phone and glanced at Ian Forest. He had given up the pretense of respecting her privacy and was studying her with obvious concern.

"Was that about Ryan Cody's daughter?"

"Yeah. Listen, I've got to run."

He nodded, accepting this. "We'll talk again soon. I'm assuming that this morning's unfortunate events have increased your interest in my investigation."

"You got that right," she muttered as she stalked from the room.

Ian followed her out of Sylvia's house. She locked the door, then turned back to face him.

He no longer stood behind her.

Gwen looked up and down the drive. There was no sign of him. The stone walkway that led from the driveway to the house was lined with flowers, but there were no nearby bushes, nothing to offer concealment. A small copse of birch trees stood to one side of the walk, but the slender white trunks couldn't hide a squirrel, much less a man.

She walked over to her car and peered in the window. No, he wasn't in the car, either. To all appearances, he had simply disappeared.

"I don't have time to think about this," she muttered as she took off down the drive.

Her frustration soared when she noted the compact car parked at the gate, blocking her way out. She hit the gate opener, pulled her car to an abrupt stop, and stalked through the resulting dust cloud, loaded for bear.

A small, slender woman got out of the car. Wavy dark hair

spilled past her shoulders. Her big eyes were a dark mossy green, and her aquiline nose reminded Gwen of an ancient cameo. She struck Gwen as an oddly patrician woman, a countess in blue jeans.

"Officer Gellman?" she inquired. "I'm Teresa Moniz. Carmine's wife."

Gwen's ire washed away on a tide of uncertainty. Carmine Moniz was one of two policemen who had died at Winston's. A lot of people blamed her for that. Most likely his widow had her own grievances to air.

"I need to talk with you," Teresa said quietly. "I believe it might be important."

Gwen studied her. There was no anger in her face, no accusation in her eyes. "What is this about, Mrs. Moniz?"

"Teresa, please. This is about an investigation you might be working on."

"Which one is that?"

"I don't know," the woman said candidly. "What I have to show you has some significance to you, but I don't know precisely what it might be."

"Look, I don't have time—"

"I see things, Officer Gellman," she said, breaking quietly but firmly into Gwen's dismissal. "Things that I can't always explain, that most people won't accept." Her pine-forest eyes searched Gwen's face. "Something tells me you might understand that."

A moment of recognition passed between them, a flash of something approaching kinship. Gwen had experienced something similar once before, in a New Age shop. The woman who ran it had a plump, former-prom-queen face, enough silver jewelry to set off the metal detectors at Logan Airport without moving out from behind the register, big blond hair dyed the color of a Twinkie, and more psychic energy than any one small woman should be able to hold. The jolt of recognition had startled Gwen, but the proprietor took it in stride. "Hi, honey," she'd said, as if greeting an old friend. "The tarot decks are over on the far shelf." Not bothering to ask what Gwen had come in to buy. Not needing to.

So Teresa Moniz was psychic. Gwen wondered if she'd warned her husband of danger that December night. Or if ever since she'd spent sleepless nights staring at the ceiling, wondering why the little flashes of insight never seemed to come when it really counted.

"I'm listening," she said cautiously.

The woman handed Gwen a piece of paper. On it was a sketch of an oblong design that looked like a roughly drawn garden maze.

"Do you recognize this?"

A faint, sick suspicion rose in Gwen's throat like bile. Something very like this had been carved into Lauren Simpson's body. "What is it?" she asked.

"I believe it's a representation of the Caer Sidi."

"The spiral castle," Gwen translated. "The link with the Annwn, the Celtic Otherworld."

Teresa smiled faintly. "You've studied."

"Not really. For a while I dated a guy who was obsessed with King Arthur, Glastonbury, all that. He showed me pictures of the Tor, claimed there was a terraced maze leading to the top."

"So they say. The symbol has been used for thousands of years, from Crete to Ireland."

"And you're showing this to me because . . ."

The woman's face turned somber. "Do you know what was done to my Carmine? To Tom Yoland?"

Gwen responded with a curt nod.

"When they called to tell me, I had to see for myself." She held up the design. "I drew this. It is what they cut into his body."

Gwen added this new layer to the puzzle. A terraced maze, layers within layers. The symbol was disturbingly fitting.

"You know who did this," Teresa observed.

"I might," said Gwen.

"And yet you look surprised," she noted.

"The people I'm thinking about are freaks, but I wouldn't have pegged them for cultists."

"That might not be the best way to describe them," Teresa said thoughtfully. "Ignorance can be as deadly as fanaticism. Sometimes, when people first become aware of a reality beyond the five basic senses, they act like greedy, stupid children. They try to wrest powers they cannot possess from ancient symbols they do not understand."

"It still sounds like ritual murder."

Teresa gave her an odd look. "But my husband and his partner were already dead."

Gwen just held her gaze. Understanding washed over the woman's face. "There were others," she stated softly. "That is how they died?"

"Yes."

"In a way, it has a sick sort of logic," Teresa said. "In the killer's mind, he might have been leading them into the next world. Or perhaps opening the door to the Otherworld."

Gwen shrugged impatiently. "I don't care if he thinks he was bringing about the second coming of Pee Wee Herman."

"You should," Teresa said gently. "You do. If for no other reason, knowing why a thing was done will often help you find the person who did it."

Spoken like a good cop's wife, someone who'd listened and understood. Gwen conceded the point with a curt nod.

"I'll keep this in mind. Right now I'm on my way to an appointment, but once this case is settled, I'll start working on what you showed me."

No acknowledgement registered in Teresa's eyes, no sign that she heard a word of this. She stared past Gwen, her face pale and set. Her lips shaped a word: *linchetto,* or something similar to it.

Gwen darted a look over her shoulder. There was nothing back there worthy of alarm.

"Hello?" she said pointedly.

The woman's gaze snapped back to Gwen's face. "Sorry," she said faintly. She manufactured a smile, pasted it more or less in place. "I won't keep you from your appointment."

"Okay," Gwen said, waiting for her to move.

They stood facing each other in silence for several moments. Then Teresa took a chain from around her neck and handed it to Gwen.

Gwen regarded the twisted horn charm for a moment, then handed it back. "Someone recently gave me one of these."

Teresa folded Gwen's hand around the charm. "Keep it. Wear it."

She turned and hurried to her car. Gwen added the charm to the growing collection in her jacket pocket. She headed out of the city, joining the rush-hour traffic going south into the East Bay. Twenty minutes later, she pulled into the Cody's tree-lined street.

Dianne met her at the door. She'd been crying. Her eyes were red and puffy, and her mascara had run like black tears. "It's on my computer," she said without preamble.

To Gwen's surprise, Ryan Cody came up behind his wife. He stood in the doorway as if uncertain whether or not to block the way.

She met his gaze. "Do you have a problem with me being here?"

His lips firmed into a thin, disapproving line, but he stepped aside. Gwen followed Diane into a small, book-lined study.

The e-mail in question filled the computer screen. There was no text, but two photos shared a split screen.

On the right-hand side was a picture of Meredith. She was barely recognizable as the same bright, confident girl in her Christmas portrait. She sat on the floor, her arms hugging her knees close to her naked body. She appeared to be unhurt, but tears streamed down her face, and her eyes were wide and dark with fear.

On the left side was a picture of Gwen, in an identical pose. Both photos were done in shades of brown, like old-fashioned photos, faded with age.

Portraits in sepia, Gwen thought grimly. Suddenly her vision of the blue frame house made a great deal of sense.

She turned to Ryan Cody. "Was it you who sent my pictures to your wife?"

He glanced at his wife, then cleared his throat. "Yes."

"How did you get hold of them?"

"After you came to my office the first time, I had a background check done on you by a consultant connected with the law firm. He was very thorough."

"I'll need to talk to him," Gwen said. She noted the flash of alarm in the man's eyes. "Is that going to be a problem?"

"He is adamant about maintaining his anonymity," Ryan Cody said carefully, "and he is in possession of a considerable amount of sensitive material vital to several ongoing cases."

"So what you're saying is that you won't give up one of your law firm's valuable assets even if that might help me find your daughter?"

"No, I'm saying that even if I gave you his name—and without going into detail, there are reasons why I can't—he wouldn't talk to you."

Gwen let that go for now. "Tell me about the Underhill club."

He shot another quick look at his wife. "It wasn't my idea to join. Membership was a gift."

"Considering the fees involved, that's a substantial gift. Who was it from?"

"Our law firm's silent partner likes to have something on the attorneys. It keeps us in line," he said bitterly.

"Is that why Meredith was taken? To keep you in line?"

"In a manner of speaking. I was going to quit the firm."

"Why's that?"

"Different values," he said shortly.

"And you're just figuring this out."

He grimaced. "Unfortunately, I've known from the beginning

what was required. The firm has a very unusual recruitment policy. They only approach lawyers who either share their values or can be persuaded to practice them."

"And how did they find you?"

"Through the Internet," Dianne Cody said bitterly. Her blue eyes held an arctic chill as she regarded the man she'd married. "Apparently it's not as anonymous as most people think. People seldom consider the possibility that the filth they wallow in might cling to them."

Gwen got the picture. "So there was some kind of tracer on one or more of the sites you frequented."

"That's right," he said.

"And I don't suppose you could report this, seeing that child porn is illegal."

He nodded, looking thoroughly miserable.

"So, why the change of heart?"

"Meredith," he said, his voice barely audible. "My daughter is about the same age as some of the girls on that site. When I made the connection, it changed things." He seemed sincere, but questions remained.

"Why haven't you assured whoever's holding Meredith that you'll stay with the company? That's what most people would do under the circumstances."

"That's what I did." He thrust one trembling hand through his hair. "They told me that they'd keep her a while anyway, just to make a point. Apparently they've done this before. They keep the kids three or four days, just to prove they can."

"But after four days, I came into the picture," Gwen observed.

"That's right." Ryan Cody glanced at his wife. "If she hadn't come to you, hadn't complicated the situation, Meredith would have been home by now."

Dianne turned white. "Don't you make this my fault, you son of a bitch!"

Gwen stepped between them. "This can wait until after Meredith gets home. Let's keep focused, okay?"

The woman folded her lips into a thin, tight line and conceded with a curt node.

"So, what's the new deal?" Gwen asked Ryan. "What do these people want from you now?"

"If I successfully defend a murder suspect, I'll get my daughter back."

The hair on the back of Gwen's neck prickled. "You wouldn't be talking about Carl Jamison, would you?"

He looked at her in astonishment. "How could you know that?"

Gwen took a long, shuddering breath. She pointed to the pictures on the screen. "See how the photos are done in shades of brown, like an old-fashioned portrait? The photographer is signing his work."

"You know who took this?"

She nodded. "The same guy took both pictures. The whole portrait in sepia thing is his trademark. He thinks it's artistic. The clients don't seem to like it, but he always makes prints for himself. Whoever sent this knew I'd recognize the photographer's trademark, and they put my picture with Meredith's so you'd be sure to contact me."

"I'm following you so far," Ryan said. "But what does that have to do with Jamison?"

"Both things are messages," Gwen said softly. "The pictures tell me where to go. Jamison is both bait and threat."

"How both?"

Her gaze moved from Ryan to Dianne, and in them was a silent apology for the words to come. "It's bait, because they know I'll come after Jamison. Threat, because I know what he'll do to Meredith if I don't."

Dianne caught her breath in a sob. Her husband tried to take her in his arms. She shrugged him off and went to stand by the window, her back to the room and her arms hugging her chest.

Gwen walked over and put a hand on the woman's shoulder. "I know it doesn't seem like it, but this is good news. They want me to find Meredith. The game has changed. Ultimately it's me they want, not her."

Dianne nodded. "What's going to happen to you?"

"A better question," Gwen said quietly, "is what's going to happen to *them*."

The woman placed her hand on top of Gwen's and gave it a quick, grateful squeeze. She walked quickly out of the room, not looking back.

Gwen turned to face Ryan Cody. "You want to know what I think about all this?"

He lifted an eyebrow in silent inquiry. She stepped closer, so they were almost toe to toe, and leaned in as if confiding a secret.

"I think you know a lot more than you're telling me. In fact, I think you're a lying sack of shit."

Color rose in his face. "I haven't told you any lies," he said evenly. He grimaced and qualified, "Not today, at least."

"Gee, thanks for making that distinction. But you haven't told me the whole truth, either."

He stepped back, looking thoroughly miserable. "I've told you everything I can."

She shook her head in disgust. "I just promised your wife that I'd walk straight into a trap and bring her daughter out, and that's the best you can give me?"

"I'm sorry," he muttered.

Her scathing glare raked him up and down. "You'll get no argument from me."

She stalked out of the house and punched Damian O'Riley's number.

"Go," he said, by way of greeting.

"It's Gwen," she told him. "Did you get the fingerprint report for me?"

"Girl, you just gave that to me, what? Yesterday?"

"Sorry to rush you, Damian, but I really need it. Now would be a good time."

"If I'm talking, I'm walking," he told her. "I'll be at the station in ten, fifteen tops. Getting you a name is gonna cost me, but I can get it fast. One of the techs is a crazy Lakers fan. He drops everything and runs the print, I forget he bet against the Celtics."

"Thanks. Anything on the DNA?"

"Not yet. I'll let you know as soon as something bounces." He paused. "I heard about Frank Cross."

"Yeah, the news is probably making the rounds. Listen, I have to go."

She hung up abruptly. She didn't want to talk about Frank. On the other hand, it didn't seem right, not having the time to grieve.

There was too much going on for Gwen to make sense of it all: the mysteries surrounding Frank's death; the strange, almost holographic vision. Then there was Ian Forest's ridiculous claims, his sudden disappearance, the weird connection she felt with him. And not just with him, she added. There was that odd, almost magnetic pull that had first drawn her attention to Ryan Cody's attorney—

An image flashed into mind: Wallace Edmonson handing her leather jacket to her. There was something about the way he held his hand directly afterward: thumb and forefingers pinched, as if holding onto something small. Or thin.

Heart pounding, Gwen hit the speed dial for Marcy's private line.

"Marcy Bartlett." Her tone of voice said, *I'm with a client, so this had better be pretty damn important.*

"Sorry, but this can't wait," Gwen said. "Wallace Edmonson is Ryan Cody's attorney. I need to know everything you can tell me about him. By yesterday, if possible."

"I see," Marcy said crisply. "Within the hour?"

"Thanks."

Gwen hung up, drove toward Zimmer's house. There was a car in the drive; her luck was starting to look up. She found a parking place a few yards down the road. Her phone rang while she was pulling in.

"Got a name," Damian said without preamble. "Your man's one Thaddeus Zimmer."

"That's what I needed to know." Her voice sounded grim even to her ears.

"Damn. You into something where a little help might come in handy?"

"I'll be fine. Thanks for the name."

Gwen turned off the phone and slipped into the house through the back door. She moved quietly up the stairs to the room where she'd seen his computer. Zimmer was seated before it, downloading pictures from his camera.

"Hey, Tadpole," she said, using his favorite nickname and putting a lot of little-girl seductress into her voice.

Zimmer let out a startled yelp and spun toward her. In a heartbeat, he was out of the chair and bolting for the door on the far side of the room.

She got across the room first and seized him by his collar. One of his flailing hands managed to find a desk lamp. He swung it wildly. Gwen released him and ducked under the blow. Still in crouched position, she leaned to one side and kicked up high. Her foot sank into his gut, knocking the air out of him with a satisfying *whoosh*. The little weasel doubled over, making a sound that was somewhere between a gasp and a whimper.

Gwen grabbed a handful of his hair and dragged his head up. "Where's Meredith Cody?"

The man's eyes bulged so wide she could see the whites around them. It took him a while to gather enough breath to frame a response. "Who?" he wheezed.

Gwen glanced at the computer screen. A dozen or so photos were displayed in thumbnail versions. Even from several paces away, she could recognize Meredith's photo from the pose and the sepia tones.

She spun him around to the computer and stabbed a forefinger at the picture. "That's her. When and where was this taken?"

"Today. I took it this morning," he babbled.

A wave of relief coursed through Gwen. As of this morning, Meredith Cody was still alive. Gwen hadn't been too confident of that.

"Where was it taken?"

"Here," he said. "He brought her here. I told them no, I don't have a studio here, but he offered a lot of money."

"Who?"

The little man shrugged. "I don't know his name. He's one of Tiger Leone's boys."

That news set Gwen back on her heels. Whoever sent Meredith's photo to Dianne Cody knew a great deal about Gwen. They probably came across the Tiger Leone connection while unearthing her hard-to-find dirty pictures. What didn't make sense is that one of Tiger's boys, and whomever he was currently reporting to, had a connection to Meredith Cody.

But the connection was there. Tiger had presented himself as a player, but he'd been working for someone else. Captain Walsh had been very eager to cover up what happened at Winston's, and he showed up at Cody's office for a repeat performance. It seemed likely to Gwen that whoever had held Tiger's leash had something going with Walsh and Cody. But what?

The only thing she could think of was the two clubs, Winston's and Underhill, both of which catered to sexual fantasies. Perhaps Ian Forest and Tiger Leone answered to the same person?

Gwen dragged her thoughts back to Zimmer, who was watching her with an expression of anxious expectancy. "Can you contact this guy? Tiger's boy?"

"By e-mail, sure."

"Do it."

He brought up his mail program and opened a new message. "Whom should I say is calling?" he asked, making a weak attempt at lightness. The look on Gwen's face stole the sickly smile from his face.

"Tell him GiGi took the bait. He'll know."

The man's head bobbed. His fingers tapped for a few moments, then hit Send. "Okay?" he asked hopefully.

"I'll wait for the response."

He looked distressed by this prospect, but his only response was an unhappy nod. Gwen took out her phone and turned it on. She had one missed call, Marcy's number. She hit the callback button.

"Here's what I've got on Edmonson, Wallace Earl," said Marcy, hitting the ground running. "The name didn't ring any bells, so I had Jeffrey makes some calls. There are no attorneys by that name licensed to practice in Rhode Island. But Simmons, Fletcher, and Rye, Cody's law firm, employs a Wallace Earl Edmonson on a contract basis, as a consultant."

"A consultant," Gwen repeated, replaying her earlier conversation with Ryan Cody. He'd said that a consultant working for the law firm had dug up the pictures of her. "Do you have an address for this guy?"

"Nothing. It looks as if he works off the books. Is this a dead end?"

A beep came from Zimmer's computer. He opened a new e-mail message, nodded avidly to Gwen.

"Doesn't look like it. Talk to you later." She hung up the phone and turned to Zimmer. "Read it."

He sent her a furtive glance. "It says, 'Inform Ms. Gellman that we will contact her tomorrow at midnight.' That's all."

"Print out both e-mails. This one, and the one you sent," she said, figuring that Frank might be able to trace the e-mail back to its source.

Then she remembered. Grief swept over her, rolling her under. Swallowing hard, she took the printouts from Zimmer.

"We're finished here, right?" he said hopefully.

"Yeah," she said in a dull tone. "We're finished."

CHAPTER

Twenty-one

∾ The long, long day was dragging its heels toward midnight when Gwen stumbled into her office. The light on the phone machine greeted her with frantic blinking. She hit the playback button and threw herself into one of the wingback chairs to listen.

"This is Jason Cross, calling for Gwen. I'm in Providence. For now, I'm staying at my father's place. I also wanted to let you know that the wake is tomorrow night at St. Brendan's in East Providence. Call me when you have a chance."

Gwen let out a long sigh. The thought of going to Frank's wake was hideous enough without the prospect of confronting her former coworkers. She hated them judging her. It was even worse to think about them judging Frank.

"Gwen, this is Kate Myers," announced the next caller. "I have the autopsy results for you. Cause of death was confirmed as drowning. There was a significant blood alcohol level. I checked with the crime lab, and the only prints on the glass belonged to Frank Cross. In short, I didn't find anything to contradict the police report indicating an accidental drowning. If that's not what you wanted to hear, I'm sorry. I spoke to Garry Quaid about the other issue we discussed. He'll get in touch with you."

Gwen massaged her throbbing temples. Oh yeah, that's what she needed—one more thing to think about.

"Good news," Damian O'Riley's voice cheerfully announced. "I found a private lab that's been doing a shitload of DNA testing over the past year and a half. All the samples were numbered. The client didn't want an ID, just wanted to verify that the DNA was human."

"Weird," Gwen muttered.

The phone clicked off. Gwen dragged herself out of the chair and up the stairs. She peeled off her clothes and stood under the shower until she felt some of her energy returning. Wrapping a towel around herself, she padded into the kitchen. She opened the fridge and studied the contents. Nothing looked particularly exciting, so she settled for one of the apples she always kept in a big bowl on the low shelf.

Even though it was well past midnight, she dialed the Cody's home number. Ryan Cody picked up after the first ring and gave his name in a crisp, impatient tone.

"You sound wide awake," she commented. "What's going on? Insomnia? Guilty conscience?"

In the tense silence that followed, Gwen could almost hear him counting to ten. "I'm assuming you called for a purpose."

"Tell me about Wallace Edmonson."

"What do you want to know?" he asked, his voice wary.

"You introduced him as your attorney, but he isn't a member of the bar. Apparently he is a consultant at Simmons, Fletcher, and Rye. By any chance, is he the same consultant who dug up those pictures of me?"

Ryan's silence was all the answer she needed.

"How does he fit into this?" she asked.

"Edmonson works for Simmons, Fletcher, and Rye, but he also works for the silent partner. He's the messenger for whoever has Meredith."

"So the other day in your office, when you met with Walsh and me, why was he there? You couldn't find a real attorney at Simmons, Fletcher, and Rye?"

"He said he wanted to meet you, take your measure."

"And you do whatever he tells you."

"In this situation, it seemed prudent."

Gwen had to give him that. "Okay, so Edmonson is the go-between. Is there anything else I should know?"

"That's everything," he said miserably. "Have you found any information about that photographer?"

"I found the guy, yeah."

"That's good news." He sounded a little brighter, almost eager. "Did he tell you where Meredith is being held?"

"He doesn't know. Apparently they brought her to his place for the pictures. But he was able to set up a meet. Tomorrow at midnight. Nice dramatic hour, right?"

"Another whole day," he said, sounding deeply worried. "I suppose there's nothing we can do until then."

"Wrong," Gwen told him. "You can give me Edmonson's phone number and address. I plan to have a talk with him."

He hesitated. "It probably won't do much good. I doubt he'll see you."

"Who knows? And if he does, I might pick up a few bits and pieces of information that will help me deal with the people who have Meredith. Anything beats going in completely blind."

"I suppose you're right." He gave her the phone number and an address on the East Side.

Wallace Earl Edmonson lived less than mile away from Sylvia and Gwen. On impulse, Gwen tossed her towel aside and reached for a pair of jeans.

Perhaps he was experiencing a middleman's dilemma, wanting out but not seeing a way. Unless he was a completely soulless bastard, he had to want a quick resolution and the safe return of the girl to her parents.

Edmonson's house was an old, partially restored Victorian, perched on one of the hills overlooking downtown. Lights blazed in several of the front windows.

Gwen went up to the door and rang the bell. Edmonson answered. He didn't look particularly surprised to see her.

"I assume this is about Meredith Cody," he said.

She nodded. "It's a nice night. Would you like to talk about it outside?"

A faint smile twitched at the corner of his lips. He stepped back and gestured her in.

The renovations suggested by the house's exterior were even more in evidence here. Old plaster was being torn from the walls, a stack of wood for new wainscoting was heaped in one corner. The furniture in the rooms on either side of the hall had been pushed to the middle of the room and draped in white sheets. The wooden floor in the hall had been sanded down, ready for refinishing.

"My study is upstairs," he said, nodding toward a long, curving flight. "I apologize for the inconvenience, but there is no comfortable place to talk on the lower floor."

She let him go first, following him up into a room that probably hadn't been redone in a century.

Gwen paused in the doorway, halted by a strong sense that she didn't want to go further. She pushed through it, and the sensation disappeared.

It was a remarkable room, even to her untrained eye. Bookshelves lined one wall, old books dusty against the dark wood. The furniture was also dark: carved mahogany tables, deep burgundy upholstery on ornate Victorian pieces. The room was remarkably well preserved. The small-paned windows were slightly cloudy—probably the original leaded glass. A crack ran up the plaster of one wall, but other than that, the room looked much as it might have appeared to its first occupant.

The only oddity in the room was a tall wood and glass case, such as might be found in a museum. In it was a single gem, displayed on a silver pedestal against black velvet.

Gwen moved closer, curious. To her surprise, the blue gem lit up when she was a few paces away, blazing like the azure heart of a candle's flame. Most likely the light shone up through the stone from the pedestal, but the effect was both beautiful and startling.

"Motion sensors," Edmonson explained, smiling. "It's an alarm, connected to a private security company."

"Got the Hope Diamond on rental?"

"Hardly that. It's a crystal—a family heirloom, valuable in its own way. Can I offer you a drink?"

"Sure."

He poured two snifters of brandy, took a sip from one, and handed one to her. The gesture struck her as strangely medieval.

"Proving it isn't poisoned?"

Edmonson smiled faintly. "You would be surprised what assurances some of my visitors require." He sipped from his glass again, then set it aside. "Please, take a seat."

Gwen settled down on a Victorian settee that was every bit as uncomfortable as it looked. Her host poured himself a second snifter of brandy, this one from a cut-crystal decanter. He took a seat across from her and idly swirled the amber liquid. His private stock, Gwen concluded, not sure whether to be insulted or amused.

"You have concerns about Meredith Cody," he said. "I've been assured that she is alive and unharmed, and will remain so until the arranged time."

"Do you know where she's being held?"

"I do not. As you might have surmised, my role in this is to carry information."

"That's what I'm looking for," Gwen told him. "The people who have her want something from me."

Edmonson nodded, his eyes on her face. "Yes, that is my conclusion as well. Do you know what that something might be?"

"You seem to know a lot about me. You first."

He shook his head regretfully. "I wish I could tell you more."

Gwen set her brandy down on a small oval table with a raised piecrust edge. "Ryan Cody said that you wanted to observe me. Would you like to share your impressions?"

"Not just yet."

"Don't like making hasty conclusions, do you? How long do you think it will take you to make up your mind?"

A faint smile curved his lips. "In this case, three days."

She waited for him to elaborate, but he didn't divulge the reason for his private amusement. Like the good brandy, it apparently wasn't for general consumption.

Gwen glanced at the grandfather clock in the corner. She'd been here for fifteen minutes and was no further ahead than when she walked through Edmonson's door.

She rose to leave. "Don't bother," she told him, when he started to follow. "I can show myself out."

Gwen drove her car around the corner and parked. She took a hideously illegal phone scanner from her trunk and walked back toward Edmonson's house, carefully keeping to the shadows. She turned on the device and crouched down to listen and observe.

Fifteen minutes, she repeated silently. A quarter of an hour passed between the time she activated the alarm guarding the blue gem and her departure from Edmonson's house. Yet there had been no response: no phone call from the security company. She'd watched him like a cat, and would swear that he didn't do anything that might deactivate the alarm.

She held her position for nearly an hour. No phone calls came or went from the house. No rental cops dropped over to check. The lights winked out, one by one, leaving the house nearly as deeply in the dark as Gwen.

Either Edmonson needed a new security service, or he was lying through his teeth about the glowing gem. Most likely everything he'd said about Meredith was a lie as well, including his claim of being a "go-between."

Wouldn't her visit here be of interest to the people who wanted her? Edmonson didn't consider it worth a phone call.

Either he wasn't serving his superiors faithfully, or he didn't *have* any. Gwen wasn't sure which option was worse news for her and Meredith.

Sunlight touched Gwen's face with warm, gentle fingers. She woke with a start, sitting bolt upright in her bed.

She felt strangely disoriented, as if the place in which she woke up was not where she expected to be. A few moments passed before she separated the pounding of her heart from the thumping coming from downstairs.

She was still wearing the jeans and shirt she'd thrown on to go to Edmonson's house last night. She barely remembered falling into bed. With a shrug, she raked her hands through her hair and went downstairs to answer the door.

A tall, thin man leaned against the door as if he required its support to stand upright. His narrow face was seamed with lines and deeply tanned. Since his clothes appeared to have been selected at random from the Salvation Army reject bin, Gwen guessed that the bronzed skin wasn't due to a spring cruise. It was hard to guess his age, since his weathered face would owe as many lines to the sun as to the passing years. His dust-colored hair was shaved close to his head. There wasn't enough of it to indicate whether it would grow out ash brown or gray. He looked vaguely familiar, but Gwen couldn't quite place him.

He peered through the glass. "You Frank's girl?"

Suddenly Gwen remembered where she'd seen the man. Several years ago, he'd been one of Frank's informants—a street person who, when he was sober, had a knack for overhearing very interesting conversations.

"George?" she said in disbelief. Last time she'd seen him, his hair had been twisted into matted dreadlocks that hung past his shoulders. "You look good."

He lifted a hand and smoothed it over his shorn hair. "Yeah. I cut the dreads off. No way to comb through the fuckers."

One of Gwen's last conversations with Frank fell into place. "I heard you got your own place."

"Yeah, but it didn't work out. I've been staying over at the shelter for a while. Brought you something."

He held out a large manila envelope with her name written on it in Frank's neat block printing. Gwen's eyes widened.

She opened the door and snatched the envelope. Her hands shook as she opened it and pulled out the folder. A glance confirmed that it was indeed Frank's notes on the investigation Ian Forest had instigated.

Gwen lifted her eyes to George's expectant face. "What took you so long?"

He flushed and dropped his eyes. "Frank gave me a twenty to hand-deliver the envelope to you."

"Let me guess: you drank the twenty and lost track of time."

"Yeah," he mumbled. He glanced up. "You gonna tell him?"

She shook her head, not sure she could get out the words.

"I suppose he ought to know," he mused. "Him being my sponsor and all."

"Sponsor?"

"We go to the same AA meetings. He's a good guy. Keep me mostly sober. Sometimes he sends a little work my way."

Gwen seized his arm. "When did you pick up the envelope?"

He looked at her quizzically. "Late," he remembered. "Had to be close to midnight."

That was an interesting piece of information. According to what the coroner said, the time of death wasn't much after that.

"Did he leave the envelope and the money out for you, or did you see him?"

"Took it right from his hand. Look, I'm sorry I was late getting it to you—"

"Don't worry about that," Gwen said, cutting him off. "When you saw him, was he drinking?"

"No!" He sounded deeply offended by the suggestion.

"Did you by any chance have a drink over at his house? Maybe leave a bottle there?"

"Are we talking about the same guy? He was my sponsor, for chrissakes. If he knew I had a drink, he'd kick my ass. You're not going to tell him, are you?"

Gwen just shook her head. When he turned to leave, she caught the sleeve of his jacket.

"Frank's dead," she told him. "Thought you might want to know."

He looked stricken. "When? How?"

"He drowned." Gwen left it at that. "The wake is tonight at St. Brendan's, if you want to come."

"Yeah. Okay," he mumbled. He ambled away, shaking his head in disbelief.

Gwen waited until he'd gone down the drive and disappeared

from sight. She went into her office and opened the envelope with shaking hands.

Frank's notes were concise, clear. Some of the information she already knew, if not in such detail.

A family was killed in a car crash out on Route 6, near Johnston. There was nothing suspicious about the crash. There was an extremely heavy rainstorm, and visibility was poor. The car was going too fast for the weather conditions. It probably hydroplaned, which would explain why it ran off the road into a tree. All three occupants of the car were pronounced dead at the scene: James and Ruby Avalon and their infant daughter, Tess. The accident occurred shortly before midnight on April 30, 1971.

Gwen shuffled the papers to the next page, and her eyes widened. The next report had nothing to do with the car accident. It concerned the murders of David and Regina Gellman, her parents.

Their bodies were discovered by a neighbor, Nancy Smithers, on the morning of May 1, 1971, after she heard the baby crying and went over to investigate. Mrs. Smithers found the back door unlocked and standing open. The parents were both dead, the baby unharmed. Police speculated that the parents surprised a burglar, who killed them, then panicked and left without completing the robbery. No arrests were made.

There was a picture in the file. On the back was penciled in Frank's neat, concise printing, *David and Regina Gellman. Photo obtained from Nancy Smithers. Mendel's peas?*

"Mendel's peas?" Gwen repeated.

She flipped over the photo and studied the images of the

young couple. These were her parents. It was strange that she should feel no recognition, no sense of kinship.

Regina Gellman was a short woman with strong features and dark eyes in a small, square face. She wore her brown hair in a shoulder-length flip, one of those big-hair looks that required a lot of teasing and several coats of hair spray. She stood in profile to show off her very pregnant belly. David Gellman stood behind her, smiling proudly. He was considerably taller than his wife, long and lanky. His hair was a rusty shade, and his brown eyes showed up darkly against a redhead's pale, freckled skin.

"Mendel's peas," Gwen murmured, puzzling over the cryptic message. The answer came to her suddenly, and she sat down on the front step, hard.

It referred to a well-known study in genetics. She'd first heard the term during high-school biology, when her teacher had assigned a family tree based on eye color. It was supposed to help the kids understand genetics. Gwen had blown off the assignment. It was easier to take a failing grade than explain she didn't know her grandparents' names, much less their eye color.

An old grievance bubbled to the surface. Why the hell did teachers keep assigning family trees? Most of the kids she grew up with were lucky to know their fathers' names. You'd think that after a few years in the classroom, teachers would figure out that very few people grew up in Beaver Cleaver's neighborhood.

But she recognized that thought for what it was: a digression, an attempt to distract herself from facing the questions in the folder.

It was also a rant that Frank had heard from her on at least two occasions. When he wrote "Mendel's peas," he was almost certainly thinking about eye color and family trees.

Both of Gwen's parents had brown eyes, which were genetically dominant. Hers were blue. That wasn't impossible, but you'd be hard-pressed to find a bookie who would give you decent odds on it.

She put the picture down and continued reading. The Gellmans had no living family members. The baby, Gwenevere, became a ward of the state.

This, Gwen knew all too well. She shuffled the pages again. What she read on the next page made her very glad that she was sitting down.

The Gellmans' time of death was estimated to have occurred between eleven and midnight. Driving distance from the Gellman home to the site of the Avalons' crash, fifteen minutes.

A coincidence, Gwen told herself. But Frank obviously thought there was a connection between the two ill-fated families, and his instincts were nearly as good as her own.

Gwen snatched up her phone and dialed Ian Forest's number. She was well accustomed to letting the phone ring, but after a dozen rings or so she was about to hang up.

"Yes?" demanded a male voice. Impatient and slightly out of breath, as if he'd had to run to answer the call.

"Is this Ian Forest?"

"Gwen," he said flatly. "This is not a good time."

"That's a fucking understatement!"

"What happened?" he said, his voice sharpening.

"I got your file from my friend Frank. He sent it over by

messenger shortly before he died. If someone comes over here looking for it, I'd at least like to know why."

"Yes, of course. I'll be right over."

She started to object, but the line had already gone dead. Muttering curses, she ran upstairs for a quick shower.

Five minutes later, she stepped out of the shower. She scrubbed her hair with a towel, then wrapped it around herself and walked into her bedroom.

The blinds were down, and the west-facing room was still filled with shadows. Gwen wasn't prepared for one of them to shift and stand.

She let out a startled yelp and snatched a tall brass lamp from the dresser. The shade dropped away, unheeded. Her towel, likewise.

"Come on, you son of a bitch!" she snarled. She hefted the lamp and waggled it like a Louisville Slugger preparing to launch a fastball.

"I've had quite enough for one morning, thanks all the same," announced a familiar voice.

Gwen lowered the lamp a few inches, not yet stepping out of the batter's box. "Forest?"

Her uninvited guest reached for the wall switch. Light flooded the room.

At the moment, Ian Forest didn't look capable of offering much of a threat. A large bruise darkened his face from cheekbone to jaw, and a trio of butterfly bandages secured a neatly dressed cut on his forehead. He held himself carefully, probably favoring ribs that were bruised or even cracked.

Gwen put the lamp back on the dresser. "You look like shit."

His smile turned into a wince. "And you look like an angry hedgehog."

Her hands went to her wet hair, smoothing it down over her ears. "Sit down before you fall. What the hell happened to you?"

He lowered himself gingerly to sit on the unmade bed. "I made the acquaintance of a . . . new colleague."

She laughed, short and hard. "Must have been a hell of a job interview. Sorry I missed it."

"You sound angry."

"You think?" she retorted. "My best friend looks into your missing heiress and bumps into my childhood. Oh, and he ends up dead. Let's not lose sight of that."

"I assure you, that wasn't part of the plan."

"No? Well then, what exactly *was* the fucking plan?"

A pained expression crossed his face, one that had little to do with his injuries. "There's no need for you to be vulgar."

"Maybe there's no need, but there's definitely an inclination," she shot back.

He studied her for a moment, his eyes neutral. "Perhaps you'd like to dress first?"

Gwen looked down, remembered that she was naked. She yanked open a drawer and pulled out a short black dress of stretchy jersey. She pulled it over her head and stalked over to Ian, hands fisted on her hips.

"I'm dressed," she said curtly. "And you're stalling."

"Why don't you tell me what you know."

She ran down the facts, quick and sparse. He listened without comment or reaction until she reached the end of her recitation.

Gwen's eyes narrowed. "How much of this is new to you?"

"Very little," he readily admitted. "What conclusion have you drawn?"

She took a deep breath. "I think James and Ruby Avalon were in danger, and knew it. In fact, I think they were running when they died. Maybe whoever was chasing them found the Gellmans instead."

"And the baby girls?" Ian asked softly.

Gwen wasn't ready to go out on this particular limb. "One was luckier than the other. I'm not sure which."

"Indeed." Ian rose carefully.

She moved to block his path to the door. "Forget it. You're not leaving until I get some answers. Who was after the Avalons? What was the connection to the Gellmans? And who the hell checked all three Avalons out of the city morgue?"

He returned her angry gaze coolly. "I believe that's what I hired you to discover."

"Technically, you haven't hired me. No money changed hands. We didn't even set a fee."

Ian reached into the inside pocket of his jacket and took out a thick envelope. He tossed it onto the bed. "I trust this will cover your services."

Her eyes narrowed. "There's no need for you to be vulgar," she said, throwing his own words back at him.

An expression of exasperation crossed his face. "That was not what I intended to imply. When we come together, it will not be a business transaction."

"When? *When?*" she repeatedly heatedly.

He inclined his head slightly, a gesture that fell short of

apology or concession. "Perhaps you prefer the word 'if.' And perhaps you would consider carrying this."

Again he reached into his coat. This time he brought out a handgun. Holding it by the barrel, keeping his eyes on hers. He placed it on the bed.

"The weapon is clean. Custom-made, not registered."

"In short, illegal. Jesus Christ!" she burst out. "What the hell are you thinking?"

"I assume that's a rhetorical question, but I'll answer it nonetheless," he said softly. "I'm thinking of the rather shabby gentleman lying dead just outside your gate."

She stared at him for a moment, then dived for her phone and hit the speed dial for Frank's number.

"Jason, this is Gwen Gellman," she said, speaking before he had a chance to say hello. "Is everything okay there?"

"Yes," he said slowly. "I mean, considering the circumstances . . ."

"Right. Listen, I know you wanted to stay at your father's place, but it might be a good idea for you to check into a hotel while you're in town."

"What's this about?"

She took a deep breath. "Your father was helping me in an investigation. A messenger just brought over his notes."

"That must have felt strange," he said quietly.

"Yeah. Yeah, it did," she agreed. "The thing is, he was looking into a family that died in a car crash about thirty years ago. Their bodies disappeared from the morgue."

"That's . . . creepy," he agreed, "but I'm still not following your line of thought."

"My point is, someone was willing to go to great lengths to keep people from taking too close a look."

A short silence followed. "You don't think my father's death was accidental, do you?"

He was quick, Gwen noted. "There's that possibility. It wouldn't hurt to play it safe."

"I'll be fine," he said calmly. "But I appreciate the warning."

"Don't appreciate it. Take it," she told him. "There's more. Someone just found the messenger. He was killed, right outside where I live. . . ." Her voice trailed off as she realized that Ian Forest was no longer in the room.

A chilling thought occurred to her: perhaps it was Ian who killed George.

She quickly dismissed that notion. George could barely hold himself upright. He couldn't have dealt the damage she'd seen on Ian's face. The timing was all wrong. There wasn't enough time between George's departure and Ian Forest's arrival for those bruises to darken or that cut on his forehead to receive such expert care. Finally, why would he give her a gun to protect her from himself?

Of course, that led to an equally disturbing question: why would he hire her to uncover the secrets of her own childhood?

"Gwen? *Gwen?*"

The concern in Jason's voice suggested that he'd been trying to get her attention for a while.

"I'm here," she told him.

He let out an audible sigh. "You had me worried. Have you called the police?"

"Not yet. I want to take a look myself before I call it in."

Before she called in a homicide, she wanted to make damn sure there was a body.

"You called me first," he said, sounding both surprised and pleased. "We haven't met yet, and you were concerned about me."

"You're Frank's kid," she said. In her opinion, that said everything that needed explaining.

"And you're looking out for both of us," he said, showing that he got it. He fell silent for a moment. "You're sure my father's death wasn't accidental?"

"All I'm missing is the proof."

"Let me know if there's anything I can do to help you find it."

"Deal."

She hung up and dialed Quaid's cell phone. He answered after several rings and mumbled something that might have been "hello."

"It's Gellman. Kate said you had some information for me."

"Right. I was going to call you after I woke up."

"That's the usual sequence," she agreed. "So what's up?"

"I worked through the night," he grumbled. "I got in three hours ago. You're expecting me to think clearly?"

Gwen sighed. "Don't think. Just talk."

"Give me a minute." There was a rustling sound that suggested he was crawling out of bed, and a soft snap that was probably Quaid shaking the wrinkles out of a discarded shirt. Gwen heard the faint sound of a zipper. She smirked. Somehow she wouldn't have figured Quaid for a guy who'd have to get dressed before he could talk to a woman on the phone. It's a good thing Kate was used to being around stiffs, otherwise she'd have shown him the door long ago.

"You remember Landers?" asked Quaid. "He transferred to Providence shortly before you left the job."

"Big guy. Receding hairline. Always had food stains on his ties," Gwen remembered.

"That's him. After you left, he got your old computer. Last week he spilled a cup of coffee over it and shorted something out. He got a major ass-chewing and an upgrade."

"An upgraded ass on that body? There's a waste of plastic surgery."

"Jesus, I should be the one who can't keep focused at this hour!"

"Moving along."

"Yeah. So O'Riley asked for the old machine for parts. It was a piece of crap, so no one thought anything of it."

"This will eventually have a point?"

"The kid took the hard drive out and took it to a friend of his who repairs computers. This guy pulls up all the files, including things that were deleted. O'Riley went through the recovered files and found one of the reports you submitted during your undercover work at Winston's."

The elation Gwen expected to feel didn't come. She had worked for months to try to clear her name. She'd dreamed of returning to the force, getting things back to the way they were.

Now, she wasn't sure that would ever be possible.

"To be honest, I'm not sure what to do with this," she said slowly.

"Yeah." Quaid sounded as troubled as she felt. "If Walsh is dirty, this won't be enough to nail him."

"There's that. Also, I've got so much going on right now that

I can't begin to think about this. Which reminds me: I need a fairly complicated favor. Got a pencil?"

"Hang on." There was a faint rustling. "Okay."

"There was a car crash on April 30, 1971, in Johnston. It wiped out a family of three: James and Ruby Avalon and their infant daughter, Tess. The bodies disappeared from the morgue."

"Yeah, Kate mentioned something about that. What do you want me to do?"

"See if there are any personal effects on file. In particular, I'm looking for driver's licenses, anything with a picture."

"I don't know, Gellman. Going back thirty years? If there is anything, it's probably buried in a warehouse somewhere."

"Your rookie seems to have the nose of a bloodhound. Maybe he'd be willing to do some looking."

"Probably. Can I go back to sleep now, or is there something else?"

"No, I'm good. And Quaid? You've been a big help. I owe you."

"No. You don't."

The words hung in the silence, heavy and final. "Guess you're particular about who you take help from," Gwen said quietly.

"That's not it."

A short, frustrated sigh came over the line. Apparently, the explanation didn't come easily, or maybe it required more words than the taciturn man liked to use at one sitting. Gwen waited for him to decide.

"You wouldn't take the blood test after the Jamison bust," he said. "I figured maybe there was a reason."

Gwen saw where this was going. "You thought maybe there

was a little something in that vial before I spit wine into it. You thought I was trying to frame the Jamisons, or maybe just close the case without much caring who got the blame."

"Yeah. The evidence we had up to that point just didn't support them as suspects. You hooking up with them looked too planned, or maybe too random."

"I can see how it would look that way."

"And some of the questions IA was asking sounded pretty reasonable."

"You couldn't stand by and watch innocent people get framed by a dirty cop," she concluded.

"That's about the size of it. But you were right, and I fucked up. Later, you gave me hell over the report I filed, but you never went up the ladder. Why not?"

"That's not what partners do."

"Yeah." He sighed heavily. "O'Riley pointed that out, believe you me."

She remembered that Quaid's new partner had been in Lauren Simpson's hotel room when she and Quaid aired that old grievance. "The kid giving you shit?"

"You could say that." He chuckled briefly, without much humor. "Feels damn familiar."

He hung up with his usual lack of ceremony. Gwen listened to the dial tone for a moment, then quietly replaced the receiver. To her surprise, she realized she was smiling.

❧ Gwen walked the perimeters of Sylvia's property, steeling herself for the sight of George's body. There was no sign of him, nothing to support Ian Forest's claim. All she found was some broken branches on the back side of one of the rhododendron bushes that lined the side wall.

She took out her cell phone and dialed his number. "It's me," she said flatly. "The gift you left me? I'm not carrying it with me. Explain to me one more time why I should."

"It's quite valuable. Silver, and very fine workmanship," he said, establishing that he knew she was referring to the gun.

"And?"

"There are some flowering bushes alongside the street. Along the wall, not far from the ground you'll see some broken branches. That's where I found the derelict gentleman."

"I looked. He's not there."

"Yes, I know. I thought it might be better if he found a less conspicuous resting place."

"You . . . persuaded him to move along?"

"That's right. You're calling very early. I don't suppose you've had a chance to get much work done."

In other words, did she call the police, with nothing but Ian's claim to back her up, to report a dead man on Sylvia Black's property? How stupid did he think she was?

"I thought I'd take a walk first," she said curtly.

"Good thinking."

Gwen's mind whirled with questions, but she knew better than to ask any of them on a cell phone. At least, not directly. "The thing we were discussing this morning, about those three people checking out early?"

"Yes."

It was an answer to her question, not an acknowledgement. He was admitting that he had something to do with the disappearance of James, Ruby, and little Tess Avalon from the city morgue. "How did you—"

"They were my friends," he said, breaking in before she could say too much. "Their privacy was important to me. To all of us."

"To all of us," Gwen repeated. "Are you going to tell me what you mean by that, or is that another one of those things you hired me to find out?"

He chuckled. "We'll talk later. In the meanwhile, keep the gift."

Gwen considered his suggestion as she walked back to her apartment. She had a weapon, legal and registered. Why did Ian think she'd need another? The silver gun was a little fancy for a throw-down piece.

On impulse, she picked up the gun and slipped it into the inside pocket of her jacket. The gun was small and lighter than it looked.

She glanced over at the wall clock. The start of the business day was still a couple of hours away. With all that had happened this morning, it didn't seem possible that she'd only been awake for a little over an hour.

On her way out, she took Sylvia's extra car keys down from the hook by the door. Her landlady was still in the hospital and wouldn't need her car today. She didn't mind if Gwen took her car every now and then, an arrangement that was convenient for the occasions, such as this one, when Gwen wanted to observe someone who might recognize her blue Toyota.

The black sedan started with a sedate purr. Gwen patted the dashboard affectionately. Too bad it was only a mile to Wallace Edmonson's house—she wouldn't mind driving something that didn't wheeze and shake whenever the speedometer crept over sixty.

She made short work of the distance and found a parking spot about half a block from Edmonson's house. She settled in to watch and wait.

After a few minutes, a silver car pulled out of the driveway. Apparently Edmonson was also getting an early start.

Gwen followed at a careful distance. Edmonson headed out of town, driving against the flow of morning traffic toward Lincoln, a nice little town—bedroom community, mostly—to the northwest of Providence.

He pulled into a medical office park with several multisuite buildings and parked in front of the building farthest from the road. Gwen pulled into a space two buildings away and watched as Edmonson got out of the car and walked around to the back of the building.

A sharp rap on the passenger window startled her. Her head

snapped toward the sound, and her hand slid toward the inside pocket where she'd hidden Ian's pretty silver gift.

Damian O'Riley peered in, grinning.

Muttering an oath, she unlocked the doors and gestured him in. He slid into the car, nodded approvingly at the soft leather seats.

"Nice ride. Your PI gig pays pretty good, does it?"

"The car's not mine. What are you doing up here?" she demanded.

"I got a call from the tech at the DNA lab. She was freaking out over the results of this last sample. Thing is, it wasn't human."

"So what was it?"

"Nothing she'd ever seen. She asked me to come up before the office opened. Sounded real nervous."

Gwen grabbed his arm. "Wait a minute—the lab is here? In this office park?"

"Yeah. Isn't that why you drove up?"

She drew a long breath. "No, but I can see how they might be related. Let's go talk to your contact."

Damian headed for the same building Edmonson had approached. A woman's scream, sharp and terrified, rose from one of the offices. There was a muffled crash, and the woman fell abruptly silent.

Gwen broke into a run. She beat Damian to the front door of the office suite and wrenched it open. He moved to the doorway, gun out, scanning the room.

"Clear," he said, and stepped inside.

She followed him in, moving cautiously into a large reception area. A set of double doors on the left led to what appeared to be a hall lined with offices. On the other side of the room was another door leading to the lab area.

Gwen peered inside. The lab was not what Gwen might have envisioned. There were neat shelves of glass vials, but most of the room was devoted to computer stations and other electronic equipment.

She glanced at Damian and shook her head. No one in the lab. He tipped his head toward the left, indicating that they should check the offices.

Two young men burst through the double doors like a sudden storm. Gwen leveled her gun the one closest to her, noticed he wasn't carrying.

She tossed her weapon aside a moment before he barreled into her. Dipping into a defensive stand, she turned her shoulder toward him. He hit hard, and she used his momentum to send him flying over her shoulder.

Damian's reflexes weren't quite as quick. The other guy slammed into him before he could get off a shot. Gunfire rang out, and the light fixture overhead shattered and sparked.

From the corner of her eye, Gwen saw Damian go down under the second guy. The two men began to grapple and roll, fighting for control of Damian's gun. She couldn't offer much help. Her guy had gotten to his feet and was circling in.

For the first time she got a good look at him. He was young, probably not far out of his teens. His face was still little-boy cute, and his blond hair was a little too long to be fashionable, even allowing for the recycled Seventies styles that seemed to be plaguing mankind.

She turned with him, ready to attack if he started working

his way toward the gun on the floor. Instead, he lunged for a backpack and darted out of the door.

Gwen went over to finish the other fight. The second man—also young, also blond—had gotten the upper hand. Damian still had control of the gun, but the blond kid had his gun hand pinned to the floor with both hands.

She got behind him and fisted both hands in his hair. With a vicious tug, she pulled his head back as far as it would go.

"Let go of my friend, and I won't break your neck," she offered.

His hands came away from Damian's arm and slowly lifted into the air.

"Get up, slowly."

The young man did as he was told. Damian also scrambled to his feet.

"I got him," he said grimly. He pulled the blond kid's hand down and cuffed them behind his back. He glanced over at Gwen. "The other guy?"

"Long gone." Gwen went over to reclaim her gun.

As she reached down for it, a muffled thud sounded behind her, immediately followed by the clatter of metal against the hardwood floor.

She spun, gun in hand, in time to see Damian sink to his knees, both hands clutching his gut. His mouth worked like a landed fish trying to suck enough oxygen from the too-thin air. His handcuffs lay on the floor beside him, open and empty.

The second man darted through the reception area and out into the parking lot. Gwen let him go. She tucked away the gun and pulled Damian to his feet.

He stared at her, incredulous. "Shoulda shot him," he wheezed.

"That might have been a little hard to explain. Come on—let's find your contact."

Damian looked uncertainly in the direction the blond kids had gone. "Call for backup?"

"And tell them what?" she demanded. "We don't know who those guys were or what they were doing here. Neither of them were armed. For all we know, they were dropping a lab-rat parent off to work on the way to school, saw a couple of strangers with guns, and ran."

"Should check it out," he said.

"We will. But think: you're out of your jurisdiction, looking into an unofficial case. Walsh would put your nuts through the office shredder."

Damian responded with a reluctant nod and started down the hall, picking his way through the broken glass.

A faint moan came from the office ahead to the left. Gwen shouldered past him and hurried in.

The room had been trashed. File drawers yawned open; papers were scattered over the floor. A chubby, dark-haired woman was on the floor, curled up amid the debris. She clutched her stomach and rocked slightly back and forth—short, pained movements that probably hurt as much as they comforted.

Gwen crouched beside her. "How badly are you hurt?"

The woman whimpered and shied away. O'Riley lowered himself to Gwen's side, wincing from the effort.

"Jennifer, it's Damian. Don't worry about the white girl—she's with me. You're safe now."

266 / ELAINE CUNNINGHAM

She uncurled enough to look up at the young cop. The terror glazing her eyes began to thaw.

"Hurts," she croaked, touching her throat. A mottled necklace of bruises was starting to show.

"Any other injuries?" Gwen asked.

She shook her head. "He hit me," she said pointing to her abdomen. "Couldn't breathe."

"It'll pass," Damian said, sending a rueful glance at Gwen. "Hurts like a bitch, though. You move around some, it'll help. Ready to try?"

"Okay."

They helped her up and maneuvered her over to a chair. "I'll call the paramedics," Damian offered.

She clutched his arm. "Don't," she pleaded, her eyes wide with panic.

Gwen was beginning to understand. "You did the DNA testing off the books, didn't you?"

The woman's head bobbed glumly. "Those men took everything," she said, speaking more clearly now. "The samples, the reports."

"Trust me, it could have been worse," Gwen said.

"Yeah? They took the money I was paid to do that last test."

"You're still a long way from worse. Money's okay, but it's hard to spend it when you're dead," Gwen pointed out.

The woman paled. "Will they come back?"

"That depends. Do you think they got everything they came for?"

She hesitated, then nodded. Gwen gave her a reassuring smile. "Then my advice is to call the police. Tell them the truth—or at least, selected pieces of it. You came in early to get some work done, when it was still quiet. Two guys broke in and trashed the place. They roughed you up and took your money. It'll take a while to clean up this mess and figure out whether or not anything else is missing. And I'm sure your bosses will understand when you tell them you want to take some time off, maybe go away for a while."

Fear edged back into the woman's eyes. "I do?"

"You do," Gwen said succinctly.

The woman nodded slowly. "Is it okay if I don't mention you were here? That might be kind of hard to explain."

"Understood." She glanced at the young cop. "See if you can find the bullet you squeezed off."

"On it," he said, heading out into the hall.

Gwen pulled up a chair and sat down across from the woman. "What can you tell me about the man who hired you?"

"He never gave me his name, but I can describe him. Tall, dark hair. He wore a suit, and his haircut looked expensive. His eyes are what you might call deep-set, and his face is so thin the cheekbones cast shadows." She grimaced. "Does that last bit make sense?"

"Yeah, it does," Gwen said, bringing Wallace Edmonson's face to mind. "It's a good description. When did this guy pay you?"

"This morning, just before the other men came."

Gwen rose and placed a hand on the woman's shoulder. "We'd better get going. Are you sure you're okay?"

The woman shrugged. "He took the sample, and all the tests I ran on it," she mourned. "He wouldn't tell me what it came from."

Gwen had an uneasy feeling—nothing specific, just an itch at the back of her mind. "What type of sample was it?"

"A couple of hairs. Dark. Not very long. They *looked* human, but one had a skin tag attached and the DNA was definitely not human."

An image came vividly to mind: Wallace Edmonson, taking her jacket from her that day in Ryan Cody's office. His hands skimmed the collar as he hung it on the coat tree. One of them came away, thumb and forefinger pinched together. It was a tiny detail, one her eye had caught and her mind filed, judging it to be of little importance.

"When did he bring in the sample?"

"Last week. He wanted it ASAP. I told him three days."

Three days, Gwen repeated silently, remembering Edmonson's strange little smile when she asked how long he planned to take to come to any conclusion about her. Three days.

The woman let out a long, greedy sigh. "What I wouldn't give for a chance to do more tests on whatever that thing was!"

Gwen edged her hand away from the woman's shoulder. "All things considered, it probably isn't a good idea to talk about that."

"I know," she said glumly. "No one would believe me, anyway."

"I'm having a hard time with it, myself," Gwen muttered.

She strode out of the building, eager to put as much distance as possible between herself and the mad-scientist gleam in the woman's eyes. She met Damian outside the building.

"Quaid called," he said. "He wants you to meet him at noon in the Arcade, first floor."

Gwen glanced at her watch. She had time to stop by the hospital to see Sylvia. The problem was, she didn't know what to tell the older woman about Ian Forest. She had no idea who or what the man was, but the answer was becoming increasingly important. Increasingly personal.

"Whatever that thing was," Gwen murmured as she pulled out of the parking lot.

Sylvia had been moved to a private room. She was sitting up in bed when Gwen walked in. Her gaze shifted to Gwen's face, and her eyes were huge and apprehensive. The book she'd been reading fell unheeded from her hands.

Gwen picked up the book and placed it on the nightstand. "How are you?"

The older woman lifted one expressive brow. "At the risk of sounded clichéd, you tell me. Sit, please. You're hovering."

She shut the door and pulled a chair close to the bed. "I don't know what to tell you, Sylvia. I talked to Ian Forest. I even showed him that painting of you. He recognized it, and he claims that he's the same man you knew years ago."

To Gwen's surprise, this seemed to come as good news. Sylvia smiled faintly and relaxed against the pillow. "What do you think?"

"I'm not sure what to make of this."

"Did he offer any explanation?"

"Nothing that made sense."

"Indulge me," Sylvia suggested.

Gwen shrugged. "He said something about being a member of some Elder Race."

The older woman laughed, not derisively but with surprise

and delight. "Oddly enough, I should have expected that explanation from Ian."

"I don't get it."

Years seemed to fall away from the woman's face as she remembered. "We were very close for a time. It was a business arrangement, yes, but it became something very close to a love affair. These things happen." She shrugged, as if admitting to a professional error.

To some extent, Gwen could relate. "Is that why it ended? It got too personal?"

"In a way. It was Ian who ended the relationship. He said he had gotten fond of me in a way that went far beyond his expectations. He said that we were too different. He made it very plain that he was not talking about class or social standing. It was something more fundamental, and ultimately insurmountable. I didn't question him too closely. I don't know why, but I believed him."

"He can be convincing," Gwen said, remembering several times when she felt overly inclined to see things his way.

"It makes perfect sense to me," the older woman went on. "Ian, a remnant of some Elder Race. Yes."

"Sylvia, you know that's impossible."

Her friend shrugged again. "Oddly enough, I don't find myself concerned with 'impossible.' It's an enormous relief to know that I'm not having delusions. *Nothing* real, impossible or not, could be as frightening as that."

Gwen replayed those words over and over as she drove downtown. There was a certain truth to them. For much of her early life, she'd wondered if there was something wrong with her. She'd been very young when she learned not to speak of things other people couldn't see or understand.

Later, she'd read several books about psychic phenomena, about belief systems that included some sort of mysticism as part of their worldviews. None of them seemed to fit her, but it was a comfort to know that odd flashes of insight were not all that uncommon. People like Teresa Moniz were proof of that.

But psychic moments were one thing; Ian Forest's claim to being a member of another race was something else.

Something else, echoed a small voice in her mind. *Not human. Three days.*

The Arcade came into view, its tired Greek facade a contrast to stolid brick buildings lining both sides of the narrow street. Gwen pushed her troubled thoughts to the back of her mind. Quaid might have come to terms with her on one level, but she couldn't see him getting his head around this new development. Hell, she didn't know what to make of it.

She found a parking place on a side street a few blocks from the Arcade. The building was one of the architectural oddities scattered around Providence: classical in design, Victorian in detail. A historical landmark, seeing that it was the first enclosed shopping mall in the country.

Inside, it resembled an oversize glass conservatory. The buttery scents of a bakery greeted her. She strolled through the lower gallery, caught sight of Quaid standing in front of a sandwich shop. He held two white bags. Good man, she noted approvingly.

He strode toward her and handed her one of the bags, as well as two small cards.

"I lucked out with the info you wanted. There was a file, and it had these licenses for James and Ruby Avalon. Neither of them were legit, but you did say you wanted pictures."

Gwen nodded dumbly, her eyes fixed on the tiny photo of Ruby Avalon. The woman in the picture had an abundance of dark-chestnut hair, and very large, very blue eyes in an angular face that reminded Gwen a little too forcefully of a Siamese cat.

"She looks a lot like you," Quaid observed.

"Yeah."

She shuffled the card behind the second, and her eyes widened with a second shock. James Avalon's face was also familiar. He was dark and lean, with deep-set eyes that seem fashioned to hide secrets. He had a craggy bone structure, all peaks and hollows.

Gwen's gaze flashed to Quaid's face. "I've got to go," she said. She turned on her heel and rushed from the Arcade, picking up her pace on the street until she was running to the car. She whipped Sylvia's sedate black car around with a screech of wheels and headed for Wallace Earl Edmonson's house.

When he answered the door, she simply held up her hands, a license in each. He studied the pictures on them for a long moment, then moved aside to let her into the house.

She followed him upstairs into the Victorian study. He poured a snifter of brandy from the cut-glass decanter and handed it to her.

Gwen took the glass and swirled the amber liquid as he had done the night before. She studied it, then set the glass aside. The look she sent Edmonson was not friendly.

"Today I rate the good stuff," she observed. "Gee, I wonder what's changed."

"Drink it," he suggested. "I'm assuming this comes as something of a shock."

"I'm not sure what 'this' is. Not all of it, at least. What's your relationship to James Avalon? If that really was his name."

"He was my brother," he admitted. "And no, that wasn't his real name, any more than Wallace Earl Edmonson is mine."

"Family secrets?"

"You might say that. We lost track of each other many years ago. I tried to find him, but it's not an easy task to find someone who doesn't want to be found."

"He was in trouble."

"Yes, and unfortunately, much of it was of his own making. He kept moving, using a number of assumed names. I came to Providence following a lead, only to learn about the accident. After the funeral, I decided to stay."

"Do you know who he was he running from?"

Edmonson frowned. "That, I cannot say."

"Whoever it was caught up with them," Gwen said softly. She rose and began to pace. "The night your brother died, another family was killed, not far from the crash. The couples were about the same age, and they both had baby girls. I'm not sure how they knew each other."

"Hospital records, birth announcements," he said softly. "It's not difficult to find others who have a child the same age as your own."

"I guess." She stopped at the window, stared out over the city below. "I know this sounds crazy, but I think James and Ruby Avalon stopped at the Gellmans' house and switched babies."

"I agree," he said.

Gwen spun to face him. "You do?"

"You look too much like your mother for it to be otherwise."

She crossed the room and sank back into the chair she'd vacated. "They must have known that someone was after them that night. They left me with strangers, hoping to save my life. I'm alive because another baby died in my place." She glanced at Edmonson. "I'm not sure how I should feel about that."

"There's nothing you can do to change it. Your parents did what they had to do to ensure your survival."

"And three innocent people died. But they couldn't know that would happen," Gwen murmured, more to herself than Edmonson. "They couldn't know that whoever was chasing them would find the Gellmans instead."

He came over and poured a little more brandy into her glass. "How did you piece this together?"

"You know that I'm a private cop. Someone hired me to find the heir to a family fortune. It couldn't have been a coincidence that he hired me to find myself."

"I'm sure it wasn't."

"Then what's the point?"

"Perhaps he wanted you to learn something important about yourself, something you would not believe if anyone told you outright."

"Go on," Gwen said cautiously.

"Would you like to see this fortune of which your client spoke? I believe it will explain a great deal."

She nodded. To her surprise, he went over to the display case holding the blue gem. He unlocked the case and took a piece of black silk from the floor of the case. Using this like a pot holder on a hot plate, he picked up the gem. He carried it to Gwen and handed it to her, still wrapped.

Curious, she tumbled the stone into her hand.

Immediately the room filled with emerald hues and the undulating shapes of mountains and glen. It was another near-holographic vision, far more vivid than the disturbing glimpse of Zimmer's blue house. This was more like a separate reality, imposed over one more commonly seen. Gwen could still make out the room, but the details were muted, as if it were the shadow and her vision the substance.

She turned her attention to the wild place her vision showed. Mountains rose above a deep, mist-filled glen, and a dry streambed undulated through the heart of it. Rocks filled the streambed, and the ground surrounding it was rough and stony. As she watched, some of the larger stones began to roll and then to leap. They tumbled together, heaping up into a stone cairn. Like a movie, playing in reverse.

Finally the structure stood, tall and mournful and somehow forbidding. Gwen watched as the vision slowly faded, then turned her gaze toward her . . . uncle?

Edmonson's face was aglow with wonder and triumph. "You have your father's gift in full measure. In fact, you're stronger untaught than he was at the height of his powers."

He sent her a comforting smile. "I can tell by your expression that you do not understand what you just did. Our family is ancient, with secrets that have become half-remembered legends. There were stories of a treasure—Celtic gold that some of our people hid from marauders. I believe that the site you just marked is a place I have been seeking for many years."

"That's impossible," Gwen said.

"Perhaps, but you have done it all the same. You have one of your father's gifts: the ability to Remember, to know things your eyes have never seen. Your mother had an affinity for rain. It's likely she called the storm the night she died, either out of fear or in a deliberate attempt to slow their pursuers. A tragic irony that she died of her own magic."

Gwen leaped to her feet. "I don't believe a word of this."

"But you do," he said, moving to stand between her and the door. "Why do you think that you, a woman past thirty, look like a young girl? What other explanation can you find for some of the things you can see and do? Have you never noticed patterns to these occurrences? Your Qualities ebb and flow with the tides of the moon, the turning of the year. Beltane approaches. Do you know what that means?"

"It's a Celtic holiday," Gwen said impatiently. "May Day. A spring festival, fertility and so on. So what?"

"It is also the traditional time of the changeling. In ancient times, the Elder Races hid their babies among the common folk."

This, Gwen also knew. Stories of changelings were common in mythology and folklore, and, by extension, fantasy novels and games. But this was real life. *Her* life.

With a faint, choked cry, she pushed past him and fled from his house.

Twenty-four

The sun was setting as Gwen walked into the funeral home across from St. Brendan's church. A wax-faced funeral director showed her to the back room that had been rented to wake Frank Cross.

A few people milled about, looking as if they were trying very hard not to check their watches too often. There were only three baskets of flowers in the room, but the smell was cloyingly sweet. Perhaps the scent permeated the house itself, along with the weight of remembered grief.

Gwen noted a few familiar faces, people who'd worked at the station before Frank retired. Some of them nodded to her, not warmly but with a certain sympathy. Losing a partner was one of the toughest things any of them faced, and in this issue, the sense of community extended even to someone as far outside the fold as she.

Gwen walked into the room and up to the casket. She was aware that the murmur of voices behind her had stilled to near silence.

The painted form in the casket bore little resemblance to the man she'd known. His hair was aggressively neat, for one thing. The side part was ruler-straight, and the natural wave had been smoothed right out of it. Frank usually styled it with a towel. His big hands looked soft and waxen, and some idiot had put clear polish on his nails. They'd dressed him in what he'd called his "funeral suit;" navy blue, off-the-rack, forty-eight long. Gwen didn't think this was quite what he had in mind when he'd coined the phrase.

You have the ability to know what your eyes have never seen.

Wallace Edmonson's words echoed through Gwen's mind. She didn't believe him—not everything he'd said, anyway—but she owed it to Frank to test Edmonson's claim. She'd heard the whispers on her way in: he'd finally drunk himself to death, fell off the damn boat. Frank deserved a better eulogy than that.

For Frank, for herself, she had to know the truth, even if it meant filling the room with unexplainable images.

Blinking back tears, Gwen reached out and lay the back of her hand against Frank's cheek.

No vision came to her call. There was nothing of Frank in that box, in this room. The secret surrounding his death was not hers to see.

Fucking useless, Gwen raged. Whatever she was, it wasn't anything that could be of use to Frank.

She turned away and walked quickly from the room. A dark young man came over to her in the hall. "Gwen."

That was Jason Cross's voice. Gwen pulled up short, regarding him with surprise.

Frank had mentioned that Jason's mother was part Wampanoag, but she wasn't prepared for him to look so different from his father. He was several inches shorter than Frank, probably no more than five-foot-ten or so, and more slightly built. His hair was almost black, his skin tanned. There wasn't a hint of his father's broad, bluff features in his fine-boned face.

"You sound like your father," Gwen said.

He smiled faintly. "That's good to know. God knows there isn't much of a resemblance."

"He didn't look like that," she said shortly. "That's not Frank. I mean, it *is*, but . . ."

"I understand."

She took a long, steadying breath and looked around at those who'd come to pay their respects. No wake was a good time, but in this case, people seemed profoundly uncomfortable.

"They don't know who to talk to, where to offer condolences," Jason observed. "I'm a stranger. Word spreads, so by now most of them know I'm his son. But what do you say to someone who hasn't seen his father in—God, how many years?"

"More than twenty," Gwen said.

"Yeah. I don't even remember him. Don't know much about him." He looked at Gwen, his expression rueful. "You're the one they should be talking to."

"Don't hold your breath."

"Problems?"

"You might say that. I left the force over a year ago. It wasn't a no-fault divorce."

"I'm sorry."

Electronic music began to play in the background, mournful stuff from the musical wasteland between a real pipe organ and whatever the hell it is they play at baseball games.

"Shit," Gwen muttered. "Frank would have hated this."

"Then that's something else we would have had in common,"

Jason said softly. "I understand that later, some of his former colleagues are going.to lift a few glasses to his memory."

She met his gaze and noted the faint, ironic smile. "Not exactly appropriate, under the circumstances," she agreed.

"So tell me, what kind of send-off would Frank Cross have wanted?"

Gwen considered. "He was a quiet guy. Not much for groups or parties. Probably I did him a disservice by pulling him out of the water. He loved the bay. That's where he'd want to be. At the very least, that's where he'd want to be remembered."

"Then let's go."

Jason held out his hand. After a moment's hesitation, she took it and walked with him out of the funeral home. Once they got outside, he didn't seem inclined to let her go. She gently tugged her hand free and pointed toward the blue Toyota. "That's my car."

"My condolences."

She wasn't expecting the teasing, and it brought a surprised grin to her face. "It gets me where I'm going. Eventually. Do you need a ride?"

"That should probably be my line. Thanks, but I've got a rental. I'll meet you back at his house, all right?"

"Sure."

She headed over to Frank's bungalow. To her surprise, Jason had gotten there first. A compact car with rental plates was parked in the drive. The house looked different. The scraggly lawn had been trimmed, and the missing shutter had been dug out of the shed and rehung. Jason Cross was obviously making himself at home. Gwen wasn't sure how she felt about that.

She went around back. Jason was on the dock, untying the row boat. He looked up and greeted her with a little smile. She hopped into the boat and took her place in the backseat.

"Do you mind changing places?" Jason asked. "I'd like to row. I've been doing too much sitting and really need the movement."

"If you're not used to rowing, it'll chew up your hands," she warned him.

He showed her his palms. His hands were slim and long-fingered, but there were impressive calluses on his fingers and across the upper palms. A thick ridge lined the outer edge of each hand.

"Holy shit," Gwen murmured. She gave up the backseat, knowing herself outclassed. "What are you, a lumberjack?"

He grinned and took up the oars. "Close, but I like to think I work with a little more finesse than that. I do some carpentry."

"Martial arts, too, by the looks of your hands."

His eyebrows rose. "Good eye. Most people wouldn't spot that. Have you studied?"

She shrugged. "I started training when I was twelve. I was small for my age, and I routinely got the shit kicked out of me. Later, when I started kicking back, they thought the training would be good for anger management."

"Was it?"

"Not really, but I did learn how to leave fewer bruises."

He winced. "You must have been a handful for your folks."

"They died when I was a baby. I was raised by the state."

"I know some guys who grew up in the system. It can be quite an education," he said.

His matter-of-fact comment was a refreshing change from

282 / ELAINE CUNNINGHAM

the awkward silence or pitying glance that usually met this
history.

"Do you still study?" she asked him.

"I practice. And I teach. A lot of kids these days need something to give them focus and exercise."

He turned out of the cove, rowing south with long, smooth
strokes. The moon was waning, but the night was exceptionally
clear and bright. Each dip of the oars sent silver ripples skitter-
ing across the dark waters. A chorus of frog-song rose from the
reeds along shore.

"When do you have to head back home?" Gwen asked.

Jason rested his chin on the oars and gazed out over the
peaceful bay. "You know, I've been thinking of staying here."

"Can you relocate, just like that?"

"Yeah. In fact, it's good timing. The guy I was sharing the
apartment with was thinking about moving in with his girlfriend. This way, they won't have to look for a new place."

"What about your job?"

"Not a problem. What I do, I can do anywhere. Enough
about me. I'd rather hear about my father."

She started at the beginning, at least as she knew it. That
meant her first few months on the force, and Frank's struggle to
turn a kid into a cop. Back then, she'd had a bad attitude and a
fondness for suspects who resisted arrest. Before long they'd
found a rhythm, one that suited them both.

The stories poured out, good memories, mostly. She and Jason laughed a lot. He asked a lot of questions. Good questions.
Gwen appreciated the way he could move from one idea to another without needing a map.

"Tell me about this case my father was working on."

She considered this and decided, why not. He was Frank's son and had as much of a right to the truth as she did. Maybe more. And he was quick—he might see things in the narrative that eluded her. He taught martial arts. If problems came up, he could probably handle himself.

So she gave him the details. After, because he asked, she also told him about Meredith Cody. He was quick to point out the connections between the two, things she'd already seen. Nothing new, but it was good to hear someone come up with the same conclusions.

A distant rumble of thunder caught her ear. She glanced up at the sky. A dark cloud was rolling in from the ocean, swallowing the stars as it came.

"It's sort of early in the season for thunderstorms. We'd better get in."

He turned about and rowed the boat to the dock. He hopped out and tied the rope with a quick, expert knot, then extended a hand to Gwen.

Because she liked the guy, she let him help her out of the boat. He'd figure out on his own that she didn't need or want girlie treatment.

"Are you in a hurry to leave?" he asked. "I could use a cup of coffee."

"Decaf?" she asked.

He looked at her in feigned horror. "Good man," Gwen said approvingly.

They went into the kitchen. Out of habit, Gwen took down the coffeepot out and measured the grounds. Jason got out the mugs and milk. It was easy, companionable. Familiar. Precisely the balm her heart needed.

Talk became more general. Books, movies, music. To her delight, Jason's musical tastes ranged nearly as widely as her own. He joined her in mourning the loss of Frank's collection of early rock. They both liked R&B and jazz, folk and Celtic. They listened to classical music but drew the line at Stravinsky. Opera was out, but musicals were negotiable on a case-by-case basis.

All too soon, she set down her second cup of coffee. "I have to go. It's almost midnight."

He smiled. "I think I've heard this story."

"No pumpkins await. I have to meet someone."

His smile faded, and his dark brows met in a V of concern. "At this hour? Do you want some company?"

"If someone was with me, the appointment wouldn't happen."

He regarded her in silence. Gwen waited with a touch of dread for the familiar litany to begin. Too many of her friends and boyfriends had hated her job and the risks that came with it. If Jason was going to start trying to protect her, they were going to have a problem.

After a moment he nodded. "Take care of yourself," he said, in a tone that expressed quiet confidence in her ability to do so.

"Thanks."

He stood up with her. Gwen's first instinct was to lean in for a kiss. She stopped, not sure she wanted that. Frank had never once tried to get into her pants, which pretty much made him unique among the men in her life. There was a lot to be said for a friendly fuck, but maybe, just maybe, this guy might be worth something more.

The rain was just starting when Gwen sprinted for her car. A dark coupe was parked along the road, just in front of her car. The door swung open, and a woman stepped out. She was wearing a bright yellow slicker with a hood, the color of the plastic coats and duck boots that grade-school children used to wear on rainy days.

Gwen's skin started to crawl even before the woman slipped down her hood to reveal a mop of curly red hair. Sandra Jamison regarded her with a reptilian smile. She gestured to her car. "Get in."

Gwen shook her head. "No fucking way. I'll follow you in my car."

"That's not the plan. If you want the kid, you'll do what we tell you."

"I want the kid, but she needs a way to get home."

"And you plan to drive her?" The woman laughed. "You really think you'll walk away this time?"

"Not really," Gwen said casually. "But if my friend in there notices that my car is still parked outside, he's going to get curious. I don't want any interference. Meredith Cody goes home. The rest, we'll wait and see."

The woman hesitated, then shrugged. She got back into her car and headed out of town. Gwen followed her to Seekonk, just over the border in Massachusetts, and parked in front of a small, white motel. Sandra took the time to swing the car around and back up close to the door.

Gwen didn't have to ask why. When the door was opened and the lid of the trunk up, no one could see what was moved from the room to the car.

She followed Sandra into the room, dreading what she would find.

Meredith Cody was tied to the bed in the same way Gwen had found Lauren Simpson: ankles crossed, arms spread out wide. She was gagged, and her blue eyes were glazed with terror.

Carl Jamison sat on the bed beside her, writing on her with a pen. He didn't have a knife out, yet. Apparently the freak didn't like to work freehand. His brother, Kyle, leaned against the wall, watching with hungry eyes.

"The Caer Sidi," Gwen said, remembering the name Teresa Moniz had used for the old design.

Carl Jamison looked up at her, startled. "You know?"

"I know it's an old design, a path to the Celtic Otherworld."

"It's much more than that. There is power in this world, things that people like you can't begin to imagine."

Gwen laughed. She couldn't help it—his portentous announcement was just too ironic, coming as it did from this pathetic wannabe.

He sent Gwen a hate-filled smile and took a knife from the table. He flicked the blade open and drew it lightly along one of the pen lines on the girl's thigh. Meredith shrieked against the gag.

Gwen instinctively started forward. Sandra Jamison seized her by the hair and pulled her to an abrupt stop. She put a gun to Gwen's head, just below the ear.

"We'll let the little girl go, on the condition that you stay to play."

"I knew the plan coming in. Give me the details—how does this work?"

"Kyle will take her away. When we're finished with you and a reasonable distance away from here, we'll call her daddy and tell him where to pick her up."

"I don't like it," Gwen said. "But, agreed."

She turned her gaze toward Kyle. "If you touch the girl, Edmonson will know."

A strange expression crossed the man's face, and he shot an inquiring look toward his brother.

Carl got off the bed and came toward her, knife in hand. "What do you know, bitch? What do you know about the Elders?"

"I know that sacrificing virgins is not the way to become one," she told him. "You'll never be an Elder. It's in the blood—and not the blood you spill."

The expression on his face told her that her shot had found its mark. He backhanded her, sending both Gwen and Sandra Jamison tumbling to the floor.

"What do you know about it?" he raged, looming over them both.

His wife scrambled to her feet, put some distance between herself and Carl. But Gwen calmly raised her hand for him to help her rise. It was a deliberately haughty gesture, something he might expect from a person about to lay claims to Gentry.

"I know because I'm an Elder."

Carl Jamison stared at her for a long moment. He took her hand and raised her to her feet, his manner almost courtly.

"The Elders don't age," he said quietly, his eyes studying her face. "When did you become a cop?"

"Fifteen years ago," she said. "But you probably knew that. Your lawyers went over my record after your arrest. Hell, they crawled up its every bodily orifice with a microscope. You know I joined the force before you were out of high school. And right now," she concluded softly, "you're having a hard time reconciling all that knowledge with what you see on my face. How old do I look?"

"Sixteen. Eighteen."

"But you're still not convinced. I can change that. Give me your knife."

Sandra Jamison let out an exasperated hiss. "She's crazy! Why are you listening to this?"

"Keep the gun on her," her husband said, not taking his eyes from Gwen's face. "If she opens the knife, if she takes a step from where she stands, shoot her."

He closed the knife and handed it to Gwen.

Immediately the room filled with color—a red haze, as if the air itself was filled with blood. Faintly glowing lines formed on the floor, spiraling up toward the ceiling, taking the shape and the path of the ancient maze.

For once, the power came to her call.

Words formed in her mind, and Gwen said them aloud. "Stephanie, Claire, Veronica, Kim, Lauren."

She spoke them slowly, solemnly, like the knelling of a bell. Naming the women who had died to fulfill Carl Jamison's insane, impossible goal.

The color and lights faded away, but there were shadows against the wall that were not there before. The Jamisons stared at her in awed silence.

"We can't kill her," Carl said softly. He sounded disappointed, like a kid who'd just heard that he wouldn't be getting a PlayStation for Christmas.

"That's not the way to get what you want," Gwen said. She smiled, coldly and deliberately. "But if you'd managed to fuck me when you had me in that hotel room, you'd already know that."

The light dawned on the freak's face. He was crazy enough to believe it. "Then if we—"

"Yes."

"All of us?"

She glanced over at Sandra, shrugged. "Why not? Our people don't draw the same kind of distinctions."

"Our people," he repeated. Believing it. Savoring it.

"But of course this changes things," Gwen said. "I want to know the girl's safe first. Kyle drops her off, she contacts her folks, they pick her up and call my cell phone. By that time, Kyle should be back, and we can all play."

Carl Jamison stared at her for a long moment with his insane eyes. Then his lips curved slyly.

"It doesn't have to be willing. You said that yourself."

Damn. The guy might be crazy, but he wasn't stupid. "But Edmonson told you not to kill the girl," she said, hoping that this was true. "He wants her returned. If you don't stick to the deal, you'll have to deal with him."

He turned to his brother. "Get the kid out of here."

Gwen watched in silent rage as Kyle took out a needle and plunged it into the girl's thigh. Her eyelids fluttered, and she fell slack against her bonds. They didn't bother to dress her—just wrapped her in a blanket. Nothing could have told Gwen more clearly what Meredith's fate would be if things went wrong.

Carl switched off the room lights, then helped his brother load the drugged and sleeping girl into the trunk. Sandra kept the gun on Gwen, holding it against her head all the while. Gwen guessed that they wouldn't take many chances with her even if she hadn't given them a freak show. After all, she'd kicked the shit out of all three of them last time.

The younger Jamison came in for his coat, looking none too happy about missing the fun.

Which was, unfortunately, about to start.

A desperate idea came to Gwen. If she could pull up images from Carl's knife, why not the gun Sandra was holding to her temple? She'd never gotten an impression from anything unless she touched it with her hands, but it was worth a try.

She took a long, calming breath, willing herself to relax. To *see*.

The window exploded inward, glass flying in eerie silence. Sandra shrieked and shied away from the illusionary shards.

Gwen grabbed the gun by the barrel and ripped it out of Sandra's hand. She backhanded the woman with it, hitting her in the face with a crack that promised broken teeth. The woman staggered back but didn't go down.

Carl came running at Gwen, knife raised high. There was no time to shoot. She dodged the first knife slash. Sandra lunged at her from the other side, stopping her retreat.

The knife sliced her arm nearly from shoulder to elbow. Gwen ignored the burning pain and threw a punch at Sandra's nose. Cartilage crumpled, and the woman staggered back, blood pouring from her nose. She was out of the fight for the moment at least, but Carl lifted the knife for another slashing blow.

Gwen caught his wrist in both hands and twisted around so that her back was to him. She bent from the waist, throwing him over her shoulder. He landed in a staggered crouch. Gwen kept her hold on his wrist, jerking the arm up painfully high. He let out a yelp of pain, but he hung onto the knife.

Gwen slammed her foot into his lower back. He howled with agony. "Drop the knife," she said, punctuating her words with another kick.

"That's your kidney," she told him, kicking him a third time in the same vulnerable spot. "You can drop the knife or piss blood. Your choice."

At last the weapon thudded to the floor. Gwen gave the man's arm one more jerk, then released him. He fell to one knee.

"You're dead, bitch," he wheezed.

With resilience beyond anything Gwen would have thought possible, he lunged from the floor, turning as he hurled himself at her. They slammed into a small table, which overturned with a splintering crash. The lamp shattered, plunging the room into darkness.

They grappled and rolled, each desperately seeking advantage. Finally Carl pinned her beneath him. His hand slid over her blood-slick arm and sought the place his knife had opened. He dug his fingers into the wound.

Gwen screamed. A brilliant flash of lightning filled the room with sulfurous yellow light, illuminating the rictus grin on Carl Jamison's face.

Her groping hands found a pottery shard from the lamp.

She drove it into his face, pushing it into his eye until she felt the wet, sickening release.

He rolled off her, screaming and holding his face. Gwen scrambled away and seized the knife he'd dropped.

Sandra came at her, fists flailing. She plowed into Gwen and sent them both plunging to the floor. The weight of both women fell on Carl Jamison, driving the knife hilt-deep into his chest.

Gwen grunted in pain as the hilt slammed into her thigh. She heaved Sandra off her and hit the switch for the overhead light.

Carl's body shuddered and jerked, and the insane light was fading from his one remaining eye. Sandra let out a shriek and threw herself on him, sobbing wildly.

Gwen collected the gun and walked over to the woman. She put the gun to her head and clicked off the safety.

The sound turned off Sandra's weeping as if someone had thrown a switch. She carefully turned her head to regard Gwen. "Are you going to kill me, too?" she said, spitting out the words.

"Not if you do what I say," she told her. "Call Kyle and tell him there's a change of plan. He's to take Meredith to Haines Park, between Riverside and Barrington. Tell him to park by the woods just past the Little League field. You'll meet him there."

She handed Sandra a phone. The woman sent her a hate-filled glare and dialed. A man's voice answered. Gwen leaned in close enough to make sure it was Kyle Jamison on the other end. She listened as Sandra repeated the instructions and the man agreed, then she took the phone from Sandra's hand before she could add anything more.

"You can't leave her here," observed a soft male voice.

Gwen whirled toward the sound, keeping the gun steady on

Sandra's head. Ian Forest stepped into the room, closing the door behind him.

"She'll call the moment you leave. The girl will be dead before you arrive, if she isn't already."

There was truth in his words, but Gwen hesitated to kill a woman who was no immediate threat. "I could bring her along."

"No time." Ian crossed the room and took Sandra's head between his hands. He gave it a quick, sharp twist. Her neck broke with a sickening crack, and she slumped to the floor.

The casual efficiency of this execution stole Gwen's breath. Ian, however, had moved on to the next practicality. He regarded the knife cut on her arm, then tore a long strip from the bedsheet.

"You've lost quite a bit of blood, but the cut isn't as bad as it looks," he said as he bound it. "It's not very deep, and there doesn't appear to be any damage to the muscle. Can you drive?"

"Yeah."

As soon as he'd finished wrapping the cut, Gwen seized Sandra's yellow raincoat and put it on. The woman's car keys were in the pocket.

"Good idea," Ian approved. "I'll ride with you."

"Forget it. I'm on the way to pick up Meredith."

"Yes, and I'm coming with you."

There was no time to argue, so she gave in with a curt nod. The rain was coming down in torrents as they drove to the park.

"Stop here," Ian said, indicating a heavily wooded area.

Gwen pulled to a stop. "It's a half mile to the parking lot," she pointed out.

"I'll meet you there."

She left him without argument and drove to the parking lot.

Leaving the motor running, she ran over to the other car, keeping her head down. Kyle Jamison leaned across the seat and opened the passenger door.

Gwen jerked the door open before he could release it, pulling him off balance. With her free hand, she hit him just above the elbow.

He screamed with pain and lunged for her. Surprisingly strong, he dragged her into the car and slammed her head into the dash. Gwen's vision blurred. She fought back from the edge of oblivion in time to see him reach for the gun on the floor.

A lighting bolt exploded from the angry sky. The windshield shattered, sending pebbles of glass cascading over Kyle Jamison. Gwen drove her heel into his hand, shattering bone.

The driver's door opened. Gwen looked up, stunned to see Ian Forest standing beside the car.

Kyle fell out of the car, bloody from many small cuts.

"Can you help me drag him over to the tree?" Ian indicated a large oak tree that stood alone at the corner of the field.

"I think so," Gwen said.

They half carried, half dragged the man over to the tree, leaned him against it.

"What now?" Gwen demanded.

"Go back to the car. Get the girl to her parents. I'll take care of the Jamisons."

She nodded and dashed back through the rain to Kyle Jamison's car. The keys were still in the ignition. She wrenched them out and hurried back around to open the trunk.

On the way, her eye fell on the oak tree, and she came to a dead stop. Ian Forest had disappeared, taking Kyle Jamison with him.

Twenty-five

Gwen stood dumbfounded for a moment. She shook herself, adding this to the growing list of things she'd figure out when time permitted. She unlocked the trunk. The girl stared out at her, terrified.

"Your mother sent me to bring you home," she said. "And she told me to tell you that first thing off, you're going to clean up your room."

Meredith blinked. "It's true," she said. "She did send you."

"No one could make that up," Gwen said.

The girl started to smile and then to giggle. Gwen helped her out of the trunk. She staggered on limbs too long confined. She helped the girl into Sandra Jamison's car and drove directly to the Cody home.

The look on Dianne Cody's face went a long way toward changing Gwen's opinion of the woman. She and her daughter clung to each other, sobbing.

Gwen drew Ryan Cody aside. "Can you get your family away for a while?"

He nodded. "We want to keep this quiet."

"Well, an official report was filed, but I don't suppose you'll have a problem burying it."

"No," he said shortly.

"I need to have a talk with Wallace Edmonson and find out who was behind Meredith's kidnapping. Until this is finished, all of it, you and your family are going to keep looking over your shoulders."

"Thank you," he said softly. She nodded and left the family to their privacy.

The rain had stopped, and a brisk wind was blowing the clouds out to sea. Ian Forest emerged from the shadows of a maple tree and stepped into her path.

"Jesus!" she exclaimed. "How do you do that?"

He smiled. "Let's just say that it's one of those things I hired you to figure out. What's next?"

"I need to talk to Wallace Edmonson."

His smile faltered. "How do you know him?"

"He works for the same law firm as Ryan Cody. He also works for whoever was responsible for taking Meredith."

"Who told you this?"

"Cody did."

Ian looked very grim. "He probably believes it to be true. In actuality, Wallace Earl Edmonson owns and controls that company."

"So he was behind the kidnapping?" Gwen demanded.

"It seems likely. He is not one to carry messages for another."

"You know him?"

Ian's smile was bitter. "I work for him. It is part of a complex obligation that would take too long to explain."

"What was his connection to the Jamisons?"

"The earl has a hand in drug trafficking. I suppose those three had some involvement in distribution."

Gwen nodded slowly. That tied up a couple of loose ends. "So my uncle is one of the bad guys."

Ian's brows rose. "You know of the family connection. So you also know what you are."

"I'm having a hard time getting my head around it." She leaned against her blue Toyota, then suddenly stood upright. "Hey! How'd this get here?"

"I drove it over. An associate of mine will dispose of the woman's car and clean up the hotel room. Since Carl Jamison was out on bail, the assumption will be that he and his family decided to relocate."

She nodded and got into the car, wincing from the pain in her arm.

"Move over," Ian said. "I'll drive you home."

"But Edmonson—"

"Can wait until tomorrow. It's nearly two o'clock in the morning."

Gwen slid over and let him take the wheel. "I don't think I've ever been this tired."

"I would have thought the rain would revive you."

Her eyes popped open. "What?"

"Never mind. Get some sleep."

She wanted to argue, but she was just too damn tired. Her eyes drifted shut, and the movement of the car rocked her swiftly toward sleep.

———

Cᴺᴼ The pounding on the door downstairs awoke her. She crawled out of bed, still in the clothes she'd worn the night before. The pain in her arm had faded to a slight prickle. Curious, she unwound the bandage. The wound had closed to a thin pink line.

"Weird," she muttered as she went down the stairs.

A cable truck was parked in front of her office. Jimmy Almeida stood outside the door.

"I was getting ready to give up," he said with an uncertain smile. "But then, if I did, I'd just have to come back."

She opened the door and gestured him into the office. "What's on your mind?"

"You were looking into whether or not someone other than my father might have killed Joe Perotti. I told you no. The thing is, someone else might have been involved. My father fixed cars before when people asked him."

"You saw this?"

"I was a kid, maybe six, seven. I was playing in the back of the shop when this guy comes in. My father drops everything, treats the guy like he's royalty or something. He even called him the earl—you know, like duke, count, earl."

"Got it."

"He asked my father if he could fix a car so the brakes would fail if they got wet. When he said sure, the guy gave him an address. The name stuck in my mind as *something drowned*. Years later, I'm working for the cable company and get a call for a house on Alfred Drowne. It brought the old memory back, so I looked through a street atlas of Rhode Island. There's nothing else even close."

"Alfred Drowne Road," Gwen repeated.

He gave her a keen look. "Does that mean something?"

It was the address given on the licenses for James and Ruby Avalon. She shrugged.

"So when I told you my father probably killed Joe Perotti, I was leaving out a big part of the story. I don't know if it'll help you find that missing girl, but I couldn't live with myself knowing I kept quiet about something that might have helped."

"I appreciate that," Gwen told him. "Did you get a look at this earl?"

"Yeah, but kids don't see adults the same way. Thirty or fifty, they all look old and they all look big."

"Did anything in particular stay with you? Like, was he thin or heavy? Dark, blond, white hair? Did he wear glasses, or have a big nose?"

"Dark," he remembered. "Thin."

"That's good," Gwen encouraged. "How old do you remember him being? Did he strike you as a young thug? A teenager, say."

Jimmy shook his head adamantly. "I couldn't tell you his age, but he was definitely an adult. He looked older than my father, who must have been about thirty at the time."

In other words, about the age the Wallace "Earl" Edmonson looked today.

She pulled her father's license out of her pocket. "Does this look familiar?"

His eyes widened. "Yeah, that's the guy! Or at least, someone who looks a lot like him." He focused on Gwen's face. "This is bad news, isn't it?"

She placed a hand on his arm. "It answers a lot of questions. Hard questions. Thanks."

He nodded uncertainly, sure that there was more to the story. But when Gwen didn't elaborate, he returned to his truck.

She drove to Edmonson's house, but this time she didn't go to the front door. She circled around and let herself in through the back.

Her first stop was the kitchen. Apparently Edmonson didn't cook much. There wasn't much but fruit in the refrigerator, no dishes in the cupboards. Other stuff, yes: papers, books.

A familiar black shape caught Gwen's eye. She moved the papers off and slid out a notebook computer.

Heart pounding, she opened the case and turned it on. A familiar picture filled the screen—a photo of the bay Frank used as a screen saver.

Wallace Edmonson had killed her parents. He had tried to kill her. More important, he had killed Frank.

"I'm glad you know," said a voice from the doorway.

Gwen lifted hate-filled eyes. "Why?"

"You have a rare ability. Your gift will enable us to find ancient treasures hidden by the Elder Races and their followers."

She rose, stepping toward him. "Followers?"

"Naturally. Why do you think the ancient cultures worshipped at the solstice and equinox? These were times of great power."

"Let me understand this. Because I'm useful to you, you decided to keep me around. And you didn't want anyone else knowing what you were doing."

"Admirably put."

"So I'm supposed to disregard what was done in the past.

I'm supposed to forget you killed my parents, and tried to kill me, and just trust you?"

"You have excellent motivation. Your aptitude for the clan gift is remarkable, but you are completely untutored in minor things. We will both be better off if we band together."

Gwen could not believe she was hearing this. She reached into the pocket of her jacket and took out the gun Ian Forest gave her.

Edmonson sneered. "So like your mother. She was a bloody-minded bitch, too. She must have truly enjoyed killing David and Regina Gellman."

"That's not true."

He merely smiled. "If you kill me now, you'll never know."

"Don't do it, Gwen," said Ian Forest. "If you do, there will be little I can do to help you."

She glanced over at him, not terribly surprised to learn that he was still following her. There were two men with him, people Gwen had never seen.

"Have you heard enough?" Ian asked them. "The earl, known as Wallace Edmonson, has broken one of our few remaining rules: he has killed his own kind."

"It is witnessed," said one of the men.

"It is witnessed," the other agreed.

They stepped into the room and fixed Edmonson with a steady gaze. He shoulders rose and fell in resignation, and he followed them out of the house.

Ian stepped forward and gently took the gun from Gwen's hand. "You won't need this now. Once the earl is gone, his people will scatter."

"Where are you taking him?"

"He won't be found. None of them will be."

She sank down into one of the kitchen chairs. He took a seat across from her.

"Edmonson was endangering us with his greed. He needed to be removed."

"And you needed to find a means to do so," Gwen said. "That's why you hired me to look into my own past. If I found out the truth, if I could get Edmonson to admit he killed my parents, job done."

"Well put." He smiled at her. "Job well done."

She shook her head, thoughtful. "No, I don't think so. In fact, I think it's just starting."

"Oh?"

"I've spent half of my life trying to help people like me: runaways, abused children, misfits who fell through the cracks. But that's not who I am. I mean," she amended, "that not *all* I am."

"No," he agreed softly.

"What if there are other people out there like me? People who've been ripped from their lives, left to deal with a world that has no place for them, or go crazy in the process?"

She fixed a steady gaze on him, her eyes willing him to tell the truth. "There are others, aren't there? Other . . . changelings?"

"It's likely."

Gwen took this in, accepting what it meant. "Then I'll find them." She smiled suddenly, without humor. "But I'll need some new business cards. How do you like 'Changeling Detective Agency?'"

"I think," he said slowly, "that this new enterprise could very quickly become a thriving concern."

Epilogue

～ Ian Forest swaggered into the back room of Underhill, feeling better than he had in many, many years. Two men awaited him. One was the silver-haired gentleman who had been with him the day he'd discovered Gwen. The other was a young man with kind dark eyes and a killer's hands.

Ian gave the young man a dismissive glance and turned his attention back to the Elder. "I have the gem."

"Show me."

He took the blue gem from his pocket and placed it on the desk, carefully folding back the silk wrappings.

"It rightly belongs to the girl," the older man said, "but I agree that the time has not yet come to give it to her."

"She is still trying to accept what she is. For that matter, she's still trying to figure out what she is," Ian said. "But Gwen is persistent. I don't think it will be long before she's capable of using it."

"We must also be sure that she will use it in a manner consistent with our methods and goals." The older man shifted his gaze to the dark-eyed man. "I know you didn't want to retain any of Edmonson's followers, but this man is in a position to be of use to us. The girl is slow to trust. She'll be wary of anyone who enters her life from this point on."

Ian turned a cold gaze to the young man. "I don't trust him."

"Is that because you want Gwen for yourself," he asked, "or because you're still upset about losing a fight to me?"

"You overstep your place, laying a hand on one of us," Ian hissed.

The young man rose. "And you overstepped yours. You worked for the earl, the same as me, but the whole time you were working to set him up. The main difference between you and me—other than the fact that you can't fight worth a damn—is that I don't sell out my friends."

"Keep that in mind," Ian said softly. "Because judging from what I observed last night, Gwen is inclined to count herself among your friends."

"We made a good start," the man who now called himself Jason Cross agreed. "In fact, I think we'll hit it off really well."